Nina, the Bandit Queen

NINA, THE BANDIT QUEEN

JOEY SLINGER

DUNDURN
TORONTO

Editor: Allister Thompson
Design: Courtney Horner
Printer: Webcom

Library and Archives Canada Cataloguing in Publication

Slinger, Joey
          Nina, the bandit queen / by Joey Slinger.

Issued also in electronic formats.
ISBN 978-1-4597-0138-0

          I. Title.

PS8587.L5N56 2012   C813'.54   C2011-903843-9

1   2   3   4   5   16   15   14   13   12

We acknowledge the support of the **Canada Council for the Arts** and the **Ontario Arts Council** for our publishing program. We also acknowledge the financial support of the **Government of Canada** through the **Canada Book Fund** and **Livres Canada Books**, and the **Government of Ontario** through the **Ontario Book Publishing Tax Credit** and the **Ontario Media Development Corporation**.

Care has been taken to trace the ownership of copyright material used in this book. The author and the publisher welcome any information enabling them to rectify any references or credits in subsequent editions.

J. Kirk Howard, President

Printed and bound in Canada.
www.dundurn.com

Dundurn	Gazelle Book Services Limited	Dundurn
3 Church Street, Suite 500	White Cross Mills	2250 Military Road
Toronto, Ontario, Canada	High Town, Lancaster, England	Tonawanda, NY
M5E 1M2	LA1 4XS	U.S.A. 14150

For Peter Slinger, and Garth Graham,
and the Relentless Spirit of Big Trout Lake

ONE

Nina Carson Dolgoy pulled at the back of her T-shirt to make sure it wasn't stuffed into the waistband of her sweats when she came out on the porch. That's what everybody in her family called it, even though it didn't have a roof or anything. It was just flat concrete with holes in the corners where there once were posts that held up some kind of railing. The railings and everything had been stolen before Nina and D.S. and the girls moved in, and D.S. said it was good that they had been, because it would have been way too crowded if everybody was out there at once and the sides weren't wide open. What had never gotten stolen were the old broken-down washer and dryer that he and Nina hauled onto it from where somebody had left them in the hall, blocking the front door. This had made it almost impossible to push the door open when Nina noticed the house was vacant and decided they might as well live there. It was getting dark when she spotted it, and she was relieved because they'd been looking for a new place ever since the men with the bulldozer and the man from the city had showed up that morning and chased them out of their old house.

They didn't have to break in. The door didn't have a lock or even a knob, just those two clunky old white machines propping it closed. Later on, when D.S. would look around the porch, he'd say what a shame it was that somebody hadn't come along and snatched the washer and dryer, because they hardly left room on the porch for anybody, but almost two years had passed since he and Nina stacked them out there, and he was beginning to think nobody was ever going to.

The sky was getting light enough that Nina could see the outlines of the high-rise apartment towers up at The Intersection. Down here, in the part of town people called SuEz, it was still too shadowy to see much of anything. Nothing seemed to be moving anyway. Certainly not anything that might have made the weird-kind-of-music noise or the barking noise she heard. The noises hadn't wakened Nina — the heat had. Except, when she thought about it, the heat had kept her awake all night. Except, from the way she felt, it was like she'd been awake forever and was going to stay that way. So she hauled herself out of bed and went to see what was going on. It wasn't like she had anything better to do.

Across the street, JannaRose was out of her house, too. She was standing between parked cars with her head to one side, listening. The noises came again, louder now. Skittery music. Then something that sounded like barking. JannaRose flipped her hands palms-up: *Beats me.* She tipped her head back and closed her eyes. She stood like that for so long, it was as if she'd dozed off. Then she said, "It's gotta be —"

Nina beat her to it. "Cops."

JannaRose opened one eye. "— an ice cream truck." Not that she looked proud of her answer. What would an ice cream truck be doing out at this time of day? At this time of day on a school day?

"Cops."

"What about the music?"

Not long after they'd met, Nina'd told JannaRose her theory about cops. "If there are two ways to do something," she'd said, "the sensible way and the completely fuckin' stupid way, the cops will pick the one that makes you think they only take their heads out of their asses so they can blow their nose." It turned out to be the sort of thing that both women believed.

So Nina had an answer to the music question. "Undercover cops," she said. "They're using an ice cream truck to sneak up on some gangster's house."

"Freeze, assholes!" JannaRose squared into a two-fisted stance, pointing her finger at Nina.

"Mr. Freezee, assholes!" Nina said, aiming back.

It was too hot to laugh. It was too hot to bullshit around. The women drooped. SuEz would have too except it was already drooped about as much as it was possible to droop and had been for as long as anybody could remember. It was pronounced the same as the canal in Egypt and ended up called that because it's the southwest end of the part of the city called South Chester. South Chester takes in everything up as far as The Intersection, where the subway station is, and the high-rise apartment towers. North of that, it's just plain Chester. Over a long period it got so everybody just called the southwest end "Southwest," and in time this got mumbled into sounding like it was SuEz. Then it got spelled that way.

It was regarded by the people who lived there as the worst part of town, mostly because for years it had been regarded as the worst part of town by people who didn't live there. From a practical point of view, though, it depended on what your idea of "worst" was. The residents of SuEz often mentioned to each other how even the whores stayed out of SuEz because their customers were afraid to drive there. And how not much dope was dealt to the locals because nobody who lived in SuEz could afford even the cheapest stuff. This was the general theory anyway. Sometimes it included how the cops stayed out of it, too, and not because it was crime-free, except it sort of was, since nobody had anything worth stealing.

On the other hand, the people who lived there were pretty insular, and while there were plenty of reasons for them being that way, it meant they really didn't have much else to judge by.

Tootlety-tootlety-tootlety!

"I don't fuckin' believe it." Nina sounded like she was trying not to yell.

About five blocks up, maybe a quarter of the way to The Intersection, a truck with a flat nose crept out of a side street and onto theirs. Yellow lights flashed at the corners of the roof. *Tootlety-tootlety-tootlety!*

"What'll the cops go around disguised like next?" JannaRose never passed up an opportunity to stick it to Nina, because Nina was one of those people who could get really irritated when anybody noticed they were full of it. "The Seven Dwarfs?" This time, though, she took only the one small shot and dropped it. She could hardly believe the truck either.

Tootlety-tootlety-tootlety! Followed by the sharp bark of amplified words still too far off to make out. But JannaRose did have to concede one thing: It sounded like cops. The way cops would sound if they sold ice cream.

"Shit." Nina was having a hard time trusting her eyes. Up

there, when the truck pulled over to the curb, tiny figures — child-sized figures — were appearing out of houses. When it stopped in front of the little apartment buildings, the loudspeaker barked longer and clusters of the tiny figures spilled out on the walks. Grownups straggled behind them, hunched from just having crawled out of bed. But so far, everybody kept their distance. Nobody went right up to the truck. They stretched their necks almost as if they were sniffing it, not quite sure what to do.

"That truck's talking to those people," JannaRose said.

"Ice cream trucks always —"

"No. Shut up. It's —"

"'Hellllll-OH!' they say. Then they play some tinkly —"

"Shut up! Listen!" As the truck moved closer, the words came clearer. "It's talking right to those *kids*. It knows their *names*."

Every single one of their names. All of them. It called each and every one over the loudspeaker.

"I don't fuckin' believe it."

"It doesn't matter if you believe it," JannaRose said. "It's —"

"It's fuckin' insane."

"Alessandra," the truck was saying, when at last they could hear it plainly. "Come and get a Glacier Gloopster." And, "Tyree, there's a Choc-Sicle Swirler here for you. You come right over here and see." And, "Crydell, you *love* Frostie-Fudgie. We've got an extra special one just for you today....

"Lewis ... a Banana Daq-a-Quack....

"Thomas Junior ... a Killer Blizzard....

"Shabatha ... Ronell ... Kirinette ... a Mr. Nice Ice ... a Slushnut Bar ... an I Scream Dream."

Tootlety-tootlety-tootlety!

"Katie ... the Silver Shiver you've been wishing for ...

"Laraquinda … the Dilly Chiller you've been dreaming …

"Robert James … Javier …

"A Drool Cooler … a Purple Slurple …"

When a name was called, the kid got pushed forward by excited little friends hoping their names would be next. But after a few seconds of embarrassment and pride that made them go all goose-pimply, being a celebrity became way more than they could bear. They ducked back into the crowd, light-headed with astonishment.

Nina propped her hand against a car to keep from falling. Had a concrete block fallen out of the sky and landed on her head? If a concrete block fell out of the sky and landed on her head, would it feel different than this? *Ice cream before breakfast!* Simply thinking about it made her feel like throwing up. No it didn't. It was thinking about it in those circumstances that did.

"Naquacielo!" the voice barked. "Here's a Razzle Dazzle Iceberg we worked all night making especially for you!"

She half expected to see Naquacielo go floating up into the sky. Knots of children hovered, but still well back from the curb, like maybe they weren't sure it wasn't a dream and didn't want to mess it up.

"Is this legal?" she said.

"Invasion of people's privacy. There must be something like that," JannaRose said. "My kids are going to go crazy."

Nina heard herself bark back at the truck. "Fuckers!"

The truck's own barking pulled more and more people out of bed. Heads poked from windows. The glass in the front doors of the apartment buildings had mostly been busted out, and kids ducked through where the bottom panels used to be. Racing out of houses, kids skidded to a stop like characters in cartoons, never quite going past the line where they would end up under the truck's control, where they would have to put their money on the counter.

Without looking, Nina knew that four little girls in their pyjamas had come out on her porch. Five little girls. The black one and Nina's littlest, same size, same age — six — could be Velcroed together the way they kept their arms around each other every minute, every day. "Zanielle, you sleep any?" she called over her shoulder. Something about what was going on made her feel the need to emphasize how wide her open-armed maternity stretched. Both girls nodded without unfastening their eyes from the truck. "Fabreece, don't you fall off that porch."

Fabreece was her littlest. Nina had wanted a break from names out of Camelot. Guinevere, Merlina, and Lady, short for Lady of the Lake — they were fourteen, twelve, and nine years old — had come along thirteen months apart and were supposed to stop there, but the idea of getting a vasectomy caused D.S. to faint every time it came into his mind, so he'd lied to her. And she'd believed him. Maybe all the sperm he'd pumped into her over the years had turned her brain to Cheez Whiz. So after Fabreece, she had the operation while D.S. huffed around saying he was going to go to court and sue that son-of-a-bitch doctor that did his. "You do that," Nina had told him.

The truck crept to a stop just shy of where she was standing. The tootlety music stopped. "I can't get by," the loudspeaker said. It was speaking directly to her, only it wasn't the same voice that had been calling out the kids' names and rhyming off the ice cream treats it had for them. That one sounded so official, it scraped the insides of Nina's bones. This one sounded like one of the kids the ice cream was being pitched to. Through the windshield she could see the driver holding a microphone. The ice-cream selling voice must have come from a computer, one geared to something that could tell where all the kids lived and recognize them and measure their reactions.

JannaRose said it probably involved a satellite.

"The fuckers," Nina said.

The notable thing about this was, when the driver said he couldn't get by, it hadn't occurred to her that she was blocking the way.

There was scrambling on the porch as D.S. came out, followed by stupefied silence as he gradually realized that his wife was in what looked like a standoff with an ice cream truck. "What're you doing?" he yelped.

The most notable thing of all, though, was that until D.S. started mouthing off at her, Nina wasn't aware that she was doing anything.

TWO

To go from being locked in a showdown with an ice cream truck to deciding to rob a bank wasn't a straight line from A to B. It was more of a process. Some of the other things that went on between Nina and the ice cream truck that morning were also part of the process. So was the urgent need to raise money for local improvements and public works. This had to do with the swimming pool at the high school getting closed down. If she could get it reopened, it would be a good place for her daughters to burn off the aimless youthful energy that might otherwise lead them to become whores and crack addicts. This happened so often in SuEz that whenever it did, nobody was surprised. And then there was how she didn't approve of stealing. Overcoming that obstacle was part of it, too.

But because she didn't know anything at all about this process, which is understandable since it was only about to get rolling, and because she definitely had no idea that she was on the brink of getting swept up in it, when D.S. Dolgoy came out on the porch and saw her eyeball-to-eyeball with the ice cream truck in the middle of the street in front of their house and said, "What're you doing?" she didn't find it very helpful.

It didn't lead her to give a little more thought to whatever it was she wasn't aware she was doing. It didn't throw a bucket of cold, clear reasonableness over her. It didn't, because she knew that when he said, "What're you doing?" it wasn't D.S. asking a question. It was D.S. telling her, "Get the fuck off the street and stop making a fool of yourself."

More to the point, she also knew that by "yourself," he meant she was making a fool of him.

So there she was, not doing anything she was even aware of except being pissed off. And then she got told to stop doing it because it was embarrassing *him*. That was the thing that *really* pissed her off.

Fuck you, D.S.

She didn't say it out loud, though, because children were present. At least he had the blond wig on the right way around. He looked ridiculous on the porch in it and her green nightie, which was a version of the disguise he'd come up with so the welfare inspectors wouldn't figure out there was a male on the premises. He looked ridiculous in it everywhere, but not nearly as ridiculous as he looked when he got out of bed in a rush and the wig was turned around backwards. That looked idiotic, like he was peeking out through one of those Hawaiian hula dancer's skirts. It made his daughters laugh until they peed their pants.

One thing she did know for sure was that JannaRose was right behind her. She didn't even have to look around. Their friendship had reached a stage where she got subconscious signals. She always knew exactly where JannaRose was and what she was doing, the same as she always knew what she was wearing, although that wasn't difficult. A T-shirt and sweats. They used to joke about these psychic powers of Nina's. "Okay, how many orgasms did I have last night?" JannaRose would ask. "You mean real ones?" Nina would answer. It would start them laughing until they had to hold each other up.

"Stay right there." Nina barely glanced around.

"What?"

"Don't move." Whether she'd done it consciously or not, JannaRose had drifted out into the middle of the street, and if she stayed right where she was, the truck was still blocked. Nina ran up the steps and yanked D.S.'s crutch out from under his arm. He didn't particularly need it, since he was almost totally healed from the last time a customer beat him up, but he kept it around since he usually needed it several times a year. And even when he didn't — when something happened that made him nervous, he leaned on it.

"What?" D.S. said, stumbling around. The girls shuffled to stay out of his way, something that wasn't all that easy with everybody already sticking out over the edges of the porch. But they managed to do it without taking their eyes off the truck, which — it was obvious from the expressions on their faces — they knew was going to do something impossibly fabulous any second now, something far more fabulous than anything they had ever dared to dream of. They didn't look as if they would survive the wait.

When Nina dashed back into the road holding the crutch near the bottom like it was an axe, it didn't get through to her children that something else was going to happen instead. It didn't even get through to them when she hauled the crutch back over her shoulder as if she was about to take a big swing at the windshield right in front of the driver. He was the only one who reacted in any way at all.

"Hey!" he said, in his amplified twelve-year-old voice, although now that Nina was getting a closer look, he seemed even younger.

"Get out of here," she said.

"Pardon?"

"Go on. I'm counting to three." She took a practice chop, swinging until the armpit-end of the crutch nearly touched the glass.

That was when something finally got through to the girls, something impossibly horrible, far more horrible than anything else would ever be in their whole lives. They squealed in agony. "What's she doing?"

"What're you doing?" It was D.S. again, only this time it really was a question. He was getting nervous, and she had his crutch out there when he needed it more than he ever had before.

The kid leaned his head out the side window. "I can't hear what you're saying," he said.

Nina hauled the crutch back. "I said" — each word came out like it was a rock and she was heaving them to him one at a time — "get your truck off of this street."

This seemed definitely okay with the kid. It was as if he'd already decided that this miserable street in the worst part of town wasn't a place where he wanted to get into a big dispute. "You'll have to get out of the way, then," he said.

Nina rested the crutch on her shoulder. "Nope."

"Huh?"

"Turn around." She made a twirly motion with her finger.

The kid studied the situation in his mirrors. "There isn't room."

"Then back up."

The driver was really young, and a complete stranger, and didn't appear the slightest bit sure of himself, but that wasn't what made it unusual. What made it unusual was that Nina had never gotten right in *anybody's* face before, never gone full-tilt at anyone, if you don't count D.S., and that was like going full-tilt at a baggie of Jell-O. Later on she told JannaRose that through it all, she never had any idea of where what she did next or where what she said came from. She was as amazed as everybody by everything that happened. And at that moment, after she told the kid he was going to have to back out of there, she felt as if she was in one of those scenes she'd seen in movies where everything suddenly freezes. Where nobody can move at all.

Until — she was so startled, she jumped, everybody did — some guy came out of nowhere and slipped up beside her. He was wearing a grey plastic windbreaker zipped all the way up and his pants were so wrinkly and bunched they didn't even reach down as far as his socks. She'd never seen him before, that she could remember, even though it turned out he was the welfare inspector who put the ladder up every night and spied on her through the little clear spot he'd rubbed on the window to see if she had a man on the premises.

"We know what you're up to," he sneered in a menacing whisper. Her eyes popped wide open as she tried to figure out what was going on. "But it won't work. So," he sneered, "you can just forget it." And he ran away, scrunching his shoulders around his ears so nobody would recognize him.

"Who the hell was that?" D.S. shouted.

"Why don't you shut up?" she shouted back. "I'm busy."

The ice cream kid sounded like he didn't know what to do. With cars parked on both sides, barely one whole lane was open. "Back up?" he said.

"Bet you could take out one of the headlights." Whenever JannaRose got the feeling that things were going to spin out of her grasp, she tried to tone them down, so it was entirely understandable that she would suggest a moderate alternative.

Nina knew what she was getting at, but it went right past D.S. "Don't you encourage her," he yelled.

"Uh-uh," Nina told JannaRose.

"What'd she say?" D.S. shouted.

What she'd said was all JannaRose needed to hear to understand that this wasn't some spur-of-the-moment, completely out-of-her-freaking-mind moment. That Nina wasn't held in a death grip by some irrational, violent impulse. What she'd said was *Why settle for the two dollars you find on the sidewalk when you can use it to buy a lottery ticket and go for all the millions?* "Okay," JannaRose said, sounding as if she was passing every single ounce of faith she had over to her friend, and moving out of the way.

Nina hauled the crutch back again. She hauled it back farther. She hauled it back as far as she could.

D.S. groaned. But the possibility that he might do anything more than that, already slight since having his neighbours see him wearing the wig and nightie always made him worry that they might not take him as seriously as they should, became absolute zero when the man who'd snuck up beside Nina and whispered to her appeared beside the porch.

"We don't like lesbos, either," he sneered as D.S. gaped at him uncomprehendingly. "Just because there's nothing in the law about lesbos sharing a residence with a welfare recipient doesn't mean we like them." The way he wrote in his notebook made D.S. think he was trying to stab it to death with his ballpoint. "We don't like them," he hissed, and giving D.S. a menacing glare, he scampered away.

Nina clenched her teeth. She waggled the crutch. She took a deep breath. She rose way up on one toe. She squeezed one eye into a slit and took dead aim at the exact spot where the kid's nose was behind the glass.

D.S. groaned louder.

She focused every particle of her being. And swung as hard as she could.

She spun around so wildly, she landed on her butt. She'd spun around because she missed the windshield. She missed the windshield because the truck was no longer in range.

It was backing up.

It swerved one way then another, collecting side mirrors from parked cars. She wasn't surprised. She'd figured the kid was driving it for the first time that morning. It looked as if it was the first time he'd had it in reverse.

The girls came down from the porch looking so hurt that she told them they made her feel like she'd used the crutch to beat their new puppy to death. Since they'd never had a puppy, or a pet of any kind, she said it in the hopes of giving them the kind of emotional perspective that would help them deal with the far more despicable thing they'd seen her do. But they made it clear she was wasting her breath. Her shoulders sagged. Behind her, down the street where she'd kept the truck from going, there were nasty shouts. Harsh adult voices started rising above the tear-filled wails of children. The voices shouted "Ignorant bitch!" and "Mind your own business, you cunt!"

JannaRose gave them the finger, then seeing Nina making her way sadly between parked cars, hurried after her. "What was that all about?" she said.

"They" — Nina's shoulders sagged even more. "Their kids ... I guess they really wanted them to hear their names called out."

"No. *All* that stuff. With the truck and the crutch and everything."

"Yeah!" D.S. was scowling. "What the fuck was that all about?"

Nina rounded on him. "You watch your language, D.S.," she said and began herding the girls into the house with little flaps of her arms.

"Tired?" JannaRose said, plopping down on the step beside Nina. It was the next morning.

"No!"

"You were asleep."

"No, no. I was trying not to sweat. I was concentrating." Nina opened her eyes so wide they bugged out. "But I keep falling asleep."

Nina had gotten out of bed long before the electric tootles and personalized sales pitches to the little children could be heard. She'd sat outside and let her anger pump up like another set of lungs. Now, here was the truck, almost on top of her.

"Aw, shit." Knots of kids pressed right out on the road, hardly able to wait for it to stop. Every one held up a fist stuffed with money.

Her front door opened and the three biggest girls came out. A weird creature with four legs and two heads teetered across from Zanielle's house: it was Fabreece and Zanielle, still Velcroed together. When the truck called Zanielle's name out along with the names of her two brothers, the mix of pure happiness and despair on her face made Nina's insides clench. "That's you!" Fabreece said in wonderment, and they tightened their holds on each other.

JannaRose spoke sharply. "You stay right there!" She pointed across at the three kids who had tumbled out on her step. "I'm warning you!"

"Mom?" Merlina said.

"No," Nina told her, without looking around.

Then the truck spoke to them. To Guinevere and Merlina and Lady and Fabreece. And to JannaRose's Jewell and Eddie Jr. and Tyrone. It said they were missing out on some really delicious things, things they would absolutely love. Things other kids would give anything to taste. Their favourites.

JannaRose whipped across the street and grabbed her three in a bear hug.

"Mom?"

"You heard me the first time," Nina said. Today there were two people in the truck. Somebody was in the passenger seat and they didn't move from it when the driver went to the side counter to handle business.

"He's got backup," JannaRose shouted, trying to keep hold of her armful.

The truck drifted slowly past. Really slowly. The passenger was holding a baseball bat. The driver brandished one of his own. They both kept their eyes on Nina.

"Jesus," she said.

"They're wearing, like, football helmets." JannaRose sounded as if it was the most amazing thing ever. "You see that?"

THREE

Not even Nina could say exactly when the idea of robbing a bank came to her, but it looks as if it was introduced into the process when the subject of robbing banks started coming up all the time in conversation. This happened after she concluded that the only way to stop the direct-sales ice cream truck permanently would be to organize an attack on the lot where the trucks were parked overnight. This would teach the ice cream company a lesson about the economic situation in SuEz in general, and in her house in particular.

She never passed up a chance to teach economic lessons along this line, although this was the first time it had occurred to her to reach beyond her immediate family and JannaRose, who usually didn't mind as much as her children. It was hard to say which of her daughters was the whiniest, Guinevere or Merlina. But they whined in different ways. Gwinny whined about how everything that happened in the world was designed to ruin her life. Merly whined about things that Nina would have liked to do something about if she possibly could. She had no idea where to begin when it came to setting Gwinny straight, but with Merly she waded right in.

"We don't have any money," she said when Merly asked why they couldn't at least once buy some things the ice cream company made exclusively for them.

"You always have a bit," Merly said.

"But every day I somehow —"

"A little bit."

" — every day I somehow manage to come up with something for you to eat."

"Today the truck is like, 'Merlina, too bad you can't have this fabulous Pecan Frosted Freeze-O-Reeno.' That would have made me happy. You never think about making me happy."

"I don't want you to starve and get sick. So today I'll find something else for you and for your sisters."

"Who cares about them?"

"We all do."

"Fuckin' assholes."

"What?"

"Nothing."

"What did you just say?"

"Nothing."

Not that worrying about Guinevere didn't take up a lot of her time. Mainly it was because Gwinny lived so much in a dream world, even if her dreams kept bumping into the plain facts of SuEz, that it started Nina thinking about how, if the school pool was opened for kids in the summer, a lot of excess and dangerous energy could get burned off. But when she tried to talk to the authorities about it, they pointed out that the reason the pool wasn't open the rest of the year either was that the filtration system and the heater and those kinds of things were so old and worn out that they didn't work. Or they worked, but not up to the required standards, and had been condemned by the health department.

Things did start to happen, though. Immediately after Nina raised the subject, the pool's windows and doors got boarded up. And that night somebody stole the boards. Then the windows got stolen, and the doors, and more boards got put over the openings, and those boards got stolen. All the stuff inside got stolen: the lifeguard's tall chair, the safety equipment, the benches, the folding bleachers, the scoreboard from when there had been swim meets, the clock-timers, the glass out of the pool office window, the office furniture. Then the heating equipment and the filtration system. Those were substantial items. Nobody could just walk away with them. It was after the big ventilators got stolen off the roof that the windows and doors got bricked up, and this was why whoever stole the water had to smash their way through with a sledgehammer.

The ice cream truck was starting to insult the girls personally. They were getting bored and crabby and it wasn't even summer yet. Guinevere was already fourteen, and the word was that lots of girls that age, although if it was girls everywhere or just in SuEz wasn't clear — anyway, Nina heard they gave out blowjobs like she didn't know what.

She was talking about this to JannaRose, about how she'd sat Gwinny down. "And I told her that oral you-knows would —"

"Oral you-knows?"

"Oral you-knows. It's not easy to come out and say some things to your fourteen-year-old daughter."

"What'd she say?"

"She said, 'You mean blowjobs?'"

"My goodness," JannaRose said.

"Fuck you, too," Nina replied.

"At least they're better than getting knocked up."

"No! Yes! No, I'd just rather she ... why can't ... that she —"

"Good luck," JannaRose said.

"So you know what she said then? She said, 'At least with blowjobs you don't get pregnant.'"

"I cannot believe it."

"The point is," Nina said, not wanting JannaRose to get the impression she was a moron, "if somebody started giving blowjobs all over the place, guys would get really interested and start taking her here and there. And the next thing anybody knew, she'd be up in the towers working for a living." So many apartments in the towers were empty and had been taken over by drug dealers and whores that she sometimes doubted there were any that people just lived in.

"You think it might be a nutrition thing?" JannaRose said. "If all we give our kids to eat is potato chips, it might not be the thing they need to grow up to be astronauts."

Nina stared at her for a long time, but JannaRose was looking down, trying to smooth her T-shirt over her stomach, and didn't notice. Finally, Nina gave up. "So," she said, "it would probably be good to find something to keep her mind off it."

JannaRose wasn't entirely distracted, though. "Like swimming?" she said.

Nina bristled. "You don't have to say it like that."

"I didn't say it like anything." JannaRose's voice took on a flinty edge. "I just said it."

Nina let it drop. It wasn't that she didn't realize that maybe it wasn't the ideal solution. She realized it wasn't whenever she said it to herself. Even when she said it to herself, it sounded like she was a moron.

Ed Oataway never did understand why his family car had featured so prominently in whatever happened with JannaRose and Dipshit Dolgoy's idiot wife at the lot where the ice cream company parked its trucks. In fact, he'd never managed to figure out anything about what went on down there, and nobody was about to tell him. It was the same with D.S. Even Nina had eventually realized that the thing she herself originally thought was the point didn't cover everything that actually happened that night. Not when she added it all together. And to be perfectly honest, she really hadn't expected to accomplish anything. What she'd expected was the same as she expected with everything she ever did before: not much. There hadn't been a day in her life when it occurred to her to expect very much of anything, and nothing had come along to cause her to think otherwise. Then here, by accident, she'd driven off toward the ice cream company, and what happened turned out to be as far from not accomplishing anything as was possible. It was so different from everything else she'd ever done that it got her started examining a lot of things about her life that up till then she'd thought were basically no use at all.

What happened in the ice cream company parking lot wasn't really very hard to describe. On the other hand, it was terrifyingly complicated.

What happened was, she created an absolute shitstorm.

Ed Oataway's family car was complicated enough to begin with. Ed had refined his trade to where he only stole cars from people who paid to have them stolen. They did this for insurance purposes. He liked the work. There was no competition, and obviously no one was interested in calling the cops in the middle of one of his daring daylight vehicular extractions, as he called them. This meant stress was non-existent. He collected a percentage of what the individual whose car he stole paid for the job, and he held on to the car until what he referred to as the parent organization hauled it away, he figured, for the international junk trade. It was a nice little business. And it was because of the stresslessness that he'd started considering whichever of these cars happened to be waiting for trans-shipment in front of his house to be the Oataway family car. So he didn't mind if JannaRose used it to go buy potato chips for the kids' supper. Neither did he mind if she got Nina to drive for her, since JannaRose didn't have a licence and got nervous driving a car with such imprecise ownership.

The one available for the assault on the ice cream company was an old brown Pontiac that was in such terrible shape, it wouldn't even begin to turn until the steering wheel got cranked a quarter of the way around. Nina said just keeping it in a straight line was like wrestling with somebody who was having a shit fit. All the way to the ice cream factory she kept wanting to grab JannaRose by the arm and yell, *"Why would anybody steal this fuckin' thing?"* What kept her from doing it was that JannaRose was already so spooked by the feeling that something awful was going to happen that it would have really upset her. When Nina considered how nervous she was herself, she didn't want to push things any farther than she secretly planned to push them.

"What are you doing?" JannaRose's voice sounded quavery as they passed the parking lot full of ice cream trucks for the second time.

"I told you. Looking." Nina hauled this way and that on the steering wheel and bounced off the curb a couple of times when she finally pulled over. She got out and tried the gate. It didn't budge. Back in the car, she glared at the fence.

"I was just thinking," JannaRose said.

Nina glared at JannaRose.

"I was just," JannaRose said again, "thinking that here, wherever we are, in some part of town we've never been before — that if something happened. And we got killed and they stole all our stuff. How will anybody know it's our bodies?"

Nina glared at the fence.

"They sometimes use dental records, don't they?" JannaRose said. "I saw it on television."

That was when Nina decided that for sure it wasn't a scouting expedition. They were going to go ahead and do it. They might never get another chance.

"But," JannaRose said, "if you haven't been to the dentist in — I don't know. I went once when I was little. One came to the school and looked at our teeth. She was a lady dentist. But," she said, "what good will that do? I bet she didn't even keep records."

Nina decided something else, too. If they were going to do it, they better do it quick. JannaRose was getting freaky. Any minute she was going to start babbling about never seeing her kids again. About how she hadn't kissed them goodbye.

"When was the last time you did?" JannaRose said.

"What?"

"Went to a dentist."

"*I don't know, goddamn it!*"

But she didn't say it. Not like that. JannaRose would have blown to pieces right on the spot.

"I don't know," she whispered. She had to. It was the only way she could keep her voice under control.

For awhile they sat in silence. JannaRose thought they were both thinking about teeth, so it shocked her when Nina hammered her fist on the steering wheel and put the shift in drive.

"*Now* what're you doing?"

Getting into that parking lot. She almost felt as if she had nothing to do with whatever was going to happen from here on. There wasn't any actual plan. No Step One leading to Step Two leading to … Kaboom! Once again, some power way down inside her, so deep she'd only just discovered it, was in control. A force more potent than anything she'd ever known. She was perfectly capable of making herself stop breathing, except as soon as she stopped thinking about not breathing, she started breathing again. But she was doing this without thinking even slightly. Like she was just part of what was happening. If she didn't do it, it would be as if she held her breath for so long that she died. And that was impossible.

"Why are you crashing into the gate?"

She wasn't crashing into it. She was pushing it open.

The gate was built to swing open like a door, but the padlock refused to give. "Holy shit!" JannaRose watched the nose of the car press against the chain link. She watched the chain link stretch the way a balloon does when you press your finger into it. The frame of the gate started bending. "Holy shit!"

JannaRose's voice sounded like it was a long way away. Nina dropped the shift into low and stomped on the gas.

The chain link just kept on bulging. Then the balloon burst. "Holy shit!" The car jumped forward. Metal fenceposts ripped out of the ground. The gate slumped flat under the Pontiac. Long sections of fence came down on either side, and the car screeched. Bucked. *Jerked* to a stop. Nina floored it. It wouldn't back up, either. She tried rocking it, forward, back. The engine roared, metal squealed, otherwise nothing. It wasn't going to move.

"Aw, for fuck's sakes," she said.

"Holy shit!" JannaRose kept saying it, over and over.

Nina opened the door and leaned way out, trying to see underneath. It was hard to do. Broken strands of chain link fencing grabbed at her hair, scratched her face. It was this wire, combined with jackknifed pieces of the fence's frame, that had grabbed the bottom of the car. Other strands wrapped around the wheels, the axles, the muffler, all the mysterious stuff down there. Every possible thing the wire could get tangled around was held solid, every which way. She couldn't see any of this, though. The only light in the parking lot was on the wall of the ice cream factory, making it extra dark and shadowy under the car. But if she hadn't struggled to climb out the door and to stand up — because of the tangle of twisty metal that made it impossible to find steady footing, a lot of struggling was necessary — if she had just kept hanging out the door there for another second or so, she would have had a much better idea about the situation they were in. Because in just a few more seconds, a light did appear down there. A little light. A little light from a little blue flame even smaller than the flame on a birthday candle. It flickered to life and illuminated, faintly, the impossible jumble the car was trapped in. The little blue light fluttered and danced on the hot exhaust pipe, fed by gasoline that was dripping from the hole the fence wire had poked in the fuel tank. But she wouldn't have seen this light for more than an instant, because she would have been blinded by the flash. There was a deafening explosion, too, but the only sound she remembered was the sickening crack her head made hitting the asphalt when the blast knocked her down.

Vaguely … when she floated up into consciousness, she could vaguely make out a voice going "Yiiiiii-i-i-i!" Oh Jesus, JannaRose was hurt! Wait. It wasn't JannaRose's voice. It was hers. She stopped shrieking. It wasn't easy, but she forced herself. Only she could still hear it! "Yiiiiii-i-i-i!"

Now *that* was JannaRose. And now she could see her. She didn't look hurt, though. She looked hysterical. She was pressed up against one of the ice cream trucks, screaming at the flames like a crazy person.

The flames!

The whole world was in flames!

No. That was wrong. The whole world wasn't. It just looked like that at first. The only thing in flames was Ed Oataway's stupid, stolen old brown Pontiac.

It was a long walk, but Ed Oataway didn't care that it was almost two in the morning when they got back. He came out and stood in the middle of the street yelling how come his car had exploded, and what were they doing with it way over there anyway.

"Can I help it if he's missing the point?" Nina said to D.S. That wasn't what worried her, though. What worried her was that he might smack JannaRose around. But all he did was yell at Nina about how if she had any guts she'd step out there and he'd pound her head in. That was why she told D.S. not to bother going out and making him shut up, since what Ed was doing didn't matter even slightly. D.S. explained that he had no intention of making Ed Oataway shut up, because there were times when a man had to blow off whatever was putting too much pressure on his mind. What he wanted to do was advise him as a friend that he better not tempt Nina to step out there, because if she did she would break him in two. D.S. said that was why Ed wasn't about to smack JannaRose around and why he never had: she outweighed him about three to one and was half again as tall, and if he tried anything she would break him in two even quicker than Nina could.

Nina rocked her head back and forth like something had come loose inside and told D.S. that he was missing the point, too. But D.S. didn't listen, and Ed whanged him in the face so hard with one of the hubcaps that was always lying beside the curb that it knocked his wig flying. When the welfare inspector hammered on her door, Ed had gone back to yelling about what he'd do if she would only step out there, and D.S. was lying on the road moaning.

"Hey, lady," the welfare inspector hollered when nobody answered the door, "there's something about that dyke you're having an affair with that you might not know." With him and Ed both shouting, he failed to hear D.S. come up the steps behind him. Getting whanged in the face with the hubcap had started D.S.'s nose bleeding, and blood was dripping down his nightie from between his fingers. His unexpected arrival startled the welfare inspector so much he nearly jumped off the porch, but once he calmed down he spoke accusingly. "I'm making note of this incident," he informed D.S., "which has led me to observe that you are not a dyke, as I had originally thought. That buzzcut," he said, "that you have been hiding under your wig, plus taking into account your unshaven legs and propensity to engage in acts of physical violence with your neighbour, makes it clear that what you actually are is a *bull* dyke. And I wish to assure you," he said, "that the welfare department will not tolerate this, especially considering that children are —"

"Excuse me," D.S. blurbled through a handful of blood. Stepping around the inspector, he opened the door, went inside, and shut it again. After awhile the inspector went away, leaving only Ed Oataway making a fuss. And he was gone when JannaRose looked out in the morning.

JannaRose told Nina that because he was required to pay the parent company a premium for having lost the car he'd stolen, he'd driven up to visit Nina's brother Frank in the penitentiary. He hoped that Frank might have some kind of an idea that would help him out of the jam Nina had gotten him into. JannaRose was especially careful not to put it the way Ed had when he announced where he was going, which was, "to see that fuckin' lunatic woman's asshole brother."

Nina could hardly believe it anyway. From one extreme — really stupid — where JannaRose's personal safety could have been endangered because he might possibly have let his violent instincts take control of his actions, Ed Oataway had swung to the other extreme — really, really stupid. When she came right out and asked, "Does he honestly think my asshole brother might know anything about anything?" JannaRose pretended not to hear the question.

But thanks to Ed going to see him, she found out that her brother had a bank robbery lined up for when he got released, which he expected to be soon, having completed three of the eleven years he'd been doing for fraud. For awhile after that, nobody talked about anything else.

FOUR

The failure of her next welfare cheque to show up should not be understated as a factor in Nina's decision to raise charitable funds by alternative means. This made it six months in a row that she hadn't been able to cash one. "It's tough enough being a welfare queen even when the money is rolling in," she said.

She called about it, not expecting to reach anybody at the welfare department, but due to some freak circumstance, somebody answered the phone on the second day. She'd spent all the day before waiting because a machine kept telling her that her call was important to them, but the next day's breakthrough occurred when she'd only been on hold for five hours.

There was a welfare office in the underground mall at the high-rise towers, and she wasn't at all afraid of being around The Intersection in the daytime, so she could have gone in person. But every time she did, the line of people waiting trailed out the door, past the empty windows of the shops that had gone out of business, and up the stairs and out on to the street. It seemed to her that there was something pointless about getting in that line, since it was always exactly the same. It never moved. It was always the same people in the same places. Once people started waiting in that line, they never quit. She said this was because standing in it had given their lives some positive direction, maybe even a purpose. As long as they did it, they had an identity that wasn't limited to being poor and getting screwed by the welfare department. They had become the kind of people who did *something* about what was happening to them — who *actively* did something. They were seekers of justice, correctors of errors, unwilling to be victimized more than they already had been, believers in the rights of individuals, and bound and determined to get theirs. They would resent anybody who suggested they were wasting their time, resent it so much they would become a howling bloody-eyed mob that dragged whoever questioned them into the line — because the last thing they were ever going to do was leave it and lose their places — and tore them limb from limb. So no matter how careful Nina was about putting her observation into words, it would still amount to her calling them a bunch of dumb fucks, and who likes that?

The person who answered the phone put Nina through to the wrong extension which, by coincidence, turned out to be the chief welfare inspector's office, so she figured she might as well take advantage of the opportunity and complain about the welfare inspector who was spying through her bedroom window and confronting her on the street with vague threats and anti-gay slurs. She punched in her welfare ID number as instructed, and a computerized voice informed her that the registered client — "Nina. Carson. Dolgoy" — had been the victim of identity theft. It

informed her that her last cheque had been diverted and/
or intercepted and cashed by a person representing himself/
herself as the previously named "Nina. Carson. Dolgoy."
Since the caller was evidently in possession of the Nina.
Carson. Dolgoy welfare ID number, the caller was evidently
the identity thief, or the recipient of materials acquired by
identity theft, and must immediately turn himself/herself in
at the nearest police station.

Nina dropped the phone. Leaning her head against the
tamper-proof coinbox, she watched it swing back and forth
and the end of its vandal-proof cord.

Of all the things that had been going on lately, it was hard
for JannaRose to say which surprised her most, but finding
this working payphone was right up there. So was finding
it in the basement mall at the towers, considering that even
the toilets had been smashed in the public washrooms down
there, although it hadn't stopped people from using them.
And finding the same telephone the next morning, still
working, was something she never would have predicted.
But Nina said it made sense if anybody bothered to think
about it. The gangsters would want at least one guaranteed
way of communicating in case their mobile phones went
dead, and there was nobody handy to steal one from. On
the other hand, Nina had to agree that once she got through
to whatever it was she got through to, although all she got
do was punch in some numbers, the transaction went on
a lot longer than any she'd ever heard of before. If things
kept going like that, the next thing she knew, the welfare
department would be coming around to where she lived,
bringing her a nice lunch, and doing her wash.

"Identity theft?" JannaRose said.

"Somebody stole my identity and cashed my last cheque."

"But they didn't send out your last cheque because your
name was spelled wrong —"

"That's right."

"— and if you signed it, it would've amounted to forgery, and that would be a crime, and the welfare department —"

"Yes."

"— didn't want to be a party to a crime. But somebody cashed it?"

"Yes."

"Unless," JannaRose said, "they sent out another cheque with your name spelled right and you cashed it. But," she said, "you have no memory of it because you immediately lost the money, which caused you to have a stroke. Or," she said, "you had a stroke and can't remember getting the money."

"Don't stop now, sweetie pie," Nina said.

"But wouldn't that mean you must have stolen —"

"Yes?"

"— your own identity?"

"Yes!" Nina pumped her fist.

JannaRose spread her fingers over her mouth. "That's awful. How can you prove you're the you the possible replacement cheque was issued to, and not —"

Nina sighed.

"— the you that stole your own identity and used it to cash the cheque? If it was two people, you and an identity thief, then it would be your word against theirs. But," JannaRose said, "if there's just one of you, and you stole you own identity, then it's your word against yourself. And who's going to believe you?"

As screwups went, the only thing this one had going for it was that it was one Nina had never heard of before. It wasn't like she and D.S. and the girls would get evicted for not paying the rent if the cheques didn't start coming soon. They already didn't pay rent. And nobody was going to bother evicting them, since the bulldozer was about to knock the house down to make way for apartment buildings. For all she knew, it had happened while she was away phoning the welfare department.

The last time she got an actual cheque and had turned it into actual cash, she'd taken snippets of the money and hidden them around the house to keep D.S. from finding it in one lump sum and spending it on god knows what. Last night she'd been up till all hours looking for some of those hiding places, figuring maybe she hadn't found them all, since she was sure she'd hidden more money than she'd been able to track down so far, which was none. Not being able to find even fifty cents made her start to panic — her chest got tight, her ears filled with a buzzy, tingling sound. She searched the whole house twice more before giving up. If she hadn't given up, she was going to start ripping out the baseboards. That would have been poke-your-own-eyes-out insanity, because she knew she hadn't done anything like rip the baseboards off to hide it in the first place. Still, the feeling weighed on her that when she got home, she was going to turn the place inside out again.

Walking home from the towers, she squinted at their rooflines. She couldn't hear any bees, although maybe it was impossible right down there. It could be they had to travel a ways before they started making the noise that sounded like a sheet being torn in half. Or it could be there weren't any at the moment. Neither she nor JannaRose bought for one minute the idea some people had that there weren't any at all, that they were one of those urban myths. She and JannaRose mostly heard them when they lay in bed at night, unable to sleep. D.S. used to say he didn't believe they existed, because why would anybody fire high-powered rounds over SuEz and not aim them anywhere else in the city? If bullets were flying over the rest of town, there would be big complaints. Nobody else would stand for it. The police would be all over the place. Although most of the people in Nina's house said afterwards that they didn't remember, she knew full well a lot of them heard them when Frank showed up the night after he got out of jail. That's why they'd all gone outside and stared into the black sky: those ripping noises. More bees at one time than she'd ever heard. Maybe it had gotten blotted out of their memories by the shock of realizing it was the last time any of them ever laid eyes on her brother.

She slumped along, wondering if, even though you couldn't hear bee noises this close to the towers, you wouldn't at least hear some other noises associated with them that maybe didn't carry as far as her house. Then she turned around so suddenly that JannaRose almost crashed head-on into her.

"Why would anybody steal the water?" The question came right out of the blue and wiped out everything else she'd been thinking.

"What water?" JannaRose said.

"The pool water."

"What pool?"

"The high school pool. What fuckin' pool did you think?"

"Somebody stole the water?"

Nina tried to collect her thoughts. Stealing water made sense. As much sense as stealing anything else did. Oh, no it didn't. Not this water. This wasn't ordinary water. Steal ordinary water, sure. Put it in plastic bottles. Sell it to fuckin' idiots. Make a fuckin' fortune. Lots of people do that. She was always telling the girls, drink it out of the tap. "It's not the same!" Get an empty plastic bottle, fill it with water out of the tap. "It's not the same!" Who'll know? "It's not the same!" It's the fuckin' same. "It's not the same!"

This wasn't the same. This was swimming pool water. *Water out of the swimming pool.* It was *filthy*. When she thought how filthy it was, it made her want to puke. *It was water people had pissed in!* It wasn't even fresh filthy water. It

had been there since the pool got shut down — what? Two
years ago? All she could remember was how bad everybody
stank when they came out of that water. She wouldn't swim
in it. She wouldn't have let her girls swim in it.

JannaRose tried to suggest possible natural causes.
"Maybe the pool got a crack in it? Could be it leaked away.
Could be there was an earthquake."

Nina laughed. She couldn't believe anybody could be
so dumb.

"So what happened, then?" JannaRose asked.

"They smashed a hole in the wall. Ran in a hose. Pumped
it into a truck."

"How do you know?"

"It's obvious."

"Why is it obvious?"

"Because they couldn't haul it all away *without* a truck."

They started walking again, and for a long time neither
of them said anything. Somehow it was a heavier kind of
silence than Nina was accustomed to. She was already feeling
guilty for having gone apeshit about the stolen water and
implying that JannaRose wasn't terrifically bright for not
being as aware of the pool situation as she should have been.
This had come right after JannaRose showed how sweet and
loyal a friend she was — spending almost two days keeping
Nina company while she phoned to try and get action out of
the welfare department. It was to lighten this uncomfortable
atmosphere that she decided to pass along a humorous
sidelight to their attack on the ice cream company that only
she knew about. It would make JannaRose laugh and feel
better about everything. It even related to a conversation
Nina had actually considered having with JannaRose on
their way to the ice cream factory, a conversation about
Tampax and the possibility of using some to blow up one of
the trucks. But what with one thing and another —

"Tampax?" JannaRose looked stunned, although nowhere near as stunned as she would be when she thought about the significance of what Nina was saying in terms of their unspoken pact that they told each other everything the minute it crossed their minds.

"Wouldn't it have been *something?*" Nina said.

"The fuck do you mean Tampax?"

"Strung together," Nina said. "I could've slid them down into the gas tank of an ice cream truck. Once they got soaked with gas, I'd light the end. Boom! I had a bunch of them already tied together in my pocket."

"You told me you didn't even plan the thing with Ed's car. That it came to you out of nowhere. That we were just on a scouting expedition."

"Yeah. This was just in case."

"Just in *case?*"

What did this all mean? Could it be that from the start, from when they pulled away from JannaRose's house, Nina had known that if she couldn't get the gate unlocked, she'd bust it down with the Pontiac, pull out her Tampax string, and blow up an ice cream truck? Read between the lines and could it be you'd see how she had it all worked out? Read between the lines and could it be you'd see that Nina didn't count on JannaRose in every situation? Maybe it would be a good idea if she was a little more careful about Nina in certain circumstances. "Maybe" — she grabbed Nina's sleeve — "maybe it'd be a lot safer for everybody if we just wrote a letter to the mayor or somebody."

Nina blinked a very slow blink. "A letter?"

"About the ice cream company. About getting them to stop calling out the kids' names and putting pressure on everybody."

"You ever write a letter?"

JannaRose didn't say anything.

"To *anybody?*"

JannaRose looked so close to sinking right into the ground that Nina stopped herself from saying, "So who the fuck are *you* to talk about writing some kind of fuckin' letter?" Finally she just said, "I've got a feeling it would be a waste of time." And again she stopped walking. Only this time, she stood completely still, not moving a muscle. An idea as hot as a welding rod had nailed her square in the forehead. "Because," she said slowly, "because nobody," she said, "listens to people like us."

Nina closed her eyes, trying to get the idea cooled down and settled in one place. "So why bother trying to get somebody else to listen?" She grabbed JannaRose by the shoulders. "So why bother with anybody else at all?"

She started hopping up and down. "Who needs them?" she shouted. "Who *needs* them?"

Whatever was happening in her brain was making her realize something so totally contrary to anything that had ever occurred to her before that she had to struggle to keep from falling over backwards.

"What's the matter?" JannaRose had never seen anybody who looked so much like they'd just stuck themselves into a light socket and turned on the switch.

"I'm — I'm — I — it — *it just came to me.*"

"What, for Christ's sakes?"

Nina drew herself up as much as she could. She looked into her friend's eyes. She looked so deeply, it was as if she was staring right through her head and out the back. She spoke slowly, and very clearly.

"That being a welfare queen —"

JannaRose nodded. Waiting for it. Ready. "Yes?"

"That being a welfare queen doesn't have to be a dead end," Nina said.

FIVE

Maybe you had to be a welfare queen to get the full impact.

D.S. was the only person Nina knew of on their street, except for Krystal Beach who drove a courier service van, with an actual paying job. Krystal, unfortunately, had gone kind of crazy as a result of the emotional setbacks she kept suffering as a result of being stalked by both her ex-husbands. And D.S. hadn't been paid when he was off work as a result of injury. Total, the world's biggest discount store, where he worked as a greeter, said that if he wanted financial assistance for being disabled, he should sue the customers that kicked his head in.

Nina could never shake her suspicion that JannaRose and Ed Oataway were in something like a loving relationship. On the other hand, it did have a financial upside. They got a welfare combo — Ed qualified because he wasn't suitable employment material. Nobody would hire him because the half a dozen times he'd been in jail for car theft had given employers the idea that he was some kind of habitual criminal. When Nina got her innards twisted because of something or other Ed Oataway did, she'd remind D.S. that Ed's criminal record was entirely due to him being lousy at stealing cars unless the owners paid him to do it. But the plain fact was that JannaRose and Ed appeared to have feelings that she couldn't detect in any other relationships she knew of offhand.

She and D.S. certainly weren't like that and never had been. Not after the first couple of weeks anyway, when Nina stopped believing any of the lies she'd been telling herself. As far as she could figure, they'd only gotten together because everybody they knew was sleeping with somebody except them. And it wasn't as if either of them had ever been regarded with much interest by anybody else. So they drifted toward each other. There was no denying that even then he almost always had some kind of a paying job, even if none of them ever paid enough for him to move out of his mother's apartment. With Nina's welfare cheque, he could afford to live with her in her mother's apartment.

Nina always said she would rather have been able to find a job, because there wasn't a job she knew of that was harder work than being on welfare. She said that even if the job was full-time, it wouldn't have taken as much of her time as being on welfare did. Just keeping yourself on it took every bit of your attention. And if you weren't on top of it every minute, you were liable to find yourself kicked off. Even if you did manage to stay right on top of it, you were still liable to find yourself kicked off. She said being a welfare queen called for total commitment.

Jarmeel Tolbert, whose little girl was such good friends with Fabreece, worked what Nina considered to be full-time, except the work consisted of trying to get a pension for the Post-Traumatic Stress Disorder he came down with in the army. His failure to obtain a pension after having his nerves crippled in the wartime service of his nation was enough to leave him as disabled emotionally as D.S. was physically, and should by rights have entitled him to the disability payments D.S. couldn't get every time his head got kicked in. D.S. said the difference was that what happened to him at Total was in the private sector, but this never seemed to comfort Jarmeel. Neither did the welfare cheques, which was all he got. He got those for being a single parent who was raising three children he'd had by three different women who all packed up and moved out, abandoning him with the babies shortly after each one was born. Either one of these on its own — that he kept on getting married again, or that he kept on getting abandoned again — was all the evidence Nina and JannaRose needed that he should qualify for far more than the standard disability, even though the diagnosis of crazy fucker wasn't listed on any of the forms.

When he mentioned his situation to counsellors, the only thing they ever suggested was confining him to an institution, but this made him even more upset because, as he explained to them every time, what had damaged his brain in the first place was confinement to an institution — the army.

In any event, when something came over Nina as powerful as a purpose that went beyond the needs of her own girls, even though it meant they would be able to go swimming without too much inconvenience, Jarmeel couldn't avoid being affected. It didn't matter to him if the person behind the community-wide effort was the bughouse woman Dipper was married to. It was a simple case of something fitting perfectly, and what fit was an idea he'd been kicking around for some time. As far as Jarmeel could see, there was no religion anywhere that didn't take in a lot of money. Add to that how hard it was to imagine that he was the only person on Earth who had genuinely been kidnapped and probed by space aliens. Therefore, if enough of the others could be gathered together, they could easily become the foundation for a pretty good faith, one with the unique advantage of appealing to Catholics and Protestants and Jews. There were likely even Muslims who'd go for it. And if this new religion directed a percentage of its financial intake to a worthwhile community project, it would be perfectly all right with him even if, as he put it to D.S., "I don't give a shit about some swimming pool one way or the other, no offence."

In the quiet moments, when she wasn't yelling so hard at the traffic that was making her life as the driver of a ConGlom Couriers van difficult that she came close to blacking out, Krystal Beach dreamed of getting rich quick. She liked this dream because she knew she had no other choice. She was never going to get rich slow. When it came to get-rich-quick schemes, though, every single one had a flaw. It was Step Two. Step Two always required you to pay some money to the people who were operating the scheme, sometimes a lot of money. Step Two always shattered Krystal's dream. Any amount of money was too much. It wouldn't have been so bad if she was on welfare. As a driver for ConGlom Couriers, she made one-third less for a fifty-five hour week than she would have made per week on welfare. That's because she didn't have any dependants. With dependants she could have made twice as much on welfare as she did working. She was glad she wasn't on welfare, though. She despised welfare because it rewarded lazy fuckers and destroyed their initiative. And because they were lazy fuckers and had no initiative, she despised people on welfare. The thing she was proudest of was working for a living, because it gave her the initiative to be constantly on the lookout for a get-rich-quick scheme that would make it possible for her to quit work and spend the rest of her life sitting around doing nothing.

Despising welfare recipients made her life awkward, because the only people she knew were welfare recipients or crooks, and she had no use at all for crooks. It could be she'd have some different social contacts if she moved out of SuEz, but she'd never lived anywhere else and couldn't imagine it. In her dream of sitting around doing nothing, she pictured it happening in what looked like SuEz, but fixed up a bit. And with more people around that she liked, although at the moment the only people she liked were welfare recipients, but then there wasn't anybody else to choose except crooks.

True, some of these welfare recipients were different than the ones she generally despised. Even one or two of the crooks were different, such as Nina Dolgoy's good-looking brother Frank, who was rumoured to be planning to rob a bank when he got out of jail, which he was supposed to soon. And Nina would have been crazy not to be on welfare. She had four little girls to feed and wouldn't have been able to do it on whatever she could make working. Nina's husband D.S. gave Krystal a pain, but he did have the saving grace of a paying job. Krystal admired him for this. As far as she was concerned, this compensated for Nina scamming the welfare department, since nobody was allowed to live with her who wasn't a complete dependant.

She also couldn't help but admire Nina for her generosity in allowing D.S. to keep on living with her whenever he was off work as a result of having been badly injured by an enraged customer when he was on the job. Because this happened so often — Krystal estimated he was off work five, maybe six times as much as he wasn't — it meant that most of the time there was less money to feed Nina and the girls. She also knew how embarrassed she would be having somebody who looked like a transvestite around the house, but she knew that if the welfare inspectors ever discovered that it was actually D.S., Nina would be kicked off welfare and her girls would suffer. So every day she watched this courageous woman get along as best she could, subjected to both the scorn that goes with associating with an individual in a non-traditional gender role, and the anxiety that goes with knowing that at any instant her fraud could be discovered and the avalanche could come roaring down. If there was one thing Krystal couldn't tolerate, it was anybody who flew in the face of established public attitudes, but nevertheless she deeply respected people who were bold enough to live their lives their own way in spite of the prejudices of narrow-minded assholes.

Add to this the community spirit that was leading Nina to try to get the school pool opened again. Put all together, Krystal's neighbour had many of the attributes that usually allowed people who had them to look down on people who were on welfare. But she refused to. That raised Nina even higher in Krystal's estimation, and is what inspired her to decide to raise money for the pool project as well.

SIX

When it came to raising funds for Nina's project, nobody in the whole neighbourhood was quicker off the mark than her own daughters. But first they had to deal with two major questions. Three of them did, because one of the questions was whether the fourth sister, Guinevere, should be included. The other question had to do with if it was okay to keep some of the money they collected for themselves.

"Gwinny's, like, only interested in the bright lights," Merlina said.

"Huh?" Lady said.

Merlina rolled her eyes. One of the totally disgusting things about her sisters was that they needed to have every word spelled out. "The towers," she said, nodding in the direction of The Intersection. She didn't know how you could explain anything as obvious as that without sounding stupid yourself.

Gwinny was beyond hopeless. Merly figured it would be easier to communicate with a sister made out of rock, since you might be able to get something through by banging your head against her. For as long as she could remember, Gwinny's interest in how she looked — which Merlina calculated on a scale of one to ten at being about fifty — outweighed her interest in everything else in the world put together. She sometimes thought it wasn't boys Gwinny cared about. It was how the boys acted when they came around — for instance, did they make her feel like some movie star? The thing was, though, because it didn't matter who acted this way, she never noticed what kind of guys they actually were. Or maybe she didn't care. The same as Nina.

Merly kept going on to Lady about how it was when Gwinny got her first period. Apparently it was a magical, mysterious experience that made her all goopy and mooshy about how she had been carried on her heart's wings into a glorified state where love and romance would spring up out of the ground like flowers wherever she set her foot down.

"When *I* got *my* first period —" Merly said.

"It was a pain in the ass —" Lady said, wagging her head slightly, as if she was keeping time.

" — it was a pain in the ass —".

" — and that's all it was."

" — and that's all it was. What's that you were saying?" Merly said.

"Nothing," Lady said.

Lately Guinevere had been spending hours on the porch, looking up at the towers when the lights came on with an expression on her face that made Merly want to throw up, it was so totally fuckin' gack. That's what had led her to mention Gwinny and the bright lights, and try to get the other two to understand that when she said this, she meant a whole lot more than actual lights and how much they were shining.

The actual lights in the towers weren't actually all that bright from down where the Dolgoy sisters lived in SuEz, but she wasn't going to talk to Lady about this any more, because Lady already thought Merly had a head full of mouse turds.

"At least in her case there *are* boys," Lady said, giving Merly a look.

"At least I'm not a prick," Merly said.

Lately Merly had started calling Lady a prick when she got mad at her. Partly this was because she always kind of had the feeling that Lady should be her brother. It wasn't that she necessarily went around acting like a boy, but there was definitely something about her — for instance, the times when Merlina was interested in having an argument and Lady was only interested in punching her. Sometimes Lady would even punch her for no reason. Another good example was the ice cream truck. When it came by and called out their names and told them they couldn't have any of the wonderful things it had for them because their mother was a mean, ugly bitch who wanted to make their lives shitty, Lady didn't seem to care about the ice cream or why she couldn't have any. What interested her was the truck: how it was specially built to carry ice cream and keep it from melting. The way Lady looked at it, that was awesome.

The question of keeping some of the money they raised for themselves came up because Merlina imagined they might be able to wait around the corner, out of sight of Nina, and when the truck came by it wouldn't know they were her daughters. They would probably have to use fake names.

Gwinny wouldn't have wanted anything to do with the scheme, because she had her own ideas about her life and where it was heading and how she would get there, and she didn't want Merly prying into her fuckin' business about anything, any time. Lady went along with Merly, but Merly knew that if anything got too weird she would make a big fuss and cause trouble. Maybe even bloodshed. Sometimes when she wasn't interested in punching Merly, she bit her.

"How much do you think they'd give us?" Lady said, after Merly outlined her idea.

"Hundreds," Merly said. She had no idea, but considering how Lady's mind worked, it made sense to sound like they'd be getting big money. Lady liked things when she knew how they would come out exactly. That was why she spent so long reading the instructions that came with stuff. Most people who bought things paid no attention to the manuals, but Lady would memorize them. In fact, because nothing new ever came into their house, no manuals did either, so she would memorize other peoples', or even manuals that she found in the trash. Going over how things worked could keep her occupied for hours.

She thought about the hundreds Merlina had mentioned. Then she wrote the number five on the concrete step as if her finger was a piece of chalk. "Five hundreds?" she asked.

"Probably."

"Five hundreds would make Mom really happy."

"But if we wanted to, we could just give her four."

Lady stiffened. She stared at the invisible number she'd written on the step. Merlina had hoped she could kind of sneak that part of the idea in. "Four hundred and fifty?" Merlina said.

"Why not all five?"

"In case we wanted to keep some for ourselves." Lady snapped her head around and looked at her sister, and Merlina knew she was going to have to work hard to sell this angle.

"To buy ice cream with?" Merly suggested.

"That's stealing."

"It is so *not* stealing! It's just a little bit extra for us. For the work we've done to raise it."

"Why don't we just steal some money and buy ice cream with that?" Lady said. Not only was ice cream not at the top of Lady's priority list, there was no logic behind her thinking.

"Okay, okay, okay." The important thing was agreeing on the main goal.

"You're always like that, Merly," Lady said. "You're always thinking about what you can get out of something. That's all you care about." She stamped up the steps and into the house.

This didn't especially bother Merly. As long as Lady was busy being upset about the ice cream part of the plan, she wouldn't pay close attention to the other parts, which started happening more quickly than Merly was completely prepared for.

It was because Lady heard her sister talking to a stranger that she came back out on the porch. And when Merlina whizzed past holding a bunch of money, she tore into the house after her.

"Mom! Mom!" Merly hollered. "Look! For your pool!"

Nina was sitting at the kitchen table looking quite confused, as if she didn't know what to do about the hole where the back door used to be. With the door gone, the kitchen felt a whole lot bigger and a lot emptier. When Merlina pushed the money into her hands, it took a considerable effort to change from thinking about the missing door. "What's —"

"How much is it, Mom," Lady yelled. "How much did she give you?"

"What's this?" Nina looked at the money as if it was a snake that was about to sink its fangs into her chin.

"How much is it?" Lady wanted the exact details, and wanted them right then.

Nina spread the bills and held them up, all four of them. "What's going on?"

"You liar! Liar!" Lady balled her fists. Her yelling got even louder. "You lying fuckin' liar!"

There was no way Merly was going to let her get away with calling her that. She had worked out the plan, she'd gotten the payoff. "It's all —"

But there was no stopping Lady. "She's like, 'We'll get five hundred!' Five hundred, Mom! The lying cunt-face!"

Five hundred is actually what Merlina asked for. She was sitting on the steps going over the details when a man walked by and said, "If you go for drive with me, I'll give you something nice." Men did this now and then. Merly and Lady called them "kidnappers" and warned each other to be careful of them. But even though one coming by was essential this time, it was unbelievable. It had hardly been a minute since she'd discussed the plan with Lady, and here it was happening. "Hold on," she told him, nodding as hard as she could. "Don't go away." She ran into the house.

And when the time came to talk money, five hundred is what she told him. Cash in advance.

"Except this is all ... it's all he had." She said this to Lady very carefully, because it was important that she understand, having been in on the idea from the beginning.

"*Why didn't you just tell him no?*" Now, though, Lady was screaming. Bits of spit were coming out of her mouth.

"All he had for what?" Nina said. She let the four five dollar bills fall on the floor. Her face had gone white. She held Lady by the shoulder, but she looked right at Merly.

"Tell him *no?*" Merly said. "Mom needs money, and this is at least *something.*"

"Fabreece?" Nina said. Instinct told her it had to do with Fabreece.

"It was all he *had!*" Merlina screamed. "I'm *telling* you!"

"*Where is Fabreece?*" Nina screamed.

"*Up the street!*" Lady screamed, giving her sister a look that made Merlina feel like she was some kind of a shit. "*Getting put in a man's car!*"

When everything cooled down and she got a chance to go over it all, Merlina had to agree that twenty dollars wasn't very much help when it came to fixing the pool. She'd only accepted it because she was a person who just naturally got enthusiastic about things. For a minute there, she was so excited about making a deal that she kind of lost sight of the actual amount the man was offering.

Later on she did ask Lady if she personally would pay twenty dollars if, for example, Fabreece got kidnapped on her own, without any of her sisters' assistance, and that was how much the kidnappers wanted for ransom. Lady said she'd never had twenty dollars, so she wouldn't be in a position to do it. If the kidnappers knew anything about their family and all they asked for was five dollars, they'd be lucky to get that.

Merly told her she'd be happy to pay them five dollars if she could come up with it, but that was the limit.

She never could get over how the stupidest people in the world happened to be the oldest and the youngest children in her family, and later on wondered if there was a scientific reason for it that had to do with statistics, or was it always like this? If it was, she told Lady, it really didn't seem worth making all that big a fuss if either of them disappeared.

Before Nina came screaming out the door, Ed Oataway had already seen the man putting Fabreece into a car and yelled at him. As the man got in the car and started it up, Ed jumped in whatever family car it was that he happened to have on hand that day and rammed into the front of the other one, and that was the end of that.

"It's getting so hardly a day goes by that I don't sacrifice one of my vehicles for somebody or other in that fuckin' idiot family," he said when JannaRose ran up to ask what the hell he was doing this time.

SEVEN

What came out of all the visionary stuff whirling around in Nina's head was her theory that if they collected a huge enough amount of money and donated it to rebuilding the school pool, other people might feel the urge to donate some of their own. There is an official, financial term for what she imagined would kick-start this outpouring of generosity — it's called seed money — but she had never heard of such a thing and neither had anybody else she talked to about it. Some people went so far as to scoff.

"You're nuts," JannaRose said.

On top of that, if they could somehow collect enough money to get the pool going again, wouldn't people naturally start paying attention to them? Enough attention that maybe they could get somebody to talk to the ice cream company? Somebody like the mayor?

"Really fuckin' nuts."

If Nina had never heard of seed money, she never thought

of the money they'd need to get the project rolling as bank robbery money, either. Anybody could raise money any way that suited them. It just happened that this was the only one that fit her skill set. But it wasn't until JannaRose started hinting that it would be nice if Nina's brother's plan for when he got out of jail included a position that Ed Oataway might fill that the idea of acquiring the necessary money by robbing a bank began jumping up and down in the back of her mind, demanding attention. Filling such a position would get Ed out of hock with the parent company for the Pontiac a whole lot faster than the only other obvious way, which was stealing a bunch of cars from people who didn't want them stolen. Suspecting where that would lead and not wishing to see her family broken apart caused JannaRose to slam things so hard that Nina could hear it across the street. Nina figured that was probably why JannaRose was doing it, but she also couldn't help but think that behaving like that would be out of character for JannaRose unless things looked quite a bit worse than usual.

As far as Nina could see, the idea of Frank robbing anything was idiotic. It wasn't necessarily that he was too dumb — he was smarter than Ed Oataway. Even she had to admit that much. But robbery wasn't his style. Nina always believed that people gravitated to whatever they were intended to do the way quarters and dimes and so on gravitated through the right holes in those machines that sort coins at the supermarket. It was why Frank leaned toward selling driveway resurfacing to old people and then disappearing with their downpayments. If he'd wanted to squeeze out of them the rest of the money they'd agreed to pay, he'd have had to come back with a barrel of used crankcase oil to brush on the driveway so it looked decent until it dried, by which time he'd have vanished with all their money.

But for this he'd have needed a truck, and if there was one thing that ranked up there with the Law of Gravity in SuEz, it was the situation when it came to trucks. The situation was that anybody in SuEz who had a truck had stolen it in the last hour or so, and the only thing they'd be interested in was selling it — not using it to do something else. A truck was a short-term proposition. Besides that, there would have been the hard work required to brush the fake stuff on some old fart's driveway, and Frank could live without hard work every bit as well as he could live happily with just their downpayments. Sometimes he'd branch out into landscaping — design and construction. The deal there was the same as driveway resurfacing, especially the part where he told them how it would increase the value of their property. This particularly appealed to people who were going to have to sell soon and move into an old folks' home. The same business fundamentals were involved: extremely low overhead and a minimum of labour and physical risk.

Frank never cared any more for risk that Ed Oataway did. D.S. used to say that was why Frank never would have made it in legitimate business, where some customer would beat the shit out of you without any warning and you'd be sent home with no compensation, until you were healthy enough to go back to work. According to D.S., if the economy had as many downturns as he did personally, people would still be getting their groceries by sneaking up behind them and hitting them with a rock. When he first said that, Nina was on the verge of remarking, "Would you run that by me again?" but by then she'd been around D.S. long enough to realize life was too short.

It was Frank's negative attitude toward risk that made Nina think bank robbery was an extremely strange venture for him to undertake. But anybody who thought her opinion on this would have any effect on Frank's plans, or Ed's for that matter, was entirely out of touch. Frank had never been even slightly interested in his sister's opinion about anything, or anybody else's that she could think of. And Ed had by now definitely decided that Nina couldn't be a bigger pain in the ass if she was triplets, and the only thing he was interested in hearing from her ever again was maybe a cry for help when a great big hole opened up in the ground and swallowed her and she disappeared forever. "I wouldn't lift a fuckin' finger," he told D.S.

D.S. said that was entirely up to Ed. After getting a face-full of hubcap that night, he'd decided that whatever was going on between Ed and Nina was their business and he was better off staying out of it.

Then again, Frank had been locked up for three years, and who could say? Something could have happened to him the way it apparently sometimes did in jail. Nina didn't know many people other than Ed and Frank who had ever done time. They weren't all over the place in SuEz the way they were in the towers, where D.S. used to say there were three kinds of folks: the ones who just got out of jail; the ones who were in jail at the moment — probably this was the reason so many of the apartments were unoccupied; and finally the ones who were trying to think of something they could do that would get them sent to jail. Down where he and Nina and the girls lived, everybody was generally too busy doing whatever it took to get through the day to spend the time necessary to put together the sort of deal that would get the police tactical squad introducing itself by asking them to lean their hands against the wall and spread their legs. The chances of that weren't quite as long as any of them entering their yacht in the next America's Cup, but pretty close. Criminal-type things did occur, of course, but they were almost always unpremeditated.

Nina said in those cases jail amounted to a big time out. Everybody got a chance to cool off, on top of which a convict could treat the time behind bars as a developmental experience, during which they could catch up on the movies they'd missed since the TV got stolen from their house. And there were some people who just plain benefited from the routine that went with being locked away. She looked straight at Merlina when she said this, although Merly believed it was because she was the only other person in the family who realized that her sisters didn't know the meaning of responsibility.

Frank was as good-looking as the guys in those Bud Light commercials. What he wasn't, however, was anywhere near as ambitious as even the Bud Light guys. This was another thing that made his plan to hold up a bank sort of curious, because from the way Ed talked, it sounded as if there was more to it than simply getting out of jail and sticking up some branch in a plaza the way a person might if they happened to be walking by one and it occurred to them that since they were broke, they might as well whip in and rob it.

The only time he ever had anything like ambition, it had led directly to winning what D.S. called a full scholarship to Hard-Time U. He wouldn't have landed in jail if he hadn't gotten involved with a woman who was remarkable for a number of reasons that would also include, when he got out, being the registered owner of a five-hundred-thousand dollar Porsche sports car. To show how much he loved her — and this was maybe the most remarkable thing about this woman, because before meeting her, Frank was always entirely satisfied to let his girlfriends show how much they loved him — anyway, to show his love for her, he felt obliged to improve his financial standing. This led him to become a major operator, contracting to do high-end condominium developments, pave and landscape them, the whole deal. But other than make the numbers he quoted bigger, he didn't even slightly change the approach he'd used to fleece old retired people. That's why it didn't take the individuals who were bankrolling these projects long to start asking themselves what was up with this guy. Unless he was some kind of mental case who was so far off his meds that he was flying at an altitude where even birds couldn't breathe, then somebody must be shaking them down. And for some reason or other, whoever it was had sent this wiener to put his foot in the door. What made it really confusing was that they couldn't figure out how this scheme Frank was fronting was supposed to pay off for whoever was behind it, because, as their accountants said when they got them to look at the estimates he'd given them, the whole thing was too stupid for words.

Was Nina surprised? When it rained, did her roof leak? The way she looked at it, Frank was lucky he never got too many ideas, because whenever he came up with one, he'd just go with it. For instance, he'd never bothered to figure out that the difference between dealing with these people and with the old farts who made up his former clientele was that he should avoid irritating these people in any way at all. In fact, he should go to great lengths to keep them from feeling even a tiny itch.

Nina said this was because of the way he processed information. When something useful blew into his head, there was no place for it to land, so it just blew around for awhile and blew out again, like a candy wrapper. The big money in these deals was unaware of this, however, and until Frank showed up, they were under the impression that they had paid off all the necessary interests so nobody would try to muscle in on their ventures. For their part, the necessary interests were under the impression that they were the only necessary interests, so they could relax, since the only thing they had to think about was how they could muscle the big money out and take over for themselves.

Every one of these people had concluded that Frank was pissing in their soup.

Men of this calibre had long since put violence behind them as a business technique except as a last resort, but who wanted to use violence against some guy with nothing more than a smile and a shiny suit when the organization behind him was so mysterious they couldn't even get a read on it and might risk everything in a fruitless bloodbath?

These days, instead of violence, they used lawyers, but what good were lawyers when, far from being able to identify this guy's backers, all they could find out was that he appeared out of and disappeared back into the stink and misery of SuEz? So the only thing left for them was to turn the matter of Frank Carson over to the courts. Several of these individuals got in touch with the senior police officers they kept on retainer for various purposes such as corporate and government relations. The charges these police officers came up with in turn were so obviously trumped up that the judge couldn't help but assume that the accused must have done something extremely wrong. Whoever was fucking him up the ass had a lot of influence, and why else would they have gone to this much trouble? On those grounds, eleven years seemed about right.

When Ed Oataway got back from visiting the penitentiary and mentioned Frank's plans, the things that began to cross Nina's mind were quite understandable when you consider that her familiarity with her brother and his shortcomings went back to the day he was born, and then take into account the astounding things she was starting to discover about her own capabilities. She was so wrapped up in working out all the implications that she sat on the porch for ages the next morning, her legs dangling over the side, and didn't even notice the ice cream truck rolling toward her.

"Cassie," it was blaring, "you didn't buy that Marshmallow Whizzard we had for you yesterday. That makes us very, very sad, because we made it for you and nobody else. You don't really want us to be sad, do you Cassie?"

And, "Leo Lee Roy, you told us yesterday you didn't have any money to pay for your Mount Ever-Ice. And we told you to go and talk to your mama and tell her how embarrassed you would be when everybody on the street finds out why she's too cheap to buy you a treat. Here, we brought a brand-new one for you today. We sure hope you're ready this time."

And, "Trafford? We don't see you. Are you hiding, Trafford? Get out here and get this Devil's Frost-D-Lite. You don't want us to take your name off our list, do you? If we do that you'll never be able to get back on it. You'll be gone forever."

She didn't even look up when her girls came out to watch heaven on wheels go rolling by. Not even when Merlina said "Mom?" — which was something the others urged her to do every time the truck came along, because she had a gift for saying it in a way that made Nina feel like the most useless mother who ever lived, so useless it was hard to understand why the authorities didn't put her children out for adoption.

This time Nina didn't even hear her. It was because that way-down-deep-inside-her spirit that had guided her into the ice cream company parking lot — and had led her, she now finally realized, to do what she'd done in the confrontation with the ice cream truck in front of her house — it was because that same spirit that made her breath get so short and her skin tingle like her nerves were full of static electricity was speaking to her again, only with a whole lot more determination than it had those other times.

"That fuckin' moron," the spirit was saying, referring to her brother Frank Carson. "That fuckin' moron could never rob a bank."

Then it paused. And cleared its throat to make sure it had her undivided attention. And when it saw she was listening with every single part of her body, it said, very pointedly, "But I could."

EIGHT

There were things about Frank Carson's plan to rob a bank that, if Nina had known them, would have made her think twice about her own. As it was, she hardly even thought about it once.

Unless you count the conversation she had with JannaRose after JannaRose casually mentioned that she'd always thought Nina was opposed to stealing. Nina asked whatever had given her that idea, and JannaRose said it was based on everything she'd ever heard her say. This forced Nina to come up with a revised ethical position on the spot.

"Okay. When you steal something, you have it, and the person that originally had it doesn't," was how it began, and it could be it had a few rough edges, because it was put together on such short notice.

"Of course they don't have it," JannaRose said. "You stole it from them. What the fuck are you talking about?"

"What you should do," Nina continued, "is shut up and let me finish. My point isn't who doesn't have it. My point is, let's say for instance there's just one of whatever it is — the one you have that the other person doesn't have any more, meaning the one that the other person had. That now they don't."

"I don't fuckin' believe this," JannaRose said.

"But with banks it's different," Nina said. "That's because of bank insurance. When you steal money from a bank, the bank insurance pays it back right away. So it isn't stealing in the way people think of usually, where what was somebody's once is suddenly somebody else's. Now," she said, "it's more like there are two things where there only used to be one, and you happen to have one of them. And so does the bank."

"Somebody doesn't have it any more. The insurance company doesn't."

"No. It doesn't work like that." Nina was drawing a lot of diagrams in the air to illustrate how it did work. "Bank insurance isn't paid by a company, it's paid by the government. The *government!*" She underlined "government" with her index finger. "And when the government needs money to fill the gap that was left by paying off some bank insurance, it just prints more. Governments can do this any time they like."

"You don't believe this either," JannaRose said.

"I do so. Absolutely." Nina hadn't spent years listening to D.S. argue without learning a thing or two. "You ever heard of victimless crimes? Robbing banks is the biggest one of all."

It was very important that JannaRose not back out on her, and especially not because some complex issue like stealing made her start thinking. Without her for support, Nina would never have the nerve. This was one thing she absolutely did know for sure.

JannaRose backed out on her halfway through Nina's explanation of how bank insurance worked. She never exactly said she did, but it became obvious when she started hmming loudly and staring at the ceiling every time Nina mentioned anything about the trip they'd made the week before to scout out the bank.

"What about a bake sale?" JannaRose had said the morning of that expedition.

She'd been hanging back — so far back it was hard to hear her. Nina knew it wasn't because she was looking up in awe at the office buildings that rose sixty storeys and more that she was moving so slowly. She had hardly lifted her eyes off the ground since they got off the subway.

Nina turned and waited. "What?" she shouted when JannaRose got within hailing distance.

"Lots of groups have them," JannaRose said, "parents' groups. When they want to raise money. For the school. Or, you know, for trips to the zoo."

"A bake sale?" When Nina got exasperated with somebody, she had to struggle to keep from sounding as if she had doubts about their intelligence. She didn't always pull it off.

"I don't know," JannaRose said.

"Do you know anybody that knows how to bake?"

JannaRose's voice had become so faint it was barely a whisper. "I don't know."

"Trips to the fuckin' zoo. Jesus Christ." Nina had to struggle to keep from saying it out loud.

What worried her was knowing that JannaRose didn't know whether she'd be too chicken to help her rob a bank. JannaRose never said anything about this, but it was something she would more or less have made it a point not to mention even to herself. There were other things she was like this about, such as her husband Ed Oataway being a criminal. She did everything she could not to think about that, because now that they had children, if Ed went to jail again it would be The End as far as their happy family life was concerned. And how come he was in a line of crime where, even though he was extremely successful, he didn't bring in enough for them to live on unless they were both on welfare? If Nina came right out and asked her about this, JannaRose would have answered, "I don't know," so she never did.

The most important thing to do right there was reassure her. "We have as much right to be here as anybody," Nina said.

"What?" JannaRose said.

The picture most people see when they think of the city is the downtown skyline, and that's where they were, in the middle of it, right down at the very bottom of all those bank buildings. Nina felt some kind of reassurance was called for, because she knew the other thing upsetting JannaRose was that they were the only people wearing sweats and T-shirts. As far as Nina knew, JannaRose had never been anyplace where nobody else was dressed like that.

"Us being here," Nina said. "It's okay. It doesn't matter that we're the only ones wearing sweats."

"What're you *talking* about?"

"About you standing here in the middle of the sidewalk not moving."

The crowd flowed around them as if the women had been in that exact spot for years and everybody was used to them.

"I'm fine," JannaRose said. This could be considered an odd thing for anybody to say who had been with Nina on what Nina had said was going to be a scouting expedition to the lot where the ice cream company parked its trucks, making it sound as if the only thing she had in mind was checking it out. When they were getting on the subway at The Intersection, Nina had kept calling this morning's expedition a scouting expedition, too.

"Are you going to be sick?"

"No."

"Then come on."

JannaRose threw up. She stared at her dripping hand as if it was the most repulsive thing she'd ever laid eyes on. Then she looked at the puddle on the sidewalk. "I'm fine," she said.

A minute later they were through the front doors. The bank's security videotapes would show, just inside the lobby, two thirtyish women of less than average height and more than average weight, although only Nina was thirty. JannaRose was four years younger.

The one in the dark blue sweats with the white piping and the maroon T-shirt was standing facing the one in the light green sweats and light green T-shirt, holding her by both shoulders. The one in the light green sweats had her head down and was shaking it sadly. The one in the blue sweats appeared to be talking earnestly to her. The one in the green sweats threw up on the shoes of the one in the blue sweats. The one in the blue sweats looked at her shoes and threw both hands in the air. Then she dragged the one in green sweats back through the front door and out of camera range.

When JannaRose backed out on her, it left Nina with no choice but to press ahead on her own. If she didn't, the swimming pool wouldn't get fixed and her daughters wouldn't have any outlet apart from the usual ones available to girls in their part of town. But it wasn't as if she didn't have a lot of other things she could be doing, such as getting squared away with the welfare department.

"Welfare giveth, and sometimes welfare taketh away even more than —"

"Blow it out your ass, D.S."

"What'd I do now?"

"Nothing." Big time. Not a single goddamn thing.

Whether Nina was right when she said her brother couldn't rob a bank really didn't matter. The bank he would be dealing with had been pre-robbed the same way a TV dinner is pre-cooked, and any bank robbing skills he might or might not have had were irrelevant. If the loot had been a TV dinner instead of 1.18 million in cash, his job amounted to taking it out of the oven when it was ready and jumping into a getaway car with it.

That he had the talent to do this had been noticed in prison, where Frank turned out to be something he'd never been on the outside — a solid citizen. This probably wasn't surprising when you consider that for the first time in his life he didn't have to worry about making a living. Not that he'd ever worried about it, but in prison the pressure was cranked down to zero. Naturally he had to be careful about a few things. Making eye contact with other inmates when it wasn't appropriate, for example, could lead to a spectrum of possibilities running from the fatal to an invitation to get romantically involved that you had to accept even if you would rather die, which you might if you didn't. It was good for him that he couldn't be bothered to deal drugs, which would have angered drug dealers, and that he had enough good manners not to win too much at poker, because there were inmates who resented it if they were the ones who lost. Added to that were inmates who got interested in big winnings even if they never played the game, but considered themselves entitled to a cut because that's the kind of guys they were, and because they had the kind of friends who took a peculiar delight in dealing with individuals who thought this wasn't fair.

There was one guy in there who made a good living as a headhunter for a number of outside organizations. He saw early on that Frank was presentable and sensitive to his environment and that he kept whatever was on his mind to himself without being a prick about it. The guy's name was Herbert, and Herbert had a feeling that Frank would be an ideal prospect for one of his clients down the road. One thing he wrote in Frank's file was that Frank had absolutely no ambition. What this indicated to Herbert was that he might not be bone dumb, which a lot of inmates figured he was, based on the crime he'd been sent up for. You could be smart as hell and not have any ambition; it just meant you fucked the dog to a different drummer.

So Herbert listed him as a solo operator with no identifiable goals who could be valuable in an enterprise where you needed somebody you could count on to do what they'd been told and not be even slightly interested in getting creative. Frank actually made Herbert sad that his clients represented such a narrow range of employers. He could have made a ton of money selling him as one of those guys who read the news on TV. They always had truly exceptional haircuts. Herbert thought this was because they paid a great deal to get it cut that way, but here he saw Frank getting his hair cut by the same inmates who cut everybody else's hair, and his haircut always looked like one of those anchormen haircuts. Until Frank came along, it had never occurred to Herbert that those haircuts he saw on TV were the result of some inner quality.

When the opening for the job at the bank turned up a couple of months before he was due to get out, having done three of his eleven years, Frank figured it would be a snap. Walk in, wave the gun around in a threatening manner, grab a bank executive named Milner and put the gun to his head after firing a bullet into the ceiling so everybody in the place realizes it's a real gun and he means real business. Milner's personal assistant would make a big show of bustling around filling a gym bag with cash. The bank would have far more cash on hand than it usually did, because Milner would have ordered extra to supply the advance requests he had forged from a number of depositors who planned to make large withdrawals on the same day, coincidentally. When the bag was handed to him, Frank was to race out of the building and be driven to an arranged destination. Herbert was as confident about recommending him as he'd ever been about anybody. His long experience as a human resources consultant made it clear to him that here was one of those truly rare individuals. Not only could he be trusted, but when he got blown away after the loot was delivered, nobody would give a shit. He was just some fuckhead from SuEz with no connections.

NINE

Since becoming a community activist, Nina had never worked without an accomplice. JannaRose had been right there beside her when she forced the ice cream truck to back down in front of her house. She'd been at her side when she'd launched her attack on the ice cream trucks in the parking lot at the ice cream factory. It was too bad she hadn't been feeling better the day they scouted the downtown bank to see if it was suitable for robbing, but Nina understood how that could affect JannaRose's views when it came to the next stage. Sometimes you do something when you're not feeling well, and you don't want to do it ever again because it's associated in your mind with how you felt at the time.

When Nina washed her runners out under the kitchen tap after JannaRose threw up on them, she noticed that the water ran out of the first one where the top part had come unglued from the sole. When she did the other one, it was the same. She hadn't realized they were that far gone. They were from the year before last, or the year before that, and didn't smell any worse after she cleaned them than they had before JannaRose let fly. It didn't matter. They weren't visible on the famous security videotape that recorded Nina's next trip to the bank, but then it didn't get to be famous because she made some kind of fashion statement. The main thing everybody who watched the video noticed was that for a long time her forehead was down on the counter and she was rocking on it from side to side. Meantime, her arms dangled straight down. When she did finally look at the teller, she didn't stand up straight, she simply tipped her head back so her chin was almost on the counter and gave the impression that she'd just woken up and was surprised to see anybody in front of her at all. By this point, the teller had backed away and looked as if she had already decided the smart thing to do was run. Then Nina said something, or maybe finished saying something, pushed herself back from the counter, and slouched out of the picture.

She told JannaRose she'd felt like somebody in the middle of the ocean who notices their lifeboat is sinking, and the only choice they have left is to swim away. "And I never learned to swim, so forget it." She didn't mind telling JannaRose what happened — they still got along the same as before. She didn't hold a grudge. Even though she'd been abandoned and left all alone to face the toughest moment she'd ever faced, she firmly believed that when it came to getting involved in public service, JannaRose was entitled to follow her conscience the same as everybody else. Nina told her she'd started talking as she approached the counter. And it was hearing what she was saying that caused her to lean her forehead on it.

"What were you saying?" JannaRose asked. "Stick 'em up?"

"No. More like, 'Oh, fuck, who am I fooling? This is so stupid. They'll catch me. I'll go to jail. They won't believe I was doing it to fix the swimming pool, so they'll put me in jail forever. My children will starve. D.S. will get a girlfriend that will move in and abuse them. D.S. is a fuckin' sex maniac. And he does sort of have a job. So every hungry fuckin' woman in SuEz will start putting out for him and some ignorant twat will think she's died and gone to heaven because she finally gets her hands on him. The girls will start doing crack. They'll be up in the towers selling their asses for a nickel a time.'" And so on.

It came out in more or less a steady flow until she leaned her head back and looked at the teller and said, "I'm sorry, but fuck it. That's all there is to it. Fuck it. I'm sorry. Just forget the whole thing."

They caught her on the sidewalk. They ran right past her when they went charging in — the holdup squad. Somebody had pulled the silent alarm. There were ten of them with machine guns, grenade launchers, helmets. After a whole lot of yelling at everybody in the bank and pointing their weapons everywhere and making everybody lie down on the floor, the teller caught their attention and explained what happened and they all ran back outside. This could be seen on the video too: Nina standing on the sidewalk in front of the building, not too sure what to do next. Them surrounding her, pointing their weapons, and yelling that she better tell them what she was up to and not make any sudden moves or else. A few minutes of this and they apparently concluded that she was just one more aimless particle of the city's vast confusion. Maybe after making passengers on subway cars nervous with her blathering, she had expanded her repertoire to blathering in banks and making tellers nervous. Looking decidedly let down, they climbed into their armoured vans and sped away.

It only occurred to her when she was almost home that it was a good thing she hadn't been frisked, or they'd have discovered the two bunches of Tampax she had wrapped in black tape and stuck on either side of her tummy. She had imagined the teller would think it was dynamite when she pulled up her T-shirt and announced that she was going to blow the place to ratshit if she didn't get a pile of cash. She drew the line at telling JannaRose about the Tampax.

She didn't make the holdup squad's logbook, either. It called the episode a false alarm, and nobody thought about it again, except for one person.

It went like clockwork. Apart from when he fired the warning shot into the ceiling. It was the first time he'd ever fired a gun, and it was so loud he nearly shit. The chief executive of the bank was named Milner, and Frank had one arm around his neck at the time. Milner actually did shit. *Now* that *lends a touch of realism to the proceedings,* Frank thought, skrinching up his nose. Right on schedule, as set out in the agreement, Milner's assistant handed over a big Nike bag full of cash, but instead of putting the gun under Milner's chin and steering him to the door, where he was supposed to push him aside brutally, Frank took into account the accident the man had just had and improvised a little bit, pushing him aside brutally right there. Outside, he discovered the driver of the getaway car was dealing with an accident of his own, only this one presented a bigger problem than Milner's. He was in the middle of a shouting argument with the driver of a beat-up green Toyota Corolla who'd misjudged the angle when he was pulling in to the curb and ended up wedged across the getaway car's left front fender. The fender was so badly crunched that the driver of the getaway car was no longer able to get away, or anywhere else. The steering wheel wouldn't turn at all. Frank's jaw dropped. The driver of the getaway car had been trying to keep an eye out for him, and when he finally spotted him, he looked as if he was about to have such an explosive coronary, it wouldn't leave a piece of him big enough to pick up with tweezers. Frank squinted, peering this way and that, taking in the scene, checking to see if any more complications were headed their way. Then he made a big, reassuring show of getting himself completely under control. In case anybody needed proof that the recommendations of Herbert, the jailhouse headhunter, were rock solid, that did it. He made a there-there gesture to the driver of the getaway car: take it easy. He made an I'll-give-you-a-phone-call gesture. He gave a thumbs up. And finally, in a manner that was cool and businesslike, he swung along the sidewalk and disappeared into the subway station at the corner.

What the driver of the getaway car got from all this was a clear indication that the guy he'd been driving was switching to some kind of Plan B that had been carefully worked out in advance, and if nobody had briefed him on it, he wasn't surprised. That's how things went in his business. He didn't even know the guy's name. Meanwhile, the moron who'd run into him hadn't shut up for one minute, and for about the fourth time was explaining to him how, because the Toyota's passenger-side mirror was broken, he'd ended up misjudging the angle, which had caused the getaway driver to yell at least three previous times, "What the fuck does the passenger-side mirror have to do with parking a fuckin' car?" But now that he wasn't going to be driving the bank robber any more, two things occurred to him. One was that he didn't give a fuck what excuse the Toyota driver had for bending his fuckin' fender, and the other was that he should get himself the fuck out of there, too. So without a word, without so much as looking at the moron, he walked away, leaving the getaway car's motor running.

Ed Oataway was serious. The passenger-side mirror was broken, although he hadn't noticed it until after he stole the Toyota that morning. But it was too good a development not to use when he explained to the getaway car driver what had caused the accident that made it impossible for the getaway car to get away. Now, though, he was hearing sirens from all directions, and since everybody else had left, he decided there was no reason for him to stick around. So, giving the toyota a goodbye pat — it was a good car, a 1997, one he would have been happy to steal as part of his job — he headed for the subway station Frank had disappeared into.

One question about Frank had never gone away: how dumb was he really? As things turned out, it never would go away. Given the way he generally operated, there was a bit of speculation that he was no more interested in putting his brain to work than any other part of his body. His sister had always kind of suspected this might be the case, since she never considered herself to be particularly dumb. There just wasn't anything going on in her life that she could do much about, so why waste brainpower on it. To her, Frank was one more individual who'd grown up in SuEz and never thought about improving his situation because it never occurred to him that it could be improved. At least it never occurred to him until he fell in love with that high-priced whore. Although what he'd done as a result didn't qualify as even close to smart in Nina's book.

Nevertheless, he wasn't so dumb that he couldn't figure out that he might not stay alive for very long once he turned the 1.18 million over to whoever had hired him to pretend to steal it. And he wasn't so dumb that he didn't realize that if for some reason they didn't knock him off, they would at least knock him over the head and take off with all the money, including the seventy-five hundred he'd been given as an advance against the fifteen thousand he'd agreed to do the job for. Neither was he dumb enough to imagine that he'd ever get the rest of that fifteen thousand unless he had the entire bundle all to himself in a private place to make sure it was divided up fairly. And, although this might sound dumb, he really did mean fairly. He would take the seven thousand five hundred he was still owed. Then, on top of that, he'd also take the 1.165 million that was left over, since he believed that was the amount he was genuinely entitled to. He was the one who had taken all the risks, and besides, they were playing him for being dumber than a hammer that the handle fell off. Far from it. He was nowhere near dumb enough to think the people who'd hired him wouldn't have somebody other than the driver of the getaway car outside the bank keeping track of what went on.

In fact, if a train was arriving in the subway station when he dashed down with the money, he wasn't even dumb enough to think he would board it. Instead he dashed right along to the end of the platform, jumped over the barrier, and jogged along to the next station. It turned out to be a scary thing to do. The drivers of half a dozen trains that came along blared their horns at the amazing sight of an unauthorized person humping what looked like a gym bag along the rickety catwalk beside the tracks. Finally, he dashed up to ground level and ran like a crazy man. When he'd gone over the details with Ed Oataway at their final planning session, he'd said that once he was out in the street again he would know everything was going to be okay, because then he'd have all the freedom he needed to manoeuvre.

And it went like clockwork. As far as Frank could tell.

TEN

As the single father of three children who were abandoned by their mothers shortly after each one was born, Jarmeel Tolbert took his responsibilities seriously. He struggled to meet the demands this placed on him while attempting to cope with the Post-Traumatic Stress Disorder that the army refused to admit he'd become the victim of during his military service. Instead they gave him a dishonourable discharge for dereliction of duty, which meant he'd refused to obey orders and spent all his days playing video games in the soldiers' recreation centre. He said he couldn't help it. It was a symptom of his Post-Traumatic Stress Disorder.

The way he looked at it, one thing was for sure: he had been dealt a bad hand. No sooner had Post-Traumatic Stress Disorder come along as a sure-fire guarantee of a medical discharge with a full pension, than everybody who could dream up something they could blame on it was parading in front of the doctors claiming they no longer had the regulation number of marbles. There ended up being so many fake victims that when the genuine article like Jarmeel showed up, nobody was interested in believing him. The doctors said they had trouble with the idea that someone who had never been in combat could come down with PTSD. Jarmeel not only hadn't been in combat in the combat sense, he hadn't seen any other kind either, such as the kind military personnel sometimes got into on a peacekeeping mission, say, or defending the embassy from insurgents.

Jarmeel had never been out of the country. His military career consisted of changing the oil in trucks and armoured personnel carriers and such at the big base a couple of hours north of the city. He was a lubricant specialist. Like any demanding occupation, it could take its toll, so Jarmeel figured he was already on the verge of feeling stress when something happened that was seriously traumatic.

A buddy of his was working in one of the lubrication bays. He was on a dolly under a big truck changing the oil. And while he lay there watching the old oil drain out, and in contravention of every rule in the book as well as the signs posted everywhere in the repair shop, he lit a cigarette.

What happened next stuck forever in Jarmeel's mind. The *whomp!* The ball of flame that had once been a truck. The terrifying knowledge that his buddy was in the swooshing blaze under it. If Jarmeel had been there when it happened, it probably would have been even worse. But in spite of being off sick with a sore throat that could easily have become pneumonia, it was still more than he could handle. Every time he dollied under a vehicle after that, he got clammy with sweat, his hands trembled, he was swept by waves of nausea and dizziness, he couldn't breathe in, he couldn't breath out, his bowels wouldn't move for the next twenty-four hours. It was perfect. Except when he got in line at the psychiatric clinic, the other soldiers bragged of having such sensational symptoms, he knew his wouldn't stand a chance. He went back to being off sick with possible pre-pneumonia, gave the matter more thought, and eventually had a powerful insight.

If he could no longer remember what lubricants went where, like antifreeze and battery acid, it would definitely be a crippling symptom. Next he had to figure out how something like this could happen. And it came to him that it could happen quite easily if the space aliens who kept the base under constant surveillance noted that, as a result of a painful experience, one of the soldiers stationed there had become terribly vulnerable.

The instant they zeroed in on him, the aliens had taken him aboard their ship and probed him for military secrets. And here's what really scared him: up till then he didn't know he had any. But he did! All those lubricants! What they were. The grades of motor oil used in various vehicles. How long before it had to be changed. Tire pressures — Jarmeel had a subspecialty of putting air in tires. He was a walking computer with all this information in it. And they'd stolen it all and left him blank. He discovered this when he returned to Earth and all of a sudden he felt a lot lighter — exactly the way people do who have been weighed down by secrets they have been forced to keep, then something happens and they don't have to any more. What a relief! Except it wasn't really. Although he was in a weakened state after being kidnapped into space and probed, now he had to deal with the fear that if the army replaced the information, he would get taken aboard that alien ship and probed clean a second time.

"As I understand it —" the psychiatrist spoke without looking up from the pad he'd been making notes on, "your concern is that you are an, um —" he ran the tip of his ballpoint under the words, "— an intergalactic security risk."

"*My* concern? It isn't just *my* concern." Jarmeel had been lying at attention on the couch, but now he pulled himself even straighter. Patriotism glowed from deep within him. "It is my *country's* concern. It is the *free world's* concern. In fact, it is also the concern of the *unfree* world. No way these space aliens care even a tiny, little bit for the well-being of us humans, no matter what our political inclination is, no matter if we live free or as slaves bound by the tyrant's chains. *My* concern doesn't count for squat compared to these other concerns that concern me. That," Jarmeel said, "is why I hate to think it could be that I'm the one that ends up giving them the piece of the puzzle they've been rooting all around trying to find, from one end of the universe to the other. The final piece that shows exactly where our true, deep-down weaknesses lie. That allows them to finally *invade* us! That brings about domination of our world by these cruel —"

He inhaled raggedly to show that he was more familiar with their cruelty than he cared to be.

"I see," the psychiatrist said.

They all said it. Eventually. All the psychiatrists and the psychoanalysts and the psychologists and the psychophysicists and the psychometricians and the psychotherapists. Even the pro bono lawyers who defended Jarmeel and the brigadier general who was the senior officer on the court martial that heard his case.

The important thing, however, is the more Jarmeel thought about it, and in the years that followed he thought about it every minute he could spare, the more he came to believe it all must have happened: the aliens, the kidnapping, the intergalactic spacecraft, the probing, the spilling of the beans unwittingly. It had to. Because it explained everything. Originally he'd made it up, this was true. But what if making it up was a coincidence? What if something happened to you that you forgot all about because your memory tracks got wiped clean by space aliens? And what if your mind came up with a hypothetical version that filled the gap? And what if it filled it perfectly? Who's to say it wasn't what had actually happened?

Sometimes theories do turn out to be the way things are. Jarmeel never stopped telling this to everybody he met.

The people who were attracted to his new religion might not at first understand how what had happened to them was a religious experience. That would be his job as the founder — to dream up why it had been and explain it to them. If their experiences had been anything like his, they had been purified and were no longer doubled over by their burdens. This was, after all, a standard experience in other religions. And none of these other religions had anything going for them to compare with extraterrestrial probing.

The more he thought about it, the more it occurred to him that these aliens were God's messengers, hovering around, checking out the action, picking suitable candidates for salvation. For one thing, the realm they inhabited — outer space — was a lot higher up in the sky, and therefore a lot closer to God's own personal realm — heaven — than the one humans inhabited. This could be what had got them interested in the Planet Earth in the first place. All those souls whizzing up through space on their way from this world to heaven could have made them wonder what was going on. Jarmeel said that if people started using your backyard as a shortcut and you had no idea who they were or where they came from, it would be entirely normal for you to be curious, too.

Jarmeel had been going around saying stuff like this for awhile, but the first time Nina paid any attention was when he came to her house one day dressed very strangely and put a handful of money on the table in front of her.

"What's that?" she said.

"Seventy-one dollars," he said.

It was the second time in her whole life that somebody had thrust cash at her, and she was alarmed. The first time had been only a couple of days earlier when her daughter had done it, and the person doing it this time had even more screws loose than Merlina. "What for?" she said, nervously.

"It's your share."

"Of what?"

"This morning's collection at my church. Your swimming pool is our first community project."

"Holy shit."

ELEVEN

Her many failures to get rich by means of get-rich-quick schemes had given Krystal Beach some useful insights. One was that everybody who said they wanted to make her rich wanted to make themselves rich first, and if the way they did this was by bleeding her dry, it was fine with them. On the other hand, if she was typical of the people they went after, they had kitty litter for brains. But it wasn't until she began to think about accumulating wealth for purposes other than her own comfort and happiness that she began to reconsider the approach she'd been taking. It hadn't been nearly broad enough.

There had been signs of this for awhile. The most obvious was when a company with a website that promised her Riches for Eternity as soon as she completed two easy steps sent her a metal detector she hadn't ordered. Things like this happened once your name got on enough get-rich-quick-scheme lists. They not only sent you stuff like cheapo metal detectors when you had never shown the slightest interest in getting rich by detecting metal, they sent them before you sent any money to pay for them, which Krystal had no intention of doing. When these Internet companies did this and then started going after you for payment, they used all kinds of tricks to scare you, but Krystal didn't scare that easily, as the company would have known if it had seen how she'd kept on with her life after she maimed Rocky Beach in such an unfortunate manner. She'd tossed the metal detector into the back of the ConGlom Couriers van with the idea of maybe hocking it.

This, by the way, was the same van she was driving when she saw Rocky Beach's dick lying on the floor. And, as a person who went off to work every day in that van and parked it in front of her place every night, she was the most notable exception to the rule that if somebody in SuEz got hold of a truck, they would sell it, because they couldn't think of anything else to do with it.

Not long after she received it, the metal detector went berserk and could easily have startled her into causing a major traffic accident, since she had no idea what was making the shrill noise. Luckily she wasn't driving at the time, she was loading up, and the metal detector's alarm went off when she threw in one particular parcel. Unluckily, there was a mishap in the back of the van when she got a safe distance from the terminal. The particular parcel came open and what she found inside was a complete mystery to her, although parts of it looked oddly familiar. When she read what was written on the box, though, she couldn't believe it. The device was a high-pressure dildo that hooked right into your household plumbing and electrical system the way a dishwasher would.

She couldn't even imagine fencing an item like that, since she couldn't imagine anybody being in the market for it ... but wait a minute. One person was. And it was that person's doorbell she rang with an apologetic look on her face, the item in one hand and the busted box in the other. When the gentleman answered, she said she was sorry, but there had been a problem in transit, and if he wanted she would return the merchandise. And he said, "Gee whiz, there must be some mistake."

Actually, before that he seemed to be having a hard time getting his breath. The, uh, whatever it was — he hadn't ordered *anything*. No, *nothing*. The address must be wrong. And the name. Some kind of computer mixup. And what a *ridiculous* looking gizmo it was anyway. What did she suppose it was? He examined it for some time, making clucking noises with his tongue, and finally he laughed. Wasn't it just too bizarre for words? Wouldn't it just make quite the conversation piece, though, when he had friends over? But wouldn't Krystal get in trouble if he accepted delivery and whoever had really ordered it called and complained, wondering where it had got to?

No, she said. There was no problem.

What the heck then. He would take it off her hands. And he gave her a twenty-five dollar tip.

Twenty-five dollars falling on her out of the sky was the kind of thing that got Krystal's mind working extra shifts. She thought how every time she tried to get rich quick, she couldn't afford to do it. But this time she also thought that if she was the one who had the item or whatever the other party wanted, they would pay *her* for it. If that sounds obvious, it wasn't. Growing up in SuEz, the only people she'd known who had anything other people wanted and were willing to pay for were whores and drug dealers.

Doing normal business was unheard of, if you didn't count the Korean up the street who had a corner store and when anybody was in it kept saying to them over and over, "Please don't steal from me. Please don't steal from me."

That was all he ever said. Nina's daughters thought maybe it was the only English he knew. When they bought something and he gave them change, he said, "Please don't steal from me." Guinevere hated him for saying it because it made her feel dirty and cheap, since she was the only one of the sisters who regularly stole very much. Merlina explained that was how Gwinny got all the magazines she had to read to find out if there was anything about her in them. When most people stole, though, they mostly stole so they could buy drugs. So they were still working within the system.

The astonishing concept Krystal stumbled on called for turning her approach inside out.

Now she needed her own scheme. One with low overhead. Better yet, with no overhead. Even better, with no product, either. And it could be she had never heard that the easiest marks are the people who think they're too smart to get conned, but somehow or other that was precisely her target market.

Not being a natural writer, she turned to Jarmeel Tolbert, who had a way with words that was perfect for what she had in mind. When she looked at the scuba diver's mask he'd spray-painted gold and wore perched on the top of his head, and told him she thought it was excellent, he was very pleased. He said he'd been forced to improvise like this because the only spaceship-style headgear available on the market came in little kids' sizes and didn't fit him.

While the letters were taking shape, Krystal was amazed how many names and addresses of potential clients she could find on the Internet, all of them top-level executives and government officials. It was also quite educational. Until then she had no idea that the capital of Nigeria was some place called Abuja.

They all started along the lines of this one:

Chief Oniwaju O. Gdabamdosi, Ph.D.,
Chairman,
Rogomaku Heavy Industrials Group plc,
(Formerly Princess Ziwawarka Esthetics
Institute),
Acacia Park, Plot PC 2,
Opposite Kringeli Disposals,
Lagos

"My Very Dear Most Excellency Doctor,"
After that, they were all word for word the same:

I takin time out ob my busy skedule to write
you about a little problem dat have come up
wid de Administeration here in Washington,
D.C. You be de one person in de worl who
in a position to solve it and get my poor
husband out ob de biggest jam he evah been
in. Yes, dat's right. I talkin about de top man.
I be de Fust Lady and he be de President
ob de United States. In dat role I be keepin
de books and lookin after de accounts and
swattin de flies and watchin de servants so
dey don't go widdlin in de Bram Flakes dat
he be needin every morning for keepin de
Presidential bowels in workin order. Den
dere's the prunes. You not watchin em every
minute, dey slippin cat turds in among de
prunes. It be a security nightmare.
But enough about me.
Let me fillin you in on a few ob de details.

Anybody who has ever been offered Nigerian
opportunities to rake in millions and wished they had the

92

resources to take advantage of them, or who has in fact raked in millions and is expecting the Lagos African Continental Bank draft to arrive any day now, because God knows, the money order their new Nigerian friend had asked them to send as an article of good faith and to cover shipping expenses was cashed months ago — anybody in a situation like those will understand how, looking at it from the other side of the Atlantic, it made perfect sense that the First Lady's brother would get hired to do some urgent renovations to Fort Knox. Fort Knox is where the U.S. government keeps all its gold, and it wasn't just run down, it was going to fall down unless something was done quickly. Putting that much gold in even a top-secret storage facility while the work was underway was obviously a huge problem. It was almost impossible to even keep track of how much there was. Just moving it to some other location would require seven or eight hundred railway cars.

Understandably, none of this could be done through regular channels. Security reasons alone made it impossible. Therefore outside, preferably offshore, assistance was necessary. So if Dr. Chief Gdabamdosi — in this particular case — could come forward temporarily with three hundred thousand dollars, the financial status of the U.S. would be protected. In return, a number of railway cars filled with gold ingots would be shunted off on a sidetrack of Dr. Chief Gdabamdosi's choosing, which he could then collect at his convenience. How did six of them sound? Each car loaded with two billion dollars worth of gold. For a grand total of twelve billion dollars, give or take.

And they all ended:

> I be attachin a name and address which, considerin de situation, ain't my real name and address for fear ob gettin into de Wall

Street Junnel and causin a run on de banks or similar panic. But if you makin out de certified cheque or equivalent fiduciary instrument to my non-official name as shown, it gonna work out just fine. You doesn't have to worry about dat, dat's for sure. De FBI have ways ob gettin it cashed for me.

And if you evah in de neighbourhood, you just come by de White House and say Hello. We givin you a nice meal and lettin you sit in de Kennedy rockerin chair wid a big glass ob gin while de President hisself be regalin you wid stories about life at de top.

Lookin forward to your soonest reply.

Krystal's email went out to a nice, round one hundred recipients.

TWELVE

Chunk. Chunk. Chunk. Chunk, chunk. Chunk.

Nina opened her eyes.

Chunkchunkchunk. Chunk. Clang.

"*Clang?*"

Sometimes you wake up because you hear something, and it turns out that nothing is there. It was a noise in a dream. This wasn't like that. Each chunk made the mattress shake. It rattled the window.

This was definitely there.

She scuffled into the hall and put her ear against the cellar door.

Chreech, chreech — some kind of scraping. Chunk, chunk. Clank.

Really, *really* there.

She crept back and shook D.S. He farted. The mattress shook. The window rattled.

"Somebody's in the basement," she whispered. It was a

waste of time. When she looked back on it, that was a good thing. Rousing D.S. would have caused such a racket that whoever was in the basement would have rushed upstairs and murdered and raped them all.

When they looked back on it, at least three of the individuals who would have been murdered and raped couldn't remember the chunking noise — that was Guinevere, Merlina, and Lady. They only heard about it from Nina after Frank and the loot from the robbery both disappeared. Until she started reminiscing about it long afterwards, they could barely recall some of the other things — the voices yelling in the cellar, the threats, the smashed windows, some guy bouncing Nina's head off the wall, her chopping the welfare inspector's arm off. The back door, of course, they could all remember it not being there. It went missing right after Frank did and stayed that way for the rest of the time they lived in the house. Everybody remembered this very clearly, except for Fabreece. Her excuse was that she was too young to remember, but Merlina and Lady didn't buy that. They believed it was because she never paid attention.

The cellar door was bolted. Nina slid the bolt back, turned the knob, and pulled. Every hair on her body stood up. *The hinges! Jesus Christ Almighty!* The whole street would be jumping out of bed yelling "What the fuck —?"

Chunk. Chunk.

Chreech.

The same noises. Whoever it was didn't hear.

She stuck her head through the opening. She couldn't make out the stairs, the walls, anything. What would happen if she flipped on the light? Nothing. There was no bulb. Anybody going down the basement, even when some daylight seeped through the window, needed a flashlight. There was no flashlight. Those were two of the reasons nobody went down there.

She listened closely. From here it sounded like the noise was coming from the back end of the house. And now that she had her head stuck through the doorway, it didn't sound like it was coming from inside, either.

More like near the back porch. Maybe under the back porch. Nina peeked through the window over the sink. The chunking came from right below it. She could yank the back door open, leap out on the porch, and yell, "Get away from here you fuckin' sons of ..." Or she could have, if there was still a back door. Instead there was a bunch of plastic drop cloths covering the opening where the door used to be, drop cloths somebody'd stuffed under the porch years ago, before Nina and her family moved in, that were caked with brittle paint and smelled like cat piss when they got wet. They had to have been there for years, because the only paint on anything inside the house was faded or peeling. Unless they'd been stolen and somebody ditched them there. Why would anybody steal gacked-up old drop cloths? Why would anybody steal the water out of the swimming pool? When the door disappeared, she had hauled them up and hung them in its place.

The door had disappeared the night before. Not even Nina had heard anything when that happened. D.S. was amazed, because whoever stole it not only had to pry off the boards that had been nailed around it on the outside to keep people from going out and falling through the porch and hurting themselves, but had to come right into the kitchen to take it off the hinges. Who knew what else these people had done while they were in the house? "It's like in the Bible," D.S. said, "where it says that if you don't have nothing then you need not fear a thief, for no thief will steal nothing."

He was telling everybody that those were words to live by when Nina said, "How on earth did we get so lucky?"

While D.S. crinkled his forehead trying to figure out what she meant by that, Nina went back to thinking how amazing it was that nobody had been murdered and raped by the door thief while they were all asleep and helpless. And now here was this whatever it was, this chunking. That must be how she came to hear it — she hadn't been sleeping very soundly because of what happened the night before.

Through the kitchen window she saw flickering. Whoever was out there had some kind of light. And they were *tunneling!* It hit her like a runaway train. *They were tunneling through the basement wall!* Why wouldn't they have just come in through the plastic sheets on the back door? They could have pushed inside in half a second. Unless they didn't know the door wasn't there. And if they didn't, this meant *whoever was out there chunking at the foundation was somebody different than whoever had stolen the door!* The safety of her household was being threatened by two entirely different individuals. Or groups of individuals. "What the fuck —?"

Whatever it was, it was another example of how seriously things were starting to exasperate her. She'd been cut off welfare before, many times, but everybody had. Getting cut off welfare exasperated her all right, but it was the same way having a cold exasperated her. After it went away, she didn't give it another thought until she caught the next one. And D.S. had been laid off for long stretches before. It was the nature of the business he was in and of the special quality he had for being a discount-store greeter. But in the present situation, certain things were seriously different. For some reason, satellite-guided, computer-driven, pinpoint ice-cream marketing had got her boiling. Instead of taking everything the way she took everything that had made her life difficult before, she'd attacked the ice cream company. And maybe having the welfare inspector sneak around ambushing her had some kind of effect that was different than when he spied on her through the bedroom window. Maybe it was getting everybody she knew involved in a huge, community fundraising project when none of them had ever been involved in anything but their own lives before, the same as she had always been. Maybe having her house attacked by two different unidentified enemies made her feel more vulnerable than she ever could have thought possible. Maybe she didn't know exactly what it was that was doing it, maybe she just wasn't used to being really, seriously exasperated by anything, and maybe that's what had turned her from an average, down-to-earth welfare queen into some kind of raging warrior welfare queen, and one who was very, very pissed off.

She didn't give the slightest thought to what she was about to do. She wasn't conscious of grabbing the first thing her hand touched. She didn't realize it was the big old butcher knife that had a splotchy iron blade and a wooden handle that was loose. The knife was lying beside the sink where it always did, where it had been when they moved in. Hardly anyone noticed it was there any more. D.S. said it would have been easier to cut something with a toilet plunger than with that knife. Nevertheless, she hoisted it above her head and went flying out the front door and down the steps, yelling for whoever it was to stop doing whatever the fuck they were doing and leave her family alone. And she wasn't even halfway down the side of the house when she crashed full tilt into somebody running the other way.

"*Joof!*" If she'd been a bulldozer, she couldn't have knocked him flatter.

"You son of a bitch! You son of a bitch!" she yelled, stabbing like crazy with the butcher knife.

"Yeagh!" he screamed, and broke free.

"Yeagh!" Nina screamed, not because he'd broken free, but because even though he'd broken free and was running away, she still had a tight grip on him. On his arm. Jesus ... *she did!* She was still *holding his arm!* It was one thing to charge out and defend your family from lethal danger. When you did that, you realized, at least subconsciously, that you might kill whoever was threatening your security, or fatally wound them at least. But who looked ahead carefully enough to consider that besides killing and fatally wounding, there was a third possibility: dismembering? Neither does anybody give any thought to the chance that what you might end up with in your hand is the dismembered portion. Nina staggered around to the back of the house where the intruder had been digging the tunnel and hurled the arm into it, her knees buckling with the sick horror of what she'd done.

"Ow!" cried a voice from the hole. "Watch what you're doing, you fuckin' asshole!"

Nina reeled backwards as the voice took wing. "Fuckin' assholes falling on top of me. Fuckin' assholes throwing shit at me." She heard scrabbling. "I've had enough of this fuckin' bullshit." She ducked around the corner as he pulled himself out of the hole and stalked to the back of the yard and climbed the fence which, from the sound of things, collapsed, because the last thing she heard after a crash was a mournful groan followed by "Fuckin' goddamn fuckin' goddamn ..."

For the rest of the night, waves of hysterical nausea broke her sleep. It didn't matter that it had been pitch dark when she'd hacked off the arm, every time it got replayed in her mind it became more visible until it was as if the whole thing had happened in the glare of spotlights. No one was safe anymore. Terrible people who were prepared to do terrible things had her family surrounded and were driving her to do even more terrible things.

No. Wait. She was exaggerating. She had to be. It was because of the strain.

That was the most encouraging thought she could come up with. Unfortunately, it was wishful thinking.

THIRTEEN

She wasn't sure whether the banging on the front door fit into the realm of ghastly dreams or horrible imaginings. The sound of the ice cream truck babbling and tootling off into the distance suggested it wasn't the sleeping one, though. So did the sight of the welfare inspector who had been popping out at inconvenient times and making incomprehensible threats. He was standing there when she opened it. For some irresistible reason, her eyes were drawn to his sleeve. The sleeve of his plastic windbreaker. That was hanging straight down. Lifelessly. Completely empty.

Her heart started thrashing somewhere under her stomach. If the clarity of the realization paralyzed her, the paralysis was all that kept her from puking. There he had obviously been, doing nothing more than going about his business when, in the mistaken belief that he was somebody else, she had attacked him. And now here he was, back. Like those hideous ghosts she'd heard about that return to claim their former bodies or, in this case, a portion of their former —

"Madam," said a clipped voice from behind the welfare inspector. That was when she noticed he wasn't alone. That was also when she noticed that after losing a limb only hours before in a confrontation that was so violent his face and clothes were still smudged with dirt, the welfare inspector wasn't also drenched with blood and hunched over in agony. There was no sign of blood anywhere. And instead of an agonized crouch, he was smirking.

When she said, "I'm out of my fuckin' mind," it sounded muffled because she'd covered her face with her hands.

"Madam," the second man repeated, scowling at her around the welfare inspector's armless sleeve, "are you, or do you claim to be, Nina Carson Dolgoy," and he read out her welfare number. "And if you are this Dolgoy person, I am obliged to advise you that you are going to wish you weren't by the time we get through with you."

The one-armed welfare inspector smirked harder.

"Now," the second man said, "in the course of performing his duties on or about last night, a departmental employee —" he nodded toward the welfare inspector "— fell into unlicensed renovations being undertaken on this site without even rudimentary precautions to prevent such a mishap: i.e. barricades, hoardings, blinking lights, sign advising motorists to slow down, sign advising pedestrians to cross to the other side, police officer on duty, and so forth, as stipulated. Whereupon the workman therein pummeled my subordinate and threatened his life as follows...."

The inspector stopped smirking long enough to pull out a notebook and read aloud, "You fuckin' asshole. What the fuck are you doing? I'm going to kill your fuckin' ass, you fuckin' asshole."

"Causing my subordinate to exit the excavation," the other man went on, "and run for his life, whereupon you ambushed him. Employing some kind of broadsword or scimitar, you severed the Velcro straps attaching certain of his personal property to his personal self."

"Below the elbow." The inspector waggled his sleeve. "As must be specified for official purposes."

"Jesus," Nina said.

"But —" the inspector said.

"But —" the other man said.

" — give it back to me and we'll —"

" — and the department will forget the whole matter. God knows it's hard enough to recruit inspectors. If it turns out that they risk losing a prosthesis on the job, we won't get any —"

"It's not the money," the inspector interrupted.

Nina squeezed past them.

"It has sentimental value," the inspector said, following her around the side of the house.

"It was worn by his father before him," the other man said.

"It's been passed down in my family for generations," the inspector said.

Give them the goddamn thing back, Nina said to herself. *Give them the goddamn thing back. And get them the goddamn hell out of here.*

But she couldn't.

The goddamn thing was goddamn gone.

She scuffled around the hole. She scuffled around the busted fence. She shook her head helplessly. "I don't know where it went," she said.

"You what?"

"Ohhhh," the other man exhaled. "This is just like you people. Appeals to your humanity fail. Efforts to elicit your sympathy for an unfortunate fellow citizen are scorned. And as a result — it was ever thus, I don't know why we even bother any more — as a result, you leave us no choice."

The inspector smirked enthusiastically.

"Absolutely no choice," the other man continued. "We do everything we possibly can to help you, but — what a waste. And so I herewith inform you that your name will be removed immediately from the rolls of welfare recipients."

"Yowee!" The smirking inspector pumped his remaining fist.

"You can't," Nina said.

"We *can't?*" The other man sounded taken aback. "Of course we can. At least I think we can. I'm certain we can. I thought I read it somewhere." He looked at the smirking inspector. "Didn't you think we could?"

"Nope. You can't," Nina said. "Nobody can remove my name, because my name has already been removed."

"It has?" the inspector said.

"Yes, yes," the other man said. "Of course it has. We knew that. We just wanted to see if you'd — um —"

"So there's nothing you can do." Nina headed around for the front door. "To me anyway, or to my kids."

"You're wrong there, madam," the other man said. "We can hold this latest offence in abeyance until you are restored to the welfare rolls, and then take you off again immediately."

"We'll take you off every time you're put back on until you return my personal property."

"How could I get back on if you take me off?"

For a minute both men swivelled their eyes back and forth. Then the other man said, "Madam, there are matters that not even we are allowed to know. After all," he said, "we don't make the rules."

"Then who does?"

"That," the man sneered, as if Nina had finally shown how completely ignorant she was, "is classified."

"You don't know, do you?"

"Of course we do."

"No you don't."

"We do too," the inspector said. His smirk had an anxious tinge. He turned to the other man. "Don't we?"

That night somebody kicked in the basement window and got inside. When Nina yelled downstairs that whoever it was better get the hell out of there, that she was calling the cops, that there were children upstairs who were scared to death, whoever it was pounded up out of the darkness and grabbed her head with both hands as if it was a basketball and started bouncing it off the wall. He kept bouncing it while he told her to go fuck herself. And while he told her she wouldn't call the cops if she wanted to go on living. And while he told her he didn't give a fuck about her fuckin' children, that he just wanted what was fuckin' his. Then the hall light clicked on, and there was D.S. wearing her pale blue nightie in the doorway to the girls' bedroom with the four of them huddled around him. The guy looked at this tableau and said, "Ah, fuck it," and let go of Nina's head, walked out the front door, got in a car, and drove away.

"What's his?" Lady said, when her sisters got over their shock enough to start whimpering.

"Huh?" Nina said, massaging the back of her skull.

"That he wants. That he said was his. What is it?" Lady said.

"I don't know," Nina said.

The night after that, there was a brawl down there. It sounded like there were five or six of whoever they were. Gwinny began screaming, and when one of them got going, it was hard for the other three not to join in. D.S. had the look of a man who, if he started to pee his pants, would keep peeing until there was nothing left of him but a little pile of dust. Nina made him take the girls across to JannaRose and

Ed Oataway's and then sat on the floor at the top of the steps holding the butcher knife in her fist. The lights were flashing and jumping around as if there was a thunderstorm inside the cellar, except instead of thunder there were thuds and swearing and people going "Umph!" Then it got completely quiet. Then it went completely dark. When she shouted down this time, nobody answered.

The next morning she borrowed a flashlight from Ed Oataway. She'd only been down the cellar once before, when they moved in, and not all the way down, either. It was too filthy. This time, as far as she could tell, apart from the window being smashed and the big hole in the back wall, the only difference was it was filthier. The smell was horrible, but in some strange kind of way. Strange because she both knew what the smell was and she didn't. She knew it because it was the smell of mildew and mold and spilled food that had never been wiped up and feet that had never been washed and dirty diapers left in the bathtub forever that nobody cared about because nobody had any reason to care, so why bother? It was the smell inside every house in SuEz, it was the smell of the breeze in SuEz, it was the smell of being so poor for so long that the poor don't even realize they're poor. It was the way her life had smelled all her life, and it had always been there the way her life had been. But if you take some music you've known and have become accustomed to hearing your whole life and turn it up so loud it hurts, you no longer recognize the old familiar tune any more. All you recognize is loudness and pain. The smell in the cellar was the atmosphere Nina had moved through every day, except at maximum volume. It was the first time she ever noticed it.

She gagged.

Apart from that, nothing down there was very interesting. Cobwebs so thick she could have used them for blankets.

Tools somebody had brought in — shovels and things. The cement floor had heaved and cracked, but nothing suggested any serious digging. In fact, it didn't look like there had been any digging at all, other than the tunnel. There were a lot of scrapes and scuffs on the floor, what you'd probably get if a bunch of guys had been fighting — rolling around in the dirt and getting knocked down.

After she'd had a chance to think all these things over, to take all the things that had been happening to her family and fit them together with Frank and with Frank's loot, she would say that she'd never had any ambition to be a genius, but it didn't matter. Because if you took a look at the cellar that day, you didn't have to be a genius to figure out what the hell was going on.

FOURTEEN

"What the hell is going on?" she said, plunking herself on a chair right in front of Ed Oataway.

It turned out to be something he didn't care to discuss. Not there in his living room, not anywhere.

"What did you do, drive the getaway car?" Nina leaned forward like she was ready to punch his head in. "Tell me! You knew about the bank robbery."

"Not exactly," Ed said.

"*Not exactly?*" Nina said. "You knew as much about it as any other living person."

"Drive the getaway car. I didn't do that exactly."

"*What* then?" Now JannaRose was chiming in. And after a little more of this encouragement, Ed gave up and explained exactly what he had done.

The story made Nina feel as if a bunch of giant people had kicked her in the stomach all at once.

"*For how much?*" JannaRose said, getting straight to

what interested her in a way that nearly shattered the glass in the windows.

"Me?" Ed Oataway said. "A thou."

"*And you were keeping it some kind of fuckin' secret?*"

"Ex — Ex —" Nina was trying to say "Excuse me" so she could break into the conversation, but her voice had turned to sandpaper. "He — He —"

Ed stared over her shoulder as if he wasn't going to say a word. About this. About anything. Ever again.

"When you made it so the getaway ..." Nina had her eyes closed like she was doing arithmetic in her head. " ... when you made it so the getaway car couldn't get away because you crashed into it ..." The arithmetic was hard, though, and she had to go slowly. " ... but if the getaway car could have got away, it was supposed to take ..." Could that be right? She went over it again. " ... it was supposed to take him somewhere?"

Ed looked as if he couldn't even hear anything she was saying.

"The getaway car was supposed to take him somewhere? Where he was supposed to give the money to ..." She seemed to be asking herself if this really added up. " ... to somebody else?"

Ed might have looked like he was tuned out, but JannaRose was taking in every word. "What?" she said.

"*Frank wasn't supposed to keep the money!*" Nina said.

"*What?*" JannaRose said.

Nina stuck her face as far forward as it could go without her nose crunching Ed Oataway's. "*He wasn't, was he!*"

There was dead silence. It lasted about a minute. Then Ed leaned way back in his chair. "No," he said.

"The son of a bitch," Nina said. "Somebody hired him to steal that money. Then he turned around and stole it off whoever it was that hired him to steal it."

"Jesus," JannaRose said.

Ed had a reputation for not saying much, but there were a few things it would have been nice to know based on what he'd just said. A few details it would have been helpful for him to add. A few gaps he might usefully have filled in. He wasn't going to, though. "No." It was all he had to say. It was all he said.

If Ed was even more tight-lipped than usual, it stood to reason. But it wasn't because he was a deeply loyal kind of guy, or because he believed everybody he was deeply loyal to would screw him the first chance they got. And it wasn't as if he felt all knotted up inside by this loyalty, even though he could see how foolish it was to be loyal to what were, when you got right down to it, shits and louses. And what did he care about what Nina thought about him keeping his thoughts to himself? She'd made it clear a long time ago that as far as she was concerned, he never had a thought that was any use, no matter whether he kept it to himself or stuck it up his ass. And it wasn't because Frank Carson had been his best friend for as long as he could remember. Or that over the years they had often talked about making one big score together so they could enjoy their lives free of want. Or that as the years passed, Ed became more and more convinced that his best friend was working up to that big score and not letting him in on it.

He wasn't even sure Frank hadn't pulled off the big score and then gone to jail to make Ed think he hadn't pulled it off, to keep him from demanding the cut his friendship entitled him to, thus spoiling their friendship. He believed their friendship was so important to Frank that Frank was perfectly capable of doing something like that to preserve it and keep all the money for himself. It made Ed sad to realize that his best friend was such a completely fuckin' two-faced cocksucker.

On the other hand, the two-faced cocksucker was the only real friend he had. They went back to first grade. They'd dreamed big dreams from the start. That counted for something. And as far as he could see, it had nothing to do with Frank lucking into the fake bank robbery when he was in jail, or that this amounted to a bigger score than either of them had ever dreamed of. Or that Frank had offered him only a very small chunk of change for handling a minor assignment in the transportation department while clearly planning to screw whoever it was who had hired him, and take the dough, and keep it all for himself. It wasn't because Ed was bitter. He wasn't. He knew how friendships worked and, given the chance, he would have done the same thing, including not paying Frank what he'd agreed to.

No, the reason Ed Oataway didn't want to discuss this wasn't quite as philosophical. He didn't want to because when it was getting dark a few hours after the robbery, he'd seen Frank go into Dipshit and Nina's house carrying the same big Nike bag he'd come out of the bank with. That was shortly before he was kidnapped in front of their house during the raging storm of gunfire. What happened after that — the way Frank got tortured and murdered — made Ed want to puke every time he thought about it. Because if Frank hadn't shown how much he treasured their friendship by stiffing him all down the line, he might have wound up with a bigger part to play in the deal, in which case he could have ended up getting subjected to the same hideous treatment as Frank. He would be eternally grateful to Frank for this, just as he would go out of his way for the rest of his life to spit on Frank's grave for screwing him out of what, by rights, should have been his.

Apart from that, the thing that stood out in his mind was that when they were all outside that night staring at the muzzle flashes from the towers and half-assed ducking because the sky was thick with what that fuckin' bonehead Nina kept calling bees — what stood out in his mind then, and still stood out, was that when the heavies showed up and stuffed Frank into the trunk of their car, he hadn't had the Nike bag with him.

That was why, shortly after two a.m., Ed had pried Dipshit and Nina's back door loose, wrestled it off its hinges, carried it across to his own backyard and hidden it under all the scrap and stuff he had piled there. He'd discovered, however, that he wasn't used to that much physical effort and was too tired to go back and snoop around their house right then, so he stretched out on the couch in his own living room for a little rest. He didn't wake up until after daylight, and that was because Nina was yelling at JannaRose that she couldn't fuckin' believe it, somebody had stolen their back door.

What Ed Oataway couldn't fuckin' believe was the tremendous number of individuals who had been breaking into Dipshit and Nina's ever since, making it impossible for him to sneak back in. Neither was he the kind of person to see the irony in this. As far as he was concerned, Frank would have wanted him to have the money in light of what occurred, the same as he would have wanted Frank to have it if it had been the other way around, and that's all there was to it. These assholes who had started showing up out of who knows where didn't give a shit about the emotions that were at stake. The 1.18 million dollars they were looking for was the same to them as any 1.18 million dollars they could lay their hands on would have been. It was stolen money and nothing more. It didn't represent all that was left of the greatest friendship in the history of SuEz. All that was left apart from the memories.

By the time Ed thought this all the way through, Nina had gone home and JannaRose was lying down with a wet facecloth over her eyes, and there was only one thing he could do in the circumstances. He banged on Dipshit and Nina's door. Nothing happened, and he was just about to start kicking it when he heard somebody on the other side. It was Nina. She didn't open the door, though.

"What do you want?" she shouted.

"He never paid me," Ed shouted back.

"Go fuckin' fuck yourself."

"The thousand he promised. I just wanted to make sure you know that."

FIFTEEN

The cop banged on D.S. and Nina's door. Nothing happened, and he was just about to bang again when he heard somebody on the other side. It was Nina. When she opened it, he started to say something but stopped and simply looked at her. He got right to the verge of talking a couple of more times, but he kept stopping. It was as if the sight of her had whacked him on the head and all he could do was stand there, staring.

Plainclothes cops were a long way from being an everyday sight in SuEz, but then, if you asked most people, so were cops of any kind. Maybe it was like Nina said, and they were scared of that part of town and avoided it if they possibly could. Or it could be they figured that anybody disgusting enough to live there deserved whatever happened to them, and anybody who wanted something done about it could do it themselves. It definitely would have been strange if anybody ever called them, at least before Fabreece started doing it, but by then nearly everybody in her family had decided Fabreece was strange. The only reason a normal person might call was if they got nervous about the gangsters shooting everything in sight at three in the morning, but if you did, it meant your nerves had deleted every cell in your brain, because if the gangsters found out who it was, that person could forget living in SuEz any more, or anywhere else for that matter. In Fabreece's case, she now called the cops on Merlina and Lady whenever they pissed her off after they got her lost when they tried to street-proof her.

As Merlina explained it, teaching a little girl to find her way home in her own neighbourhood made extremely good sense. She also explained that anybody who thought about it carefully would think it was weird that somebody hadn't street-proofed Fabreece already. So she and Lady took her for a long walk one afternoon without telling her what the plan was, although Merlina told Lady that this was because when you really do get lost, you don't get a chance to plan for it. Then they snuck away when she wasn't looking and headed for home.

After she realized she didn't know where her sisters were or where she was, she pulled out D.S.'s mobile phone. It came as a complete surprise to Merlina and Lady that Fabreece had the phone, but it turned out she always carried it in case of emergency after she'd ended up getting taken into a car by a strange man that time. She called 911, but after she talked to them for awhile, 911 hung up. Apparently they decided it was just a little girl dinking around, and if they sent the cops racing out every time some little girl decided to see what would happen if she called 911, they wouldn't have time to deal with any of the real emergencies that came along. Meanwhile Merlina and Lady couldn't find their way to their house, and it wasn't until the next morning that somebody from their street saw them and asked what they were doing in that part of town and drove them back.

The minute they saw Nina, Merlina started telling her it was because they had street-proofed themselves that they knew to hang around near an all-night gas station in case rescuers came searching for them. Then she said she and Lady were sorry about Fabreece and hoped somebody would find her alive somewhere, too.

"Fabreece got home before dark," Nina said.

This amazed Merlina and Lady, but after 911 kept hanging up on her, Fabreece phoned Ed Oataway, who came and picked her up. "Thank God," Merlina said. "Our training did her some good after all."

"Oh, yeah?" Nina said. "Well, I'm really pissed off, and you two will be good and sorry when I find out what the fuck is going on here."

"Mom," Lady said, "Merly never even mentioned street-proofing until yesterday. Her whole idea was to get Fabreece lost forever so there would be peace and quiet for the rest of us or something."

"You are so fuckin' lying, Lady," Merlina said.

Lady said Merlina's original idea had been to do it to Guinevere, but she couldn't get her to come for a walk with them.

When Nina finally stopped yelling "I don't fuckin' believe this!" and things cooled down a bit, Merlina reminded Lady how Lady had kind of neglected to mention to Nina that when Merlina first told her about the plan, Lady hadn't exactly objected. She pointed out that if they ever did something else that involved Fabreece, and Ed didn't happen to have his phone turned on, and she could only call 911, they wouldn't have to worry because the cops would never come.

Even though a yellow linen sports jacket and a pink polo shirt — there was a black silk square in the breast pocket of the jacket — might have fooled some people, Nina knew right away that the man on her porch was a cop. That was why she didn't say anything either, not even "Yeah?" when he just stood and stared at her. The silence felt as if it could go one for a week or two, but then the cop shot a glance up the street.

"What's that?" From his tone, he didn't like it, whatever it was.

She still didn't say anything.

"That noise?" he said, and looked at his watch as if he wanted to make sure it really wasn't seven in the morning yet.

"Noise?" Nina said. She'd been hearing it for twenty minutes.

"Jesus Christ!" He edged down a couple of steps, taking care where he set his feet. He wasn't built like he spent a lot of time in the gym. He also looked kind of old for a cop. He stared in the direction of the towers. When at last he said, "It's an ice cream truck," Nina thought he sounded like somebody who had never seen one before in his whole life.

"Oh." Most of her experience with cops had involved steering clear of them, but when she couldn't, she opted for the non-committal.

"What's it doing at this time of day?" His forehead creased as if somewhere behind it he was running down a list of laws, looking for one that had to do with when it was legal for ice cream trucks to operate. He checked his watch again. "On a school day?"

"Selling ice cream?" She thought about saying this. It was fairly non-committal, but sensitive individuals might catch a whiff of smartass. Then she considered "I don't know," but rejected it, too. Just how stupid would she have to be not to know, and by coming out and saying it, she risked making the cop think she thought *he* must be stupid. Even more than he doesn't like somebody who's a smartass, a cop really and truly doesn't like it when anybody hints that he himself might be stupid. And it doesn't matter if the hint is so subtle, it's outside the range of normal human hearing.

Nina's daughters pushed into the doorway. She stuck her elbows out, and they were on the verge of whining about how they couldn't get past when they saw the man on the steps and shut up. Not even people who'd grown up there could say how everybody down to the littlest kids knew a cop when they saw one. Could be it was a sixth sense they'd inherited from all those ancestors who had lived in a part of town where everybody from outside took for granted that they were guilty of something. They had to be. Look at them. Nobody went around acting that suspiciously without a good reason.

The technical term in law enforcement for people who behave like this is assholes. Some people can earn the description, but folks in SuEz were born to it, and that's mainly why cops had no interest in the place. Imagine how crazy it made them, driving around and seeing nothing but natural-born assholes everywhere, and knowing they could get them off the street in one second flat if they could only find out what law it was the assholes had just broken. Cruising through SuEz probably caused more cops to think maybe they didn't have what it took to do the job than anything else they encountered in their careers.

A police officer with feelings of inadequacy could be dangerous, but that's not why the one on Nina's porch was. He turned back to the door and found the woman surrounded by four kids, not one of whom paid the slightest attention to him. They were trying to squeeze past their mother to see the ice cream truck. That was the only thing she seemed to care about too, but nevertheless he puckered his lips in a way that showed he was about to get down to business. Then the first amplified words he could clearly make out stopped him again.

"What's the matter with you, Terence?" the truck said, and the cop's forehead got really wrinkled.

Especially since right after "What's the matter with you, Terence?" it said. "This is a disgrace. For the last three days you haven't bought the Eskimo Blasters we made with you in mind. We stay up late every night making them just for you, Terence. And we bring one to you every morning, fresh and delicious. Do you know we throw the old ones out? The ones you don't buy. They're no good any more. They're garbage. How do you feel about that, Terence? Forcing us to throw them away when we've gone to the trouble of making them for you, and you alone. So get over here with your money, Terence! You're starting to make us angry."

And: "Shelagh — we like you, Shelagh. You're not like Gironelle and Tara, who we don't like any more. They don't come down here and buy their Glacier Gloopsters and Frozeberry Flyers. We like you because you always buy your Frosty-Totsies. You were able to buy one yesterday because you went in the jar above the stove where your mother hides her change and you found enough to pay for it. Shelagh — don't worry! After you've spent all your mother's change, she'll have something you can sell to get enough. A ring maybe, or a necklace. Right now, though, all we hope is you've got enough money for today. Because if you don't, we're going to stop liking you, too."

Until: "Look boys and girls!" It was in front of Nina's house. "This is where Guinevere and Merlina and Lady and Fabreece live!" The cop whipped his head around. "Their mother is an ugly fat pig and is mean to them. Somebody should call the welfare department and ask if they know she abuses them. It could be they're covered with bruises. Notice how they never come down where we can see them? But you stay away from them, you hear. They smell and they're full of lice."

The cop was down the steps and around to the driver's window before the girls and Nina even noticed he'd moved. He was bellowing. He was waving his arms around. He was flashing his badge. He was saying, "What the fuck do you think you're doing? If what you're doing isn't against the law, I don't give a fuck. It's as against the law as I need. And if," he was saying, "you come back on this street ever again I'll impound the goddamn truck and hold it in custody until every fuckin' thing inside it melts. Including," and here he shoved his head right in the window, "*you*, you shit on a stick."

The truck sped off, leaving him in the middle of the street with his chin stuck out. His face was bright red except for the white spots around his eyes. It was still those colours when he came back up the steps, still half shouting, "I never heard any such fffff-f-f —" To calm down he almost had to strangle himself. "I never heard of any such ... a *thing* in my life." He was worked up.

"Yes, sir," Nina said, her voice no different than before.

"Anyway, they won't try that again." With his fingertips he tugged his sports jacket closed across his stomach and tucked in his pocket square. "Now if you kids will excuse us, I want to speak to Mrs...." His voice trailed off. As the girls headed into the house, they glared at him as if he'd taken a dump on their front steps. It was the last thing he expected.

" ... to Mrs. Dolgoy ..." And again he went silent. This wasn't the way he was used to working. He didn't bully people. He intimidated them by being so completely sure about everything he did. This time, though, something was wrong. Not wrong, disturbing. Not disturbing, peculiar. Not peculiar — yeah, peculiar.

He *recognized* this woman.

It's as if he *knew* her.

Where did he know her from?

He had no idea.

To a man who'd built his career on never getting tripped up by the unexpected, if this wasn't peculiar it was … too fuckin' peculiar.

Nina waited. She could wait a long time before doing anything to help a conversation with a cop get off the ground.

He took a couple of breaths to pull himself together. "Mrs. Dolgoy, I'm very sorry, but I understand you're related to Frank Carson. His sister? I wonder if you could come downtown and possibly identify a body?"

"When?"

He'd never heard anything like it. No reaction. Just "When?" Like if he'd told her he was from the works department and they were going to shut off her water for fifteen minutes. It was so unlike anything he'd ever encountered that he had to struggle to keep his voice level.

"Now?" he said.

"Who'll take care of my kids?"

Okay. A good, practical question. He knew he was thinking too much and not simply reacting in the professional way that produced fear and co-operation in people he was interviewing, but he was damned if he could figure out what was making him do it. And if he'd had kids, he wouldn't have wanted them anywhere near this street to begin with, much less getting babysat by any of the assholes who lived on it. But what the hell.

"Isn't there a neigh —"

"They're all busy."

"Wait!" He looked at his watch again, tapping the glass. "The kids'll be at school in —"

"They'll be off sick today."

"Really? They looked fine to —"

"They're going to be off sick."

"But —"

"Because they're ashamed of what the truck said."

Oh, for Christ's sake. He supposed he could pack them all into his car. He had his own car today. A Toyota Solara, electric blue. A two-door convertible. He looked good in it with the top down, his silver hair streaming. His hair lapped over his temples, over the tops of his ears, fluffed around the back of his neck — perfect for streaming. But these were dirty little kids. Not dirty on account of missing their baths last night. There was no "on account of" about it. They hadn't had baths last night. Or any night. Or ever. They never had baths. They were born dirty, and they'd been getting dirtier every day since. They breathed dirty air, they ate dirty food with their dirty fingers, they played in the dirt. If the dirt got washed off them, there would be more dirt under it. Anything they touched would get dirty. It would get dirty and it would stay dirty. It would never, ever be clean again. And if there was one thing Detective Sergeant Robbie Toole stood for, it was this: he would defend the law as far as it was useful to him to do so, but he would defend to the death his right to fit the stereotype of a gay man who was vain about his leather upholstery. To his death, to your death, to anybody's death, it didn't matter. Sand yellow — that was the colour of the upholstery. With the electric blue exterior, it was lethal.

"Mrs. Dolgoy — you knew Frank Carson might possibly be dead, did you?"

"No."

Un-fuckin'-*believable!* She knew her brother just changed his shirt, did she? "When did you last see him?"

"The night he got out. Or the night after. Around there."

"Can you say for sure?"

"The night all the bees flew over." She looked up, as if the sky was something she didn't place a whole lot of trust in.

"Hundreds of them. Somebody said they must've been using machine guns, because some of the bees were tracer rounds."

Toole kept his mouth shut. It could turn out that she was a mental case. Then again, she might be really cagey and trying to lead him into a hopeless mush of doubtful and confusing information. Who knew what the hell she might be? Or it could be he hadn't made himself very clear when he asked the question. Never mind. You just had to let some things go by. You learned the hard way.

"It doesn't matter," she said. "It's him."

"What?"

"The dead guy. It's Frank."

"How can —"

"By the fingerprints. You checked the fingerprints. Looked them up. Saw it was Frank. Checked with the prison or something. Saw I was his only relative. Why else would you have ended up here?"

Wow! "You and Frank ..." He was about to say something about how maybe they weren't all that close, but it drifted off.

"So what do you need me for?"

She had him there. But there was one thing he couldn't figure out and this visit to the sister wasn't going to make any clearer. Who the fuck Frank Carson was that somebody would murder him in such a gruesome way? Whatever that way was, exactly. The only thing he could say for sure was that an awful lot of wacko-ness had been turned loose on some asshole from SuEz who nobody ever heard of.

That's what had made Toole curious in the first place. Nobody puts that much effort into killing somebody for no good reason. No. That wasn't completely correct. A pervert might. Or perverts, since there were two of them. How would they know which chat rooms to troll to discover each other in the first place? But that was a tiny little coincidence.

The enormous Jesus coincidence was how did they decide on this particular victim? Somebody they just happened to see walking along the street? Who just happened to get out of jail the day before after doing three of eleven? And the day they snatch him just happened to be the day somebody walked out of the Great Big One National Bank with 1.18 million dollars, withdrawn at gunpoint? And the guy dies as a result of methods that Allied soldiers used in Iraq to encourage uncooperative individuals to divulge information? And the face of the armed robber in the bank security video just happens to ID the same as the fingerprints on the tormented stiff that was found tied to a tree in the park?

Little coincidences were things Toole had no problem with. You could always find them, especially if you were prepared to exercise a little creativity. But an enormous Jesus coincidence — there never had been such a thing. Ever. And there never would be. Not as far as cops were concerned. Not as far as a cop was concerned who was serious about his work. So now the only question was whether these two creeps had been successful in persuading Frank Carson to give up the information they wanted before he — the aptness and similarity of the phrase made Robbie Toole smile when it popped into his mind — before he gave up the ghost.

That's what he was interested in finding out more than anything. In fact, it was the only thing he was interested in finding out. Because to him, being a cop was more than a job, it was a business.

As a senior member of the holdup squad, Toole believed his task was comprised of three parts: to catch individuals who carried out armed robberies, to recover the loot, and to ensure that a reasonable portion of it — when this was absolutely unavoidable — was returned to the victim. In some instances, the way he did these things depended on whether the individual was shot while fleeing. In others, the deciding factor was whether the individual ended up in custody on a charge that was quite a bit less serious than armed robbery, as a result of having arrived at a satisfactory arrangement with Toole. This was called arrest-bargaining, and Sergeant Toole was very skilled at it. And why not? After thirty-one years with the department, it was all that made his shit salary into something that vaguely resembled a living wage.

He'd found that an enhanced income was necessary after it occurred to him that he might be gay and, after thinking about it carefully for some time, concluded that he was. One financial aspect of dutifully informing the department of his revised sexual orientation was that he ended up being ten years past his due date before he made sergeant. And sergeant was as far as he was ever going to go, because none of the police chiefs he'd served under was a good fairy who would wave their wand and promote him, or raise his salary, any higher. So it came down to basic economics. Unless he made something on the side, there was no way he could afford his stereotypically gay lifestyle. Robbie Toole was essentially an honest man — certainly honest enough to admit that he was well past middle age, and for that reason alone it was impossible to do it on the cheap and have the kind of friends and home decor he wanted.

This was why he'd tracked down Frank's next of kin.

"I'll be in touch," he said. As he handed her his card, he got a momentary glimpse inside the house, and had a strange feeling that something was funny about the light in it. How it seemed to flood toward him. How it was almost as if the whole back end of the place was a gigantic picture window. Maybe even that it wasn't a window, that there wasn't anything there at all.

As soon as he was out of sight, Nina tore the card to pieces and dropped them off the side of the porch. Then she let herself think about Frank. *The dumb son of a bitch*, she thought. She wondered if it was the guys that grabbed him that did it. Somebody did. If it had been an accident, the cop would have come out and said there'd been some kind of accident. She hadn't ever been all that close to the dumb son of a bitch. And now — now that was about it for her side of the family. Everybody gone but her. She wondered how upset she was going to be. It hadn't been easy to clamp her reaction right down flat when the cop had been there. Maybe that she could do it at all was a SuEz thing. Maybe when it involved something as big as Frank getting murdered, and you clamped it down as hard as she had, it would take awhile before it rose back up and slammed you around. *The dumb son of a bitch.*

SIXTEEN

Victor didn't believe Raoul had been an interrogator at Abu Ghraib. But when somebody went around bragging about how he'd studied advanced intelligence gathering techniques at a prison in Iraq as famous as that one was for using them, Victor wasn't about to interrogate him to find out if he was lying. When the image you wanted to create for yourself was that you were a sicko torturer, then you might as well be accepted as one. If the result was the same, who gave a shit about the facts? It had been a long time since Victor arrived at the conclusion that when it came to dealing with people who had snakes in their heads, the smart thing to do was whatever had to be done, and not get them wondering about you.

He didn't believe Raoul's name was Raoul, either.

Victor's own approach to interrogation was pretty straightforward. If you wanted somebody to tell you something, and they didn't want to, you squeezed their nuts. If they still didn't want to, you squeezed harder.

Raoul was happy to pass along what he said were the latest trade tips, and if he learned them at Abu Ghraib or on some website for perverts and they worked better than squeezing somebody's nuts, it was okay with Victor. Raoul was happy about all sorts of things besides that. Victor went so far as to think Raoul was happy about everything. It was why he never stopped smiling. It wasn't a fake smile, either, or a sarcastic one. It was a big, happy smile like you'd expect from a person who felt really pleased about something. As far as creepiness went, Victor thought this was the icing on the cake. He wondered if maybe the infant Raoul's parents kept bouncing him down the stairs on his head until the smile never left his lips, and had then sent him out into the world to make it a sweeter place.

One thing Raoul made a big deal about was using ordinary, down-to-earth equipment, stuff you could find around the house or wherever. It gave the interrogator some extra whammy if he used things so familiar that most of the time people just took them for granted. "Or look at it the other way around," he said. "What if you're just getting comfortable in the dentist's chair and you suddenly notice that he's about to plunge into your mouth with a knife and fork? See how that makes it even more terrifying?" Victor took the diplomatic route and nodded appreciatively. Another example: nothing beat a J Cloth for waterboarding. The person being worked on should see it get pulled right out of the box. And be sure and to use national brand names. People identify with them, even if they reach for the economy brand when they're shopping. And, yes, he could have carried electrical wires with him, but that wasn't his style. When the cord was ripped out of the toaster and the ends were stripped in front of the guy they were going to be attached to, it had a real strong psychological effect even before it was plugged in.

Victor was pretty sure he remembered seeing stuff about ripping the electrical cord out of the toaster in a movie, but he didn't mention it.

They had Frank stripped naked. If the person being interrogated was naked, it always put him at an emotional disadvantage. You felt more vulnerable naked.

"Unless you happen to be driving a tank."

"What?" Raoul said.

"But then, how often does anybody get naked and climb behind the controls of a tank?"

"Sorry?"

Victor thought the lights behind Raoul's eyes might have dimmed a couple of watts, but the smile stayed as wide as ever. Snakes — oh, Jesus. So many of them packed in there, his skull was ready to burst.

They had also knocked Frank unconscious, and every time he came to, Raoul banged him behind the ear with the tire iron from the car. "Letting him regain consciousness, and then knocking him out again, reinforces in his mind how completely he has lost control of his universe. Furthermore, it allows you to complete your preparations without being distracted by his struggles."

I can't fuckin' believe it, Victor thought.

"What's that?" Raoul said.

"Good," Victor said. "Good. I want to get you to go over all this again later. So I can make notes."

The next time Frank woke up, he was tied to a tree. His ankles were bound with wire. His hands were tied at the wrists and raised above his head by what looked to him like an extension cord looped over a branch. They were in a wooded part of a park or something. He watched Raoul hunt around in the car's trunk with a flashlight, pull out the jump-starter cables and open the hood. Raoul attached one of the cables' clamps to the car's battery and the other end to Frank's right nipple.

"Ouch!" Frank said. "What're you doing?"

"You're not serious," Victor said to Raoul.

Evidently he was, because he attached another clamp to the other battery connection and then pinched the skin of Frank's scrotum and clamped the other end to that.

"I'll tell you where it is," Frank said, making a whole bunch of faces.

Raoul ignored him, opening the door on the driver's side.

"He'll tell us where it is," Victor said.

"No, he won't."

"He says he will."

"He won't tell us the truth."

"I'll tell you the truth," Frank said, trying to make it clear he wasn't just going to watch the proceedings like it was a TV show.

"No, he won't. He won't tell us the truth until he gets a taste of the old prune juice."

"Prune juice?" Did Victor hear that right?

"What's brown and wrinkly and a shock to the system?" Raoul asked. "A hundred-and-ten volt prune! At Abu Ghraib we loved prune jokes."

"It's in the Porsche!"

"What Porsche?" Victor sounded willing to give Frank the benefit of the doubt.

"What's brown and wrinkly and can blow your ass off?" Raoul asked. "This was my favourite."

"I'm telling you! It's all there!" Frank was yelping. Actually, he'd been sounding very agitated since the first clamp was attached.

"A prune grenade!" Raoul laughed loudly, then shook his head and went back to his normal smiling. "Pay no attention to him," he told Victor. "He'll say anything to keep from experiencing intense pain."

"What's this about a Porsche?" Victor said.

Raoul slipped behind the wheel. "A day without prune juice," he said. "How about I serve him a little?"

"Let's just hear what he's got to say."

"Forget what he's got to say."

Victor closed his eyes. "Forget what he's got to say? What do you mean forget what he's got to say? You mean you don't *care* what he's got to say. You just want to give him a fuckin' jolt."

"I just want the money." Thinking about how much he wanted the money made Raoul's smile almost dreamy.

"You want to give him a jolt. If we could get it without giving him a jolt, you wouldn't be the fuckin' slightest bit interested."

"What are you getting at?" Even though it was dark, Raoul's smile gleamed through the windshield.

Frank was squirming back and forth. "The Porsche, it's yellow. It's —" He started to piss.

"I've had enough of this bullshit," Raoul said.

"You think you're some kind of fuckin' genius!" Victor couldn't believe he was blowing up like this. It was embarrassing. Why was he going to bat for some asshole he'd been hired to squeeze 1.18 million dollars out of? He grabbed Raoul's sleeve. "You want to do this no matter what."

"The Porsche is in the garage at her building. Her name is Junetta —"

"You hear that?" Victor was jerking Raoul's shoulder.

" — Solito. She lives at —"

"Yeah?" Victor moved toward Frank, hungry for every word. "She lives at?"

" — at —"

"*Jesus Fuckin' Christ!*" Victor threw his hands in front of his face. He dove to the ground, dodging a stream of sparks — maybe an actual flame. Anyway, he hit the ground to get out of the way of something that came blazing out of Frank's dick. Other blazing streams came out his ears. His eyeballs popped. Little tongues of flame from the sockets licked his eyebrows.

"Fuckin' amazing," Raoul said, switching off the engine.

Victor was on his knees, his face in his hands. He was whimpering.

"Although I worried that this might happen."

"You worried —"

"It's this eight-cylinder engine." Getting out of the car, Raoul picked up a flashlight and inspected Frank Carson, slumped dead against the tree.

"You *worried* that this might happen?"

Frank's teeth clacked. Clackclackclackclackclack. It reminded Victor of the wind-up choppers they sold in joke stores.

"Should have gone with a four-cylinder," Raoul said. "Not such a powerful charge." It is possible to tell by the sound of someone's voice whether they're smiling, even if you can't see them. Raoul sounded as if everything pleased the absolute hell out of him, despite this minor setback. Victor expected him to slap his forehead and say, "Don't that beat all?" He didn't, though. He just went on about what might have worked better. "A Jetta maybe. Imports are more precision engineered."

"What the fuck are you talking about?" Victor said. "They all use the same batteries."

"Are you sure about that? Why would they? Smaller motors. Precision engineering."

"*He was going to tell us!*"

In spite of the darkness, Victor had a clear impression of steam rising from Frank's body. At least his teeth had stopped going clackity clackity.

"Juanita something," Victor said.

Raoul pulled onto the road. "That's bullshit. He hadn't been properly motivated." He sounded like he couldn't believe what a slow learner Victor was.

"A Porsche."

"Maybe," Raoul said. "But an economy car will work better. I'd try a Jetta."

"*She has a Porsche!* The fuckin' *Juanita* woman. That's where the fuckin' *money* is."

Raoul leaned back in the seat, enjoying the sweep of night they were speeding through. "You should try to keep up with the research, my friend."

SEVENTEEN

Krystal Beach's emails caused a sensation in Lagos.

Never had so many Nigerians been offered the opportunity to get their hands on so much money. Before this, they had to start a relationship from scratch with some far-off stranger and follow up with no end of back-and-forth correspondence to persuade the stranger to pass along their life savings, or more if they could be persuaded to borrow it. Yet some of the individuals they corresponded with, after making all kinds of promising noises, still backed out, forcing the Nigerians to find another stranger to start up a friendship with from scratch.

Because so much money was up for grabs, and because word got around among the leading industrialists and officials who received the White House offer, and because these industrialists and officials had a great deal of say in how the country was run, they decided great care had to be taken to make sure they weren't in danger of throwing their investment away. And so Operation Due Diligence sprang to life. Kevin Olorgasele and J. Ridgeway Mbunzu, the two most feared colonels in the Finance Ministry, were given airplane tickets and sent to see if six railway cars filled with gold ingots could truly be obtained by paying the wife of the president of America three hundred thousand dollars cash in advance. If this turned out to be the case, they were directed to see if the six railway cars filled with gold might then somehow be obtained without paying the wife of the president or anybody else anything at all in advance, or ever. And, if that were possible, whether they might then be able to obtain a great many more than a mere six railway cars without ponying up as much as a nickel, even though everyone in Nigeria agreed that the amount she had asked for was very reasonable in the circumstances.

Kevin Olorgasele and J. Ridgeway Mbunzu were impressed by how easily their national intelligence organization discovered that the emails had been sent from the computer terminals that anybody could use for free in the public library beside the subway station at The Intersection. When they considered all the ways this location was entirely unconnected with Washington, D.C., it became obvious why it had been chosen as the secret communications centre for the Fort Knox venture. And when the owner of the email address was tracked down, the colonels were equally impressed to see how much the woman who appeared to be the driver of a delivery van for ConGlom Courier Services by the name of Ms. K. Beach behaved as if she really was the driver of a delivery van for ConGlom Courier Services by the name of Ms. K. Beach. "I say, Ridgeway, old thing," Olorgasele said, "it's bloody marvellous. The best cover I've seen in my many years in the business."

"We are dealing with a top-drawer organization, Kevin," Mbunzu agreed. "I shouldn't be at all surprised if the Agency weren't too far below the surface of this. It's something we would be wise to bear in mind."

The district where this Ms. K. Beach person lived reminded them of parts of Greater Lagos where bad things could easily happen to you even if you were minding your own business. From the looks of SuEz, they assumed that warlords and their armies must be raping and looting out in the countryside, and this had caused farm workers and the residents of remote villages to move into the city, and especially into parts of it where they could survive when they didn't have any money. The biggest difference was that the places like that over here had apparently been built by somebody who had tools.

A number of times they observed her on the sidewalk chatting with the resident of the house at the end of the row hers was in, a black man who had three children but no wives at all, as far as Kevin and Ridgeway could see. Sometimes they saw him coming and going in a cape that appeared to have been made out of a shower curtain with a leopard-skin pattern that somewhat strangely, Kevin thought, reminded Ridgeway of home. Any doubts they had about Krystal being the go-between vanished when they realized that every time they snuck around keeping her under surveillance, they saw two white men sneaking around doing the same thing. These must either be Agency operatives who wanted to make sure she came to no harm and didn't pull a doublecross, or they had got wind of the deal she was involved in between the White House and the Nigerians and were looking for ways to get some of the ingots for themselves.

Thoroughly satisfied that the gold connection was in their sights, the colonels decided it was time to quit commuting from the motel they'd been staying in near the airport, but they didn't want to move right into the middle of SuEz, because everywhere they went people stared at them. Even the two white men with the T-shirts that didn't quite cover their bellies would turn and stare at Kevin and Ridgeway in ways that felt quite alarming. And no matter where they lurked on the Beach woman's street, a throng of laughing, foul-mouthed little girls always gathered, trying to reach their dirty little hands into the strangers' pockets.

"Perhaps it is some cultural thing," Ridgeway said. "Something we do so naturally we are not even aware of it, yet it draws attention in this country."

"One thing that occurs to me," Kevin said, "is that no one apart from yourself is leading a goat on a rope." He couldn't quite keep the edge out of his voice.

For a second Ridgeway looked hurt, then he began to laugh. "Haw, haw. Your sense of humour, old sport. Ripping as always." But another reason for moving into town was that they frequently had difficulty getting a taxi with a driver who would let them bring the goat. That morning they'd been left standing outside their motel three times by cabs that sped away, the drivers cursing in Arabic about how newcomers to this country were getting stupider and stupider.

Kevin seethed at this, but silently, as he'd been silently seething ever since the afternoon Ridgeway had gone for a walk and returned to their room leading the goat. He kept silent because he was worried. Had the job become too much for his great colleague and friend? Had culture shock turned his brain to orange marmalade?

Ridgeway actually went dewy around the eyes when Kevin reacted with a baffled, "I say, I say." He'd described coming across what he'd taken for a livestock market in a parking lot surrounded by shops a few roads over. Seeing the goat, he found himself recalling visits to his grandfather's place in the green hills when he'd been a boy. His grandfather kept goats, and the sight of this one filled Ridgeway with longing for, in Kevin's condensed version, the familial home of memory.

He had asked to buy it. "The proprietor told me, however, that this was not a market, but something called a petting zoo —"

"A what?" Kevin said.

"— but we fell to haggling."

"Haggling?"

"Pardon, old love?" Ridgeway was dreamily scratching the goat between its nubbin horns.

"How much did you pay?"

"Two thousand dollars."

"*Two thousand dollars?*"

"Cash. Of course, you would have known that."

"*For a* —" Kevin struggled to regain control. A professional crisis might be brewing here. The team's fate may be threatened. "For a goat?"

Ridgeway admired his acquisition. "An excellent one, as you can see."

Kevin couldn't, not even slightly. He was a city boy and always had been. So was Ridgeway, as far as he'd known. It was extremely odd, was it not, for a city boy to be homesick for something his closest friend and colleague had never heard him refer to? All right, perhaps he had mentioned his grandfather's village. But this stinking, forsaken, flybitten … He began wondering exactly how much, when push came to shove, he was going to be able to depend on a professional partner he used to consider perfectly normal. Perhaps this strange obsession would pass. Perhaps it was some sort of jet lag. A great deal of money needed to be found and spirited away. The slightest uncertainty could be fatal.

They rented an apartment in a tower at The Intersection from a man they thought had been asleep on the floor in the corner of the lobby, but who hobbled over when they looked as if they were getting nervous about all the whores and drug dealers working there. "If you's don't need a key right this minute, you's can move in right now," the man said. For an extra fifty dollars he dragged in a bunch of furniture.

"You's want shit?" he said as he was leaving.

"I beg your pardon?" Kevin said. It wasn't until the man mimed sticking a needle in his arm that they caught on. They shook their heads.

"How about pussy?"

Kevin and Ridgeway eyed each other blankly.

"Nah." The man shrugged and stuffed the money for the first month's rent down the front of his pants. "I guess with that goat you's don't need pussy."

They stared speechlessly as he went out the door and slammed it, and they were still staring speechlessly when it crashed down flat on the floor and two men, one carrying an assault rifle, stormed in and explained that they lived next door and wanted their fuckin' furniture back. After Kevin and Ridgeway had carried it into the other apartment, the man with the automatic weapon followed them back into theirs and shot out all the windows. "You watch your asses," the man said, walking out over the door that still lay where it had fallen.

It took them a long while to get to sleep that night. They didn't feel secure, since they hadn't been able to do anything but prop the door against the frame, and the goat kept up a plaintive bleating. Ridgeway said he'd heard of animals becoming restless when a tsunami was about to strike. Kevin said if that was the case, they should at least be grateful for being on the twenty-fourth floor.

A horrendous boom split the night, scaring them so shitless that if they never fell asleep anywhere again for the rest of their lives, they would have known why. They only realized it was the unhinged door crashing flat for a second time when somebody blinded them with a flashlight. "What you motherfuckers doing in my place?" he said.

They stuttered something about not knowing it was anybody's place. About how they'd just rented it that afternoon.

"No motherfuckers rent my motherfuckin' place from nobody but me," he replied.

They described the man they'd given their rent money to. "Never heard of a motherfucker like that," he said. "*I'm* the motherfucker you motherfuckin' pay. And right now is when you motherfuckin' pay me, or —" he stopped. He shone his flashlight around. "What happened to my motherfuckin' windows?"

Kevin and Ridgeway promised to replace them. They said there had been a misunderstanding with the next-door neighbours. They promised to pay the man his rent too, but first they had to cash a money order at the bank.

"Motherfuckers expect me to believe that?"

They swore on their mothers' graves they wouldn't cheat him.

There was another explosion. The goat fell over. Lowering his pistol, the man ran his light up and down its twitching body. "Just a motherfuckin' reminder," he said. "You bring me that money by ten tomorrow morning."

Something in Ridgeway snapped. It had been building up, but watching somebody shoot his goat pushed him over the limit. He rushed at the man, hollering. In the darkness, Kevin could hear thumping and grunting. The grunting grew louder. Two more shots were fired. Then, barely visible against the black sky, and with a grunt that was almost a shriek, the man heaved Ridgeway's body through one of the blasted-out windows twenty-four floors above the ground.

"Ten o'clock." The man was gasping. "Don't motherfuckin' forget." His footsteps boomed as he strode across the door and into the lightless hall.

Kevin couldn't tell what was making him shake so violently, horror or grief, but he didn't stick around to find out. He didn't even take time to breathe before he was in the corridor himself, skittering toward the fire stairs, praying that the homicidal maniac had gone the other way. By first light he was huddled in Nina's cellar, still shaking. Nobody in the neighbourhood knew he was there, but because he'd been keeping an eye on Krystal Beach, SuEz was the only part of town he was familiar with. And with most of the back wall of the house gone, the cellar offered the most obvious hole to hide in. Besides, his mission didn't end just because of the death in the line of duty of Colonel J. Ridgeway Mbunzu, his dear and respected partner. Dear because one of Kevin's wives was one of Ridgeway's sisters. And respected because Ridgeway's wives had been so beautiful that Kevin was screwing two of them when he and Ridgeway ended up getting sent over here on assignment. It hadn't been easy for him to cheat on his friend. Not with the two of them working together most of every day, and drinking together most of every night, after which they would cruise the whore districts to take advantage of the action they got on the house all over the place thanks to making sure the taxes on the madams didn't amount to more than a small pile of monkey shit.

But could one man alone take on this Ms. K. Beach, even if he did happen to be a very good man? Should he perhaps go back to Nigeria and regain his strength by offering his sympathies and comfort to Ridgeway's widows? Would the Finance Ministry take his return as an admission of defeat and send a team of the younger men who would have become the most-feared colonels since he and Ridgeway left? If he stayed, though, and if he could pull it off, wouldn't his share of the gold be twice as much as the half he would have gotten if he and Ridgeway had been forced to split the whole thing before faking their deaths and going into extremely luxurious seclusion?

He concentrated really hard on how he might accomplish this, because when he didn't concentrate really hard, he would start noticing the smell in the cellar, which made him feel like vomiting. When that happened, he asked himself what it was about the New World that was such a big attraction. No wonder the African people they brought out had to be chained down in the boats.

EIGHTEEN

Somewhere there was 1.18 million dollars that, if she could find it, she could use to help fix the swimming pool. Then she could get on with her life.

Nina laughed every time somebody said that, but after awhile the laughter in her tank started running low and she didn't bother any more. She did wonder what the people who said it had in mind. Did they mean she could get back to doing whatever she'd been doing before the whole business of the school pool and the bank robbing and the ice cream trucks and blowing up Ed Oataway's car and her brother getting murdered came along? If that's what they meant, she wondered what it was they thought she'd been doing. If people thought getting on with her life meant she'd been heading somewhere with it, or that it had been going somewhere and she was on board, riding along, that wasn't how it worked. Her life had started when it started and then stayed right there. She got older, she got married, she had children, or once the other way around, but nothing changed. Did they think all this swimming pool and stuff was a distraction? That because of it she'd had her thumb in her bum and as soon as it was over she could put the pedal to the floor again?

It wasn't like there weren't distractions before this. Things always came along that weren't exactly ordinary, and some of them weren't welcome, either. D.S. getting the shit kicked out of him at work wasn't ever welcome. Did it count as a distraction? It happened so often that if it distracted you, the next thing you knew you'd be distracted every time one of the girls told her sisters to go fuck themselves. You'd be distracted by everything. You'd be distracted to death.

She had a hard time thinking of D.S. getting the shit kicked out of him as a part of her life she wanted to get on with, or that she'd want to if she had any choice in the matter. And if she did get on with it, or didn't, what difference would it have made? His job would have brought in a fair bit of money if he could have done it without getting the shit kicked out of him. But he couldn't. It was like he had some kind of gift for it, and for it not to happen would require cutting off some part of himself that made him what he was. Lady couldn't quite see what Nina meant by this until Merlina explained how it would be the same for Guinevere if she had to get rid of her falsies. She would no longer exist. But Lady said Merly wouldn't exist if she didn't have such stupid ideas. And Nina told them this was a perfect example of what happened when anybody tried to discuss real issues in their family, although it was probably bound to be like that considering D.S.'s influence. If he was going to have a gift, it was going to be a stupid one.

It seemed kind of strange that Total kept hiring him as a greeter, since just about everybody who knew him wished he would go away and leave them alone. They felt like that even when he wasn't around. Even his daughters did, although he'd never done anything awful to them or threatened them in any way. Nina wasn't surprised. It was the way you'd expect kids to react when their father was completely irritating, and when he was around they couldn't avoid realizing it.

For instance, if he spilled something, he'd say to whichever of the girls was handy that if she wiped it up he'd take everybody on a holiday to France. He promised them this whenever they cleared up whatever kind of mess he'd made, but instead of it becoming a joke, it only got more irritating because, say, for a class project, one of them had to colour the part of the map that was France blue, and she didn't know where France was. If she asked D.S., he'd point to where it was, and she'd colour it, but when she got to school it would turn out that the country he'd told her to colour blue was Greece or someplace. And when she got upset with him, it would turn out that he didn't really know where France was. Worse than that, he knew he hadn't known when she first asked him. That hadn't stopped him, though, because he would never let on that there was anything he didn't know. When she pointed out its actual location, he said, "I thought you just meant where it was roughly."

Or when they got on him for never saying "Excuse me" after he burped or farted and he started making it into a D.S. kind of joke. He'd shout "Excuse me!" and they would look up because they didn't know what he needed to be excused for. "For what?" they'd say. And he'd shout, "Nothing!" He did this three or four times a day for years until it got so they didn't even notice him shouting "Excuse me!" That didn't stop him, though. He'd start yelling, "Hey! Hey! Hey!" until one of them would say, not having thought what she was doing through completely, "What, for God's sake?" And he'd shout, "Nothing!"

Nobody could understand why every time he got well enough to go back to work, Total would assign him to be a greeter again. Sometimes all he'd do was say, "Welcome to Total," and a customer would punch him in the eye. But he always acted like nothing happened. "It has to do with how the customer is always right," he told his daughters. "It is the Total philosophy." He was extremely proud to be associated with a company that had a philosophy and wondered if his family wouldn't do better if they had one, too. Merlina said the only one she could think of was "Gwinny is a twat," but he said she was too young to understand the difference between a philosophy and whatever it was she'd suggested. Merly said it didn't matter, it was the only thing she truly believed.

Ed Oataway's opinion was that no matter who the people were, or where it happened, everybody who met D.S. got so irritated they wanted to kick the shit out of him. It was no more complicated than that. It got to the point where D.S. came to regard anybody who didn't actually kick the shit out of him as his friend. Ed said this was the problem he had for not having given in to the urge to do it in the first place.

As far as Nina could see, getting on with her life wasn't something that counted for much. "Trying to get through today so I can try to get through tomorrow," she said to Merlina, "does that sound like I was getting on with my life?" She enjoyed fiddling around with hard questions like this, but she didn't have much time to chew on them when she had to spend all her time rushing around trying to survive. "Maybe helping you girls survive was a life, but was it a life for you, too?"

Then she gave her head a shake. "Being a welfare queen has a lot less going for it than a lot of people think," she said. When Merly asked if that would maybe suit them as a family philosophy, it made Nina laugh.

The loot wasn't in her house. She knew that. However, not everybody knew she knew it, or if they had known, they wouldn't have believed her. This explained why the whole back wall was off. Why her and D.S.'s bedroom no longer had a roof. And why the kitchen didn't either. When the mystery home wreckers tore off half a side wall, the roof over the girls' bedroom collapsed. She moved them across the street into JannaRose's, except for Fabreece. Fabreece went to Jarmeel's to be with Zanielle. D.S. refused to sleep in the house, claiming it was impossible because the wreckers sometimes worked all night. He started spending nights in abandoned cars along the street. Everybody he knew told him it was too bad he had to do that, but unfortunately they had some problem or other with their house that made it impossible for him to bunk in with them. He said that was okay, he hated using somebody else's bathroom. Lady said that wasn't the real reason. She said it was really so he could move to a different car every night, which made it harder for the wreckers to find him when they decided to murder what was left of the family, having already disposed of Frank. When Nina screamed down the stairs that the wreckers had been scaring her children and had forced her family to move out, they yelled back, "Hey! Shut the fuck up or you'll be really fuckin' sorry."

She didn't know for absolute certain that the money wasn't in the house, but it was so logical it had to be true. Why would Frank hide 1.18 million there when he knew the next time he showed up the house might not be standing, as she'd known from the day they moved in that it might not be the next time she showed up? Look at what was happening at that very moment, and it wasn't even the city or developers.

And while the wreckers weren't about to believe anything she would have told them, she got exactly the same feeling when she explained to JannaRose, or to D.S. for that matter, that Frank hadn't been in the house long enough to hide anything. Not in a serious way, at least. He might have stuffed it behind the fridge, but what the hell. As a matter of fact, the Nike bag he brought was beside the fridge, where he'd tossed it when they went outside to see what was going on with all the bees flying over. They could hardly hear each other for the noise that filled the sky. It went up and down her backbone like a whole bunch of nailfiles. And the Nike bag still looked just as empty as it had when he'd arrived with it. But no matter how many times she went over this with JannaRose or D.S., they would nod as if they completely agreed with her views on the subject, but their faces gave the impression that they where thinking, "Well, yeah, I guess that might be possible." When Ed Oataway examined the bag a few days after Frank disappeared, he took for granted that it had been emptied after Frank arrived at Dipshit's house. He spent a lot of time trying to figure out how this might have happened, if it had happened after he stole the back door, and who had done it.

The thing that worried Nina most, though, was Guinevere, who didn't seem to be handling even the survival part of life very well. Merlina explained to Lady that this was because Gwinny was an idiot, and the main reason she was had to do with her only being interested in getting on everybody's nerves because it was taking her so long to be a big star of some kind or other. She couldn't stand it that she wasn't on the covers of any of the magazines she stole from the Korean's store. What drove Nina crazy was that she was always huddled someplace snerfling. She had to share a room! Big fuckin' deal. Everybody had to share a room. Nina had never not shared a room. It was true that the room Gwinny shared at that moment was at JannaRose's, but the kids she shared it with were pretty much the same ones she usually did. And even when the room she shared before this was in her own house, it wasn't a house they'd lived in for long. They didn't even pay rent or anything. They'd just moved in. They were always going to get kicked out. The bastards who were wrecking them out of it were changing the timing, that was all, and probably not by much.

It was also true that Nina had never had much of an idea about how to comfort somebody, or maybe what to comfort somebody about when things were exactly the same as they'd been for her. Merlina told Lady the main reason the two of them did okay was that they didn't bother dreaming, but Lady said she wasn't too sure about that. Sometimes she dreamed whether she wanted to or not. The night before she'd had a dream about truck racing. Merlina said what she meant was they didn't waste time dreaming about what their future would be like, but Lady said if her future was that she was going to be a racing-truck driver, that was okay with her. Merlina said Lady was an idiot, too, but a different kind than Gwinny, who was one of those high-strung people who caused difficulties for everybody around them even if they had to go out of their way to do it. Maybe she couldn't help it. Maybe she had some kind of a thing in her system that would land her in a mental hospital some day.

Finally Nina couldn't take the screeching and emotional tension any more. She grabbed Gwinny and yelled, "What is your fuckin' problem anyway? Do you think it's different for anybody else in this family?" Then she nearly died of shock because Gwinny doubled over, vomited bright red and collapsed to her knees with her arms wrapped around her tummy.

"She's puking blood! Jesus Christ! Jesus Christ!"

Nina and Gwinny were out on the walk, but Merlina and Lady could see from the front window that what she had vomited was the fifteen sticks of red licorice she had just stuffed into her face without offering even one to anybody else. "It comes out different colours when she eats different-coloured stuff," Lady said.

They kept watching while Nina knelt and hugged their sister really hard. Between shrieks, Gwinny said she was sorry. That she was sorry most of all because of what happened to Frank. "We shouldn't have done it," she said.

Nina narrowed her eyes. Something was missing there. "What shouldn't you have done?"

Gwinny just shook her head above the bright red puddle.

"What did you do, Gwinny?"

"Robbed him."

"I can't hear you. Did you say you —"

"She's a real, real bitch," Merlina said to Lady. What they could hear through the closed window wasn't very loud, but it was clear.

" — robbed him?"

Lady looked at Merlina. "You were like 'Its okay to take it, he's our uncle,'" she said.

"Shut up," Merlina whispered, because she didn't want Nina and Gwinny to know they were spying.

"Yes," Gwinny said. She started trembling, and her voice sounded the way it did when she was really frightened. "We diiiiid!" Then she stood abruptly and ran up the street in the direction of the towers.

JannaRose, who'd been watching from her place, came over and squatted by Nina. Nina had no idea if JannaRose had heard what Gwinny said, but it had started her own mind surging.

What on earth could Gwinny and her sisters ...
In his whole life Frank never had anything worth ...
Except when ...
Except the one and only time when ...
But how ridiculous can you ...

Except he did show up carrying that Nike bag, and for all I ...

The bag's still beside the fridge, as empty as ...

So Gwinny ...

And her sisters ...

So Gwinny and her sisters ...

Her eyes grew huge and wide. "Holy fuck."

She wasn't whispering. It was just that her voice would only come out very small.

JannaRose stood and twisted this way and that. She wasn't built to squat any more. "What'd you say?" she said.

"Gwinny — the kids — they stole something."

JannaRose didn't move. Didn't blink. Didn't do anything. It wasn't as if, because of what Nina said, she wanted to stand totally still so she wouldn't jiggle the idea around before she got it completely installed in her mind. It was that telling a woman who grew up in SuEz — you having grown up in SuEz yourself — it was that telling this woman that your kids, who at that very moment were growing up in SuEz, had been stealing was as close as you could get to telling her the sky was straight up there, over her head.

"They get caught or something?" It was the only rational thing to say. It was what anybody who knew Nina would have said.

"No. Gwinny told me."

Which left JannaRose with absolutely nothing to say at all. So they stood there not saying anything, until after awhile Nina said, not so much to JannaRose, but as if she was going over the details in her own mind to make sure she had them straight, "From Frank."

JannaRose's head snapped back as if at last, after five hundred years of incomprehension, somebody had said something in the only language she happened to speak.

"Holy fuck," she said in a low voice.

"Yeah," Nina said.

They looked up the street, as if wondering where Gwinny had disappeared to. But they didn't really look at anything. They just stood there, stunned. That's what they were doing when Gwinny whipped around the corner of the house next door, the expression on her face about what Merlina would have expected to see on the face of a fourteen-year-old who had finally figured out how to get rid of the guilt that had been destroying her personal esteem. All she had to do was rat her sisters out. And it turned out it wasn't a big problem. Already she felt a whole lot better.

"Here," she said.

"Here?"

"What we took."

Nina and JannaRose weren't exactly certain what 1.18 million dollars would look like, but sort of expected something more than Frank's shiny old leather wallet that was curved in the shape of his butt. JannaRose later told Ed Oataway it was as if a magician said he was going to pull a rabbit out of a hat, and then pulled out — Tah-da!! — nothing. Not a goddamn thing. Except for his hand, and it was every bit as empty as when he stuck it into the hat.

Gwinny gave it to Nina.

JannaRose laughed. Taking the wallet from Nina, she made a jokey show of weighing it. "Was there millions of dollars in it, honey?"

"I don't know."

As far as Nina was concerned, everything was starting to feel quite a bit stranger than whatever had happened just before it, which, whatever it was, had been really strange. "You don't know?"

Gwinny shook her head.

"You stole the wallet and didn't notice how much money was in it?"

"It wasn't me that stole it."

Merlina saw that when it came to sticking up for Merlina, one person in particular wasn't going to. "Fuck you, Gwinny!" she shouted, running out on the porch. "And who stood there and watched me? And who wasn't like, 'Don't do that!' or a single other fuckin' word?"

"What's going on?" Nina said.

"It was sticking out of his pocket when he was sitting in the kitchen," Merlina said. "All bulging way out."

"Yeah?"

"And it accidentally got nudged when I —"

"It accidentally got nudged?"

" — accidentally when I gave him a hug, and it fell on the floor."

Nobody moved for a minute or so. If a bee had flown over right then, nobody would have heard it because they were thinking too hard.

"So was there any money in it before you gave it to your sister?"

"She didn't *give* it to me."

"What?" Nina and JannaRose said it at the same time.

"She *sold* it to me."

Nina's glare was so ferocious that Merlina backed up. Nina kept glaring at her even when she was speaking to somebody else. "I didn't even look for money in it," Merly said, really fast. "I didn't know anything about any money."

"So why did you buy it, Gwinny? And what did you buy it with?"

"Things she wanted me to steal —"

"Things she wanted *you* to steal —"

" — from the Korean's store." Gwinny's eyes were shut so tight, her whole face was squeezed together. It was as if she expected Nina to smack her.

"What did she want you —"

"You really are a dumb fuck, Gwinny," Merlina said.

"Shut your mouth, you!" It wasn't until then that Nina took her eyes off Merlina and looked at Guinevere. "What did she want you to steal?"

"Nothing," Merlina yelled. "Some bubble gum."

"Excuse me," JannaRose said, and everybody turned toward her, as if relieved by the interruption. "Before I lose track here." She brushed some lint off Gwinny's shoulder. "So why," she said, "did you want to buy the wallet? When neither of you knew if there was any money in it or not?"

"I thought ..."

JannaRose nodded to keep her going.

"She said ..."

"What did she say, honey?"

"There was a condom in it."

"*Why don't you just stab me right in the fuckin' heart?*" Nina said, expecting her eyes to fill with tears, but they didn't.

"A condom?" JannaRose sounded like she couldn't believe what she'd just heard. "No. Condoms leave a round mark, like —"

"*Don't you fuckin' tell her anything!*"

" — like a big O." JannaRose squeezed the wallet, looking very doubtful. "This doesn't —"

"I know."

"*She knows!*" Nina massaged her forehead. "*Of course* she knows. Why *wouldn't* she know? *Everybody* fuckin' knows. *Fabreece* probably knows."

JannaRose unsnapped a fastener and tipped out something that was wrapped in aluminum foil. "You thought this was a condom?"

"Merly's like, 'This in here is a condom,'" Gwinny said.

Nina grabbed the little aluminum foil package from JannaRose and waved it at Merlina. "Did you think this was a condom?" she said.

"I've never seen one," Merlina said. "It could have been."

"So why didn't you open it?" Nina said, unfolding the foil.

"I didn't want to touch it," Merlina said.

"Who wants to touch a condom with their fingers? *Ewww!*" It was Lady. Merlina looked astounded. Her sister was backing her up. It was the first time ever.

"So," Nina's nose was about half an inch from Gwinny's, "you know everything about condoms, but you didn't know what this is?" She held up the key that had been wrapped in the aluminum foil.

"I know what it is," Gwinny yelled, like she'd had enough insults.

"I never knew what it was really," Merlina yelled, trying to make it sound as if she didn't know what it was when she sold it to Gwinny.

"I never saw any money," Lady yelled, but Nina just walked up the steps and into the house. "We never took any! We never knew about it!"

Nina went into the bathroom because the door still had a lock. She locked it. She opened the fist holding the key and read the name on the emblem. She'd never known for sure how you say it. Porsh? Porsh-uh?

NINETEEN

L. Roy and L. Ray Elwell were identical twins. "We've been twins for seventy-one years," one of them would say.

"Since we turned five," the other would come in with. "Before that we didn't look the least bit alike."

"In fact, we weren't even related."

"Those were the good old days."

"Tell the truth, would you want to look like him?" And they'd point at each other and laugh their asses off. There was nothing L. Roy and L. Ray enjoyed more than their little jokes, and they'd been enjoying that one, and updating it, for a long, long time.

They called their operation a "service centre." This was another one of their jokes. It was actually a chop shop that everybody else just called Elwell's. There was no sign on it. They'd inherited it from their father. They'd learned how to be mechanics from the men who worked for him. From him they learned how to run a business, which he'd done by sitting in his office on the front seat out of a 1949 Hudson Hornet and listening to the radio until it was time to go home and listen to the radio. There had been changes around Elwell's since then. Now L. Roy and L. Ray sat on the front seats — they each had one, they were bench seats — out of 1974 Dodge Dusters, watching TV until it was time to go home and watch TV.

Another change was that nobody worked for them. They rented out service bays and hoists to mechanics who ran their own operations. Some had been at Elwell's for years and had many clients. Some only needed a place to work on a car for a couple of hours, often late at night. Some had their own tools, some rented what they needed from L. Roy and L. Ray. Frank Carson was just a little kid when he started hanging around. That's all he did for a long time, hang around. It was all he did anywhere, since he didn't go to school much, but Elwell's was where he did it the most. Nobody there minded. He was quiet and always happy to run out for cigarettes or coffee or whatever. By the time he was a teenager he was sweeping floors, jockeying cars. Taking them apart and putting them together again, though — that's what turned him on. His ability to do it impressed everybody around the place. The thing was, it was the only thing that turned him on, not being particularly interested in girls at that age either, and L. Roy and L. Ray found this the slightest bit peculiar.

"He was like a classical piano virtuoso that only wanted to fool around with the piano's insides," L. Roy said.

"What would an old bullshit hound like you know about classical piano virtuosos?" asked his brother.

"Old and *cultured* bullshit hound," L. Roy replied.

"The only thing that was ever cultured about you," L. Ray said, "was the specimen the doctor sent to the lab to see if you got the clap from Phyllis Whatsername."

"Fennaty. Phyllis Fennaty. And it turned out I wasn't the one that got it. Not that I was surprised. I couldn't believe anybody would've touched her that didn't have a dick made out of asbestos."

"That was always the way," L. Ray nodded sadly. "Left the dirty work to me."

Not that the Elwell brothers didn't appreciate that there was something attractive in how the parts of a car fit together and worked, but if it was going to hold their attention for long, taking cars apart and putting them together again needed a purpose beyond the simple pleasure of doing it. Such as money, for instance. Doing it for money was a real good purpose, to their way of thinking. So what was with this kid?

Everybody was starting to wonder, including the pimps and drug dealers Frank got to know because they could afford to have top-of-the-line automobiles stolen for them, and came to Elwell's when they needed maintenance and repairs. A lot of plain, ordinary car thieves did too when they needed to make modifications — changing serial numbers and external trim so the vehicle no longer precisely resembled the listing in the police computer and at the licence department, and so on. Even though he wasn't old enough to have a driver's licence, it wasn't long before Frank could do this a lot better than any of the guys who worked regularly at Elwell's. He could strip a Lexus down to its components in under two hours — twice as fast as anybody else. This made a car like that even more easily marketable when you considered the cost of replacement parts through the more usual channels, and when it came to luxury vehicles, it was considered by many individuals in the trade to be a less risky proposition than selling them in roadworthy condition. But Frank didn't care about any of this. L. Roy and L. Ray got the impression that he only cared about it when he discovered that nobody wanted him to put the car back together again. When that happened, he went around sort of depressed, like he was living only half a life.

It wasn't until girls entered Frank's picture that he changed, and even then it wasn't in the direction of the talent so many people had seen in him, although he did keep working around Elwell's for awhile to pick up a buck or two. And nobody would have given it a second thought that he got to be one of the smallest of small-time con-men — nobody from SuEz ever expected anybody from SuEz to do particularly well in any line of work — if he wasn't ignoring so much other potential. L. Roy and L. Ray had never found anybody they were much interested in marrying, and they had no children either, and it surprised them to discover how disappointed they were when he started coming around less and less. Neither one wished to appear sentimental, since it would give the other brother too much leverage in a relationship that had as many landmines as you'd expect with a pair of aging male twins who still lived in the house they'd been raised in and still ran the family business.

However, they both admitted to being more saddened by the news of his death than by the death of anybody else they'd ever known. So heavy was their sorrow that they left the shop right after hearing about it, which happened to be in the middle of the morning, bought a bottle of rye and took it home. Their habits had become fairly moderate in the last few years, so it surprised them to discover they'd emptied it before they'd even started to think about what they might care to have for lunch. And when they did make themselves something to eat, there wasn't a dry eye at the table.

Now here was Frank's sister, walking into their office.

"Nina," L. Roy said, nodding hello.

L. Ray nodded hello, too. "Nina," he said. "We are saddened by your loss."

"Very saddened. He was like a son to us," L. Roy said.

"He probably stole even less from us than a son would have," L. Ray said.

"A son would have stole us blind," his brother agreed.

"Not Frank. Frank never stole more than he thought was fair."

"Than what he needed."

"Than what he wanted."

"Than he could carry."

"When he stole more than that, he had to borrow the truck."

"Always brought it back, though. The truck, that is."

"Yes. We're not saying there wasn't something a little —"

"— strange. Definitely —"

"— definitely a little strange about him."

They looked apologetically at Nina. "If you'll pardon us for saying it."

"With you we feel like family," L. Ray said.

But if they felt a huge upset when Frank died, the fright they'd gotten the last time they saw him alive made them wonder why the ground under their feet didn't shake so hard that all the buildings for blocks around fell down. The memory of that moment nearly flattened the two of them when Nina fished the car key out of her pocket and dangled it between her thumb and forefinger.

"Oh dear," L. Roy said.

"Oh dear, oh dear," his brother said.

"It has come back to haunt us." They shielded their eyes as if the key gave off a blinding light. "The Porsche Carrera GT." L. Roy pronounced it "Porsh."

"Pretty fancy car?" Nina asked.

"Sticker price new, five hundred thousand."

"We looked it up," L. Roy said when Nina cringed.

"Six hundred and five horsepower. About the most powerful road car ever built."

"Up there, anyway."

"We had no idea what was going on, but the first thing we thought was Frank has bit off more than he can fit inside his mouth."

"A man with a car like that is asking for trouble."

"When it is not, so to speak, his own car."

"When possibly he took it without the knowledge or consent of the registered owner."

"And when it's bright yellow, to boot." L. Ray said.

"As yellow as a canary's keister."

"We couldn't have been more worried for him. Here he was, just fresh out of jail."

"Couldn't have been fresher if you squeezed him."

"Said it belonged to a friend of his."

"A friend indeed."

"The whole place went dead silent when he drove in."

"As far as you could tell. You couldn't have heard an anvil drop. That car sounded like it was taking off for outer space."

"An almighty roar."

"Told us his friend's car needed a little work and could he borrow one of our bays to do it in."

"When he gets out of the penitentiary, he doesn't even drop by so we can say welcome home. Then he shows up with this vehicle."

"Scared the life out of us."

"Spoken like a gentleman, L. Roy."

Nina asked what kind of work the car needed.

"Alignment, he said."

"Said it had a shimmy. Hard to imagine. Hardly looked like it'd been driven."

"Worked on it one hour and nine minutes."

"Then, voom. Gone."

"Told us to put it on his tab."

"His tab!" L. Ray yipped a laugh.

No, that was the last they saw of it. Of Frank, too.

Yes, as a matter of fact. Not that it was any of their business, but yes they did get the licence. Not that there was any need to have it on record, it being Frank. Just that when a car comes in, they note the licence. Force of habit.

Did they possibly remember —

Without moving from where they sat, without checking a note, L. Roy and L. Ray rhymed off the licence number in perfect unison.

Could they maybe — with their computer —

"Run it?" L. Roy said. And still without moving, they rhymed off in unison the name Junetta Solito. And her address. And her phone number. And that she did not need to wear corrective lenses while driving. Not that it was any of their business. Force of habit.

Nina wrote it down with a stub of pencil that was on the counter, and then smiled apologetically. "I haven't got any money to pay you for this."

"We'll put it on Frank's tab," L. Ray said.

When she left, L. Roy said, "It saddened me to hear her say she doesn't have any money."

"If it's true, it will sadden a lot of people."

"What I meant was, maybe we should do something to help her out."

"In the circumstances, I'm inclined to wait and maybe see if she might do something to help *us* out."

"You would take advantage of that fine young man's own beloved sister?"

"Not unless the opportunity arises. I think he will rest easier knowing that at least his tab got paid. What was it the last time I looked, 1.18 million?"

"Hm. Maybe. At least then the poor woman could get on with her life."

TWENTY

Jarmeel Tolbert opened his church in a neighbourhood grocery store that had been abandoned for years. Inventing a religion based on being taken up into space and probed by aliens was easy enough, the hard part was figuring out how to inform other folks who'd had the same experience that he was open for business. It turned out not to be a problem. People started gathering on the sidewalk before he'd finished prying the plywood off the window. They all looked so totally happy to see him, it made him nervous. If he didn't turn out to be all they hoped their leader might be, they were going to make the best of it, and anybody who tried to stop them would be really sorry. For the first time he got a hint of the burdens the founder of a religion takes on.

In spite of the things all these people had in common, none of them knew each other. Neither did they know how they'd known where and when to gather. Until they found themselves part of the crowd, each one believed nothing like what happened to them had happened to anybody else. They'd never so much as hinted about it to anyone, to blood relatives or even spouses, because they were afraid of being called crazy. Over the years some of them had begun to think they *were* crazy. Coming together like this was a revelation.

Jarmeel opted for a fundamental doctrine because fundamentalism had been getting headlines for other religions, and he figured a religion as cutting edge as his should also talk the talk. The first fundamental was you would never be accepted as a full member unless you'd been probed by aliens. It was followed closely by the belief that when you were taken aboard an alien spaceship in outer space, you had been much closer to God geographically than anybody else who'd lived to tell about it. However, Jarmeel was fundamentally opposed to getting specific about the probing, because some things were just between you and your Lord and the aliens. He personally couldn't say what had been involved when he was probed because he was so filled with wonder by the other things that were going on. He couldn't even put in words what the effect was on him, if you didn't count his getting fired by the army and founding his religion.

It was different with different followers, though, and this led them to get into arguments that sometimes ended with people throwing furniture at each other during the worship service. Where it had been mainly spiritual with Jarmeel, a lot of folks remembered details right down to the size of the probes in millimetres and how there had been no need to sterilize them because the environment inside the spacecraft was germ-free. Because he couldn't provide first-hand data like this, some members of the congregation tended to look on Jarmeel as a person who hadn't been converted as profoundly as they had been, but he kept reminding himself that different viewpoints show up in all religions, especially during the startup. What it did, however, was leave him with a feeling that if they ever needed a martyr, he was the one they'd appoint.

Something else separating Jarmeel from the believers who could remember every tiny detail was that they got off on it. Believers who find that what are sometimes called the mysteries of their religions give them a buzz in their shorts have been a factor in all faiths and creeds forever. They're usually far more devoted than anybody else, but on the minus side they are liable to explode like volcanos and blow the foundation the faith or creed was built on to hell and gone. This was more than an average risk for Jarmeel, since the proportion of this kind of believer was upward of ninety to one in Nearer My God, which he declared was his religion's official name, despite it generally being known by his followers as the Church of Eee-Yow! They called it that because it was what they had exclaimed rapturously the moment they were first probed. It was also what they cried out when they attempted to recreate the experience using likely looking implements they bought in cooking equipment stores. Jarmeel eventually stopped being startled when they yelled Eee-Yow! at the tops of their voices when he finished leading them in prayer, and anyway it sort of sounded like some of the words that popped up in the prehistoric section of the Bible.

Something Jarmeel would really have liked to know was whether their followers scared the shit out of the founders of other religions. He'd stand in front of them and preach the word — "This ain't science fiction," he'd say, and they'd all start humming as if they'd swallowed electric shavers. "Because it ain't fiction!" he'd say, and they'd hum louder. "But it ain't science, either!" By this point Jarmeel would have to struggle with himself to keep from running like a crazy person out of the building, because the humming vibrations would spread right up through the soles of his feet until the stuff his eyeballs were filled with got jiggly. When he finally got a grip on himself, he'd shout, "What we got is built on faith!"

And they'd all start nodding. "But it's more than faith. It's more than faith because we've *seen* it. *With our own eyes! When we were out there in those alien ships!"* The thing about their nodding that spooked him was they all did it at precisely the same speed.

Nodding, humming. Nodding, humming.

"When you have seen it with your own eyes," he'd tell them, "when you have felt it deep inside you. That's when you know that what we've got here —" he'd point to his heart "— and here —" pointing to his head "—is *not* just some kind of faith-based religion. What we've got here *is space-based!* You hear? *A space-based religion!* You hear what I say?

"We don't *need* faith, because we've *got* space! *Yes we do!"*

And they'd all start doing the thing that really creeped him out. They'd go "Hoooom, hoooom." Over and over. Some of them would have their eyes rolled back until all you could see were the whites. "Hoooom, hoooom!"

Looking back on it, Jarmeel figured that a bunch of the members of his church had put two and two together. They didn't get abducted for no reason. God doesn't dick people around. God *wanted* them abducted because he had chosen them to do things he needed done that the aliens couldn't handle for one reason or another.

If the followers didn't know exactly what these things were, sometimes they would have a sudden revelation. For instance, it was revealed to quite a few of them that they should start showing up at church heavily armed. Sometimes on the subway or in the supermarket checkout line, it would be revealed that they should profess their faith by drawing their weapons and waving them around. Then the police would get called and sometimes there would be a shootout and sometimes a follower or two would end up getting killed, but at the very least thrown in jail. This understandably led them to claim they were being persecuted because of their religious beliefs.

Other religions were conspiring against them. And how was it those other, those enemy religions, could get the police and politicians to do things they wanted, while Jarmeel's followers got arrested for shooting up the movie screens in cineplexes when they showed material that was contrary to the best interests of them and their God? The more things like this happened, the more Jarmeel's followers came to see that religious toleration was nothing but a weapon the rich and powerful used to keep the meek and probed in their place. And they were going to do something about it. They had no choice. They had no choice because they were God's servants. But the reason the first enemy church they burned down was the big Presbyterian one in South Chester was because it was the closest.

TWENTY-ONE

Nina would have had a better idea about some of the things she was up against if she had been even vaguely aware that there was more to the gay lifestyle than the kind of people you slept with and how it was you slept with them. For most of her life she didn't even know there were lifestyles some people could opt for. Her failure to pay more attention to home decorating shows on TV led directly to her failure to appreciate the deadliness of the threat she faced. As for the gay people she knew in SuEz, they provided no insight. They lived the way everybody around them did — the way she did — because how else could they afford to?

One did stand out, though. That was Bootsy, and even Nina had to admit that his lifestyle was different. This was because at night he hid in the ravines down by the Parkway, sleeping on the ground or whatever. Nina's children threw trash at everybody who went by the house who was weird, unless they were too scary, but it pissed her off when they did it to him, because by and large he was as normal as all kinds of other people they didn't throw stuff at. Merlina said she didn't know what she was talking about. The way he walked was totally weird: his arms straight down so they moved only a little bit, and his hands flat out at like little airplane wings. Something she did think was weird was that from the time Lady was five or six, she would call her sisters fuckin' assholes when they threw stuff at him and would pick up whatever they'd thrown and throw it back at them. Nina didn't think Bootsy even noticed Lady doing this. It was almost like he was glad they were throwing stuff. He'd weave his hips back and forth as if he was dancing. Finally Lady would start throwing rocks, and her sisters would run away, because she could throw hard.

Right around the time he started paying close attention to Nina, Sergeant Robbie Toole discovered he couldn't stop vibrating with excitement, and he was sure this was because his senses were telling him he was on to a very profitable thing with the little round lady. At other times he was just as sure it was because his new boyfriend had moved in.

It could be that this boyfriend was more demanding than most, or it could be he gave Toole that impression because when you were twenty-eight and worked in a store that sold DVDs of old movies where the cowboy stars wore a lot of eye makeup, you were more tuned in to a lot of things and more inclined to stay up late and tear around town than when you were fifty-two and had been on the police force since you got out of college. However he cut it, Toole found himself spending far more than ever to finance a lifestyle that he was already blowing his brains out on.

If you didn't have a bunch of different drinking glasses all made of the very choicest crystal, even if you had to look through brides' magazines to find out which one the juice went in, your friends who were also participating in the same lifestyle talked behind your back. They said things like it was extremely fortunate that you weren't an astronaut because you couldn't get liftoff with a Saturn VI, which was a martini with two Viagras instead of olives, meaning it was fine with all concerned for anybody to get it on with your boyfriend whenever you weren't guarding him with your fangs bared. Then there was the china, one set for fine dining, a whole different set for when you invited people for brunch in the sunroom, and none of which was ever brought out for everyday. Then there was the silver.

He was just had a smallish two-storey house on a dead-end street near a park, but he compensated. For instance, he'd spent five thousand dollars on silk cushions for the furniture on the deck. Toole had let this drop one recent Sunday afternoon and was delighted to hear his friends sniff as he sidled on to pour Chablis for his other friends, "What will he do if there's a cloudburst, shit a brick?" "I think he must already, gold ones." "Well, I mean, how else does he manage to ..."

It had to be done. If he hadn't thrown out a figure for the cushions, they would have made one up, and it would have been below what they sold the crap for at Total Discount. Nothing beat the gay lifestyle when it came to being cut-throat.

Scarcely two weeks later, it was another party — you couldn't afford to let much time pass, or one of your friends would run your death notice in the paper. This particular night, Robbie Toole had all his very best stuff on display, not least — he was pleased to point out — Carlo. The dinner marked two months since they'd met.

And on a major occasion like that, no one who was invited expected all the guests would be participants in the gay lifestyle, but despite that, almost all the guests were astonished to find the police chief there. And his wife. And Mayor Gladly Bradley. Nonetheless, the real standouts for a lot of the guests were four friends Carlo invited who Toole thought looked as if they made their living cruising men's washrooms at convention hotels. If they did, it must have paid well, to judge by the quality of the leather they wore. Toole thought the cheesiest thing about them was how stressed they looked, as if they were having trouble keeping up the pace, and one day soon would be switching from cocaine to crack. And two of them were carrying knives. Just because Toole was crooked didn't mean he wasn't a good cop.

The police chief was there because, as a devoted Christian, he'd made a point of reaching out to the various kinds of people who somehow or other had managed to survive the internal battles to keep them off the force by reason of race, disability, and all the other things the police department was obliged by law to ignore in its hiring practices. Toole's rise to the rank of sergeant was a sure sign that things had changed, and this, his most recent chief, depended on him so much for counsel and as an in-house ambassador, that Robbie boasted of being able to work him like one of those toy cars you went vroom-vroom on the floor with and then let go and watched it speed off wherever you'd aimed it. The chief's Christianity was so intense that when he got home that night, he believed he'd lost his wallet. It never crossed his mind that it had been lifted by one of Carlo's little friends, as Toole had taken to calling them. It also never occurred to him how much shrieking laughter its contents would provoke when bouncers demanded proof of age and the chief's driver's licence started getting flashed all over town. They ran off thousands of them, laminated and everything.

"Gladly" was the nickname pretty well everybody used for the mayor, because when he'd first gotten into politics it became well known that he was glad to do absolutely anything for anybody as long as there was something in it for him. Close observers also admired his gift for smelling dirty money anywhere inside the city limits. It was what had led him, years before, to befriend Robbie Toole when Toole had started politicking to rise from the lowest ranks despite his sexual preference. Gladly had the feeling Toole had the same capable nose where money was concerned and, since he was a police officer, was often in a good position to do something more than just sniff it. Eventually they'd become each other's biggest political investment, and so this dinner was a very important event with a lot of things going on, quite apart from a number of the guests discreetly snorting the odd substance and caressing the odd well-filled crotch.

When they got a moment together, they had what might have sounded like kind of a strange conversation. The strange thing about it was they both spoke at the same time. But they had no trouble keeping track, because they'd had many conversations like this before. For one thing it saved time. Even better, it made life difficult for eavesdroppers.

The mayor said, "My finance chairman tells me that there's a little bundolo unaccounted for in SuEz. From a bank job that went funny a couple of weeks back. Two, three million. Not huge, but it's amazing nobody's tracked it down yet." He gave Toole a surprised look. "I expect somebody will soon, though," he continued. "I know I've said it before, but you can't just campaign when an election's on. You have to keep reminding voters every day in between that they can't live without you. It's good to know we could do what we could to keep your new friend from getting sent back to where was it, Guatemala? And it's always good to get a chance to talk to the chief in an informal setting. Jesus, he's a boring fuck, but you have to keep the wheels turning. Anyway, listen, I got to run."

While Robbie Toole said, "I saw you got a chance to talk to Carlo. He's very grateful and was looking forward to meeting you. His English isn't really all that bad, is it? He's been taking classes. Did he tell you about his new job? Clearing tables at Farina's was such a dead end." Toole shook his head sadly. "But once you spoke to the feds about his little immigration problem, he turned out to be the *perfect* person for a shop a friend of mine owns that does a wonderful business in CDs and DVDs, and he's enjoying the experience tremendously. And that street has picked up like crazy lately, so I'm sure he'll have a lot of opportunities to mention your name to all sorts of potential voters. No, it was Colombia. And wasn't it wonderful of the chief and his wife to come? I know he'll be pleased he had a chance to chat informally with you." He raised his index finger and wagged it a little bit. "I gather the actual amount is 1.18 million."

Then he squeezed the mayor's arm. "It was really sweet of you to drop by."

"Always good to see you, Robbie," the mayor said, putting an arm around Toole's shoulder and giving him a bracing hug. And he was through the crowd, out the door, into his limo, and gone by the time Toole could say "Dinner," just loud enough to catch everybody's attention and signal the caterer, "I believe is served." He thought it was more than just the tiniest bit interesting that the mayor's office had phoned at four thirty that afternoon to say the important meeting that was scheduled for that evening had been cancelled at the last minute, and Mayor Bradley was going to be able to make it to the party after all. Interesting, but not all that much of a mystery now. "Better get your ass in gear, old love," Toole said to himself. "Who'd have thought so many vultures have nothing better to do than circle such a pissy little pile of money?"

He'd had a good week and had been looking forward to a chance to celebrate ever since he figured out why he'd had the weird feeling that he knew her from someplace — the little round lady who'd been that asshole Carson's sister. It turned out she'd had a couple of starring roles in the Toons. Okay, one was just a cameo, but it was a killer cameo when you started to see how everything fit together. Toole loved the Toons. Young cops had urged him to smoke a joint before watching, because when they did they laughed so hard their asses fell off. But he got all the pleasure he needed out of them without assistance. Besides, he never smoked dope when he was on duty. What could be stupider than getting tripped up by chickenshit regulations when you were doing some serious lawbreaking?

The Toons were selected video clips from closed circuit security cameras that got put together every week or so on the department's in-house website. A cop might forget there was a camera in his cruiser, and everybody got to see him get out and take a leak in full colour. People who got arrested and put in the back seat sometimes did amazing things with parts of their bodies — stretching and waggling them around. The cops always said that if real movies had stuff in them like they saw in the Toons, it would make them more true to life, such as when the closed circuit caught a guy shooting another guy outside an apartment building. But if you ran the tape back further, you could see the gunman, while he's waiting for the other guy to show up, picking his nose and looking at what he picked really very closely. It's like he was thinking, *Whoa! I never saw anything like this before in my life!* The techies edited it so this ran over and over — picks nose, shoots guy, picks nose, shoots guy — until everybody was laughing so hard they were almost sick to their stomachs.

Most times, though, they were just peculiar things, and even the compilers weren't sure why they'd included them. The famous bank security tape of Nina with her forehead on the counter in front of the teller, rocking from side to side, wasn't famous because it had showed up on YouTube and everybody was talking about it everywhere, or even because a lot of people saw it on the Toons and said it should be in the annual highlight reel. It was famous because one person remembered it a few weeks after seeing it. As a result, something in his mind was triggered when he first set eyes on her. A couple of days later, he thought, *Hey!* and started going back through the Toons for the last while. When the techies dug out all the bank's videos for that day, he got to see her outside minutes after the scene at the counter. She looked as if she was having an argument with some of his uniformed brothers and sisters from the holdup squad. Whatever was happening there on the sidewalk, though, there was no mention of it in the reports. According to the squad's daily log, that call to the bank had been due to a false alarm.

Toole got the techies to do a computer search of other days around that time, and they discovered another performance by the same woman. Another performance at the same bank. This time another little round lady was with Carson's sister. They were both dressed in crummy T-shirts and sweats that made him think of panhandlers on the stairs in the subways. The tape showed the women coming in the front door. Then they stopped, facing each other. Then the other woman puked on the Carson woman's shoes. Then they ran out. It was like a bit of surreal slapstick from some old silent movie, beautiful and perfect. Toole watched that clip a dozen times. It made him laugh so hard his ass fell off.

TWENTY-TWO

The next time he dropped by, it was Monday morning, and she was still asleep when he banged on the door. Not even the sun was up. To get the conversation going, he'd decided on a breezy approach: "Where's that ice cream truck today?" he began. Like, had he shown them or what? As if the only reason he'd turned up on her porch was to prove that when he chased something off the street, it stayed chased off. But then, as she stood half-asleep in the doorway, not saying a word, he started outlining the real reason. How on two different days she'd shown up in videos at a downtown bank acting in a way that suggested she intended to rob it. Both times she got cold feet. Actually, and he sounded pleased to take such care with the fact, her feet hadn't so much gotten cold the first time as vomited on. And he sounded far more pleased to tell her that nothing she'd done was a crime. Intending to rob a bank wasn't, and neither was chickening out.

She still didn't say anything. She hadn't said anything much the last time, but this time it felt different, as if she wasn't saying anything because she'd gone deaf. It was when this occurred to him that he glanced past her and realized the wall really was gone from the back of the house. Even more of it than the last time, when he thought he was seeing things. And even though he had a sweetheart of a line ready that went "So you had this flurry of robbery interruptus," jacking around felt just too weird in the circumstances. Instead, he walked her carefully, step-by-step, through the case he was putting together.

It started with her two failures as a bank robber. Next came her brother getting out of jail. The day after that, her brother showed that at least someone in the family knew which side was up; he walked out of a bank with 1.18 million dollars. Later that day he got murdered. So his current whereabouts could be traced with ease. With the money, it was different. There was no sign of it. More than just no sign, no anything. It had disappeared like magic — poof! And there was something about this she should understand: Toole had been around long enough to know that if the crooks who murdered Frank had gotten hold of the money, it would have been mentioned here and there around town. It would be the same even if an entirely different bunch of crooks got hold of it, like, for instance, the crooks who set Frank up to pull off the robbery, if it turned out they were different than the crooks who murdered him. And let's face it, some crooks had set him up. How many guys walk out of jail and right away make a score like that? On what happens to be a day the bank has an extra-large supply of cash? The sound of bundles of stolen cash sliding into crooks' pockets is something people always heard in what Toole called the armed-robbery community. And when somebody heard a sound like that, next thing you knew, everybody in town heard about it.

But what was everybody in town hearing instead? Nothing. That's right. Nothing at all. And all this nothing everybody was hearing started coming in loud and clear at almost exactly the moment that Nina stopped trying to rob banks, and her brother knocked one over, and the money he'd stolen disappeared, leaving nothing anybody could find but his sorry-assed corpse. And here's what interested Toole as a police officer: was there some connection? Because while he was not a man of faith, if there was one thing he definitely didn't believe in, it was magic.

So, there. He'd done it. Gone pointedly and specifically through the case he was assembling. Except there was a problem. He'd only done it in his head. He thought he was saying it to her, thought he was crushing her under the relentless weight of circumstances, but he wasn't. What he'd been doing instead was staring slack-jawed at the space where the back wall once was, and the only thing he actually said out loud was, "What happened to your fuckin' house?"

No sooner had he gotten those words out than the ice cream truck came around the corner up toward the towers, chittering and chattering and going tootletly. He looked at it. She leaned her head around the corner and looked at it. And it was because they were both looking at it that they both ended up being eyewitnesses. It was too far away for them to identify anybody, but they could make out a little boy about the size of Fabreece coming out of one of the apartment buildings holding some kind of stick. They could watch as he pointed the stick at the ice cream truck. They could hear BOOM! It was so loud it echoed off the towers — Boom, boom. Everybody around the truck ran away as fast as they could, leaving the little kid on the ground where he'd been knocked over backwards by the recoil. Nina and Toole were certain they could see a wisp of smoke curling out of the truck's service window. The street was completely silent, but slowly, melting the silence like boiling water dripping on an ice cube, came the computerized announcements. Although it was still too far away for the cop to make the words out, he could get the pattering rhythm. Kids were having their names called and being told to hurry up and buy their ice cream treats or they would be in seriously bad trouble.

"Fuck me," Toole said. He grabbed under his jacket and was down the steps and running up the street, waving his gun.

"Fuck me," Nina said, her heart hammering so far up in her throat she could hardly swallow. The girls rushed out and clustered around her, with D.S. clumping behind them. "Fuck me! Did a bomb go off?" he said.

"Shotgun, sounded like," Lady said.

"What would you know about anything?" Merlina wasn't about to let whatever was happening keep her from stomping her sister into place.

"Sounded like a shotgun!" Ed Oataway shouted from across the street.

"More than you fuckin' do," Lady said to Merly, and pushed her off the side of the porch.

By the time Sergeant Toole got there, police cars and ambulances were arriving with their sirens going. Over them, JannaRose's voice rose trembling. "Whoever thought it would lead to shooting and killing? Oh God, oh God." Nina leaned her head against the doorframe and closed her eyes.

The strange thing was that hardly two hours later Mayor Gladly Bradley arrived. Investigators were still crawling all over the scene, and yellow tape had been put up to keep spectators back. He stood in the empty space in front of the truck, and while reporters and TV cameras crowded around him, he took a bullhorn and spoke to everybody in the neighbourhood, appealing for calm. It was terribly important that they all stay calm. The appeal was a personal one, from him to the residents of SuEz. But he was also speaking on behalf of the whole city. Everyone who lived there — would they please stay calm. Please don't let their emotions get the better of them. Let patience and reason prevail. And calm. Everybody should please see it in their hearts to do this.

It was strange because everybody wondered what he was talking about. That's because everybody was already about as calm as it was possible to be. If they were a little more keyed up than they would have been on an average weekday morning, it was because it was a change from what they'd grown used to. Obviously they were all surprised that a little kid had dug his father's shotgun out of a closet and opened fire. And there was a bit of argument having to do with the kid being so small and the gun so big. Some people swore he'd been aiming at the ice cream truck driver in the serving window, but he couldn't control where he was pointing and ended up assassinating the right front tire by accident. Others said no, he'd intended to take the tire out from the start and, what with being only seven years old, he'd done a good job. But these conversations never reached a point that could be described as even faintly heated.

The strangest thing, though, was that when he finished getting his picture taken and shaking hands with people around the truck, Mayor Bradley marched down the street to Nina's house and banged on the door. TV cameras followed him the whole way, but neither Nina nor anybody else she knew ever saw any of the pictures. She and D.S. and the girls were in the middle of the street when this happened, and since she couldn't push through the TV people, she had to holler, "Can I help you, sir?" It took Gladly Bradley a minute to find out who was yelling at him, but as soon as he did, he marched down the steps and shook her hand.

"Mrs. Dolgoy," he said, "it is a terrible day for the city when it starts with violence as it has this sad morning. But what very few of your fellow citizens realize is that you and your family have lately been victims of violence quite apart from this. And," the mayor said, "as a result you suffered a grievous personal loss. I want you personally to know that you and your husband, D.S., and your four daughters have your mayor's deepest sympathies, and the entire city's as well." Then he gave her a big hug and headed back through the crowd.

When he arrived in SuEz that day, it was the first time anybody Nina knew had ever seen him except on TV. When he left, nobody could think of anything that ever happened that made less sense. Except for Robbie Toole, and to him it made more sense than he cared for. Nina, though, wasn't thinking about whether it made sense or it didn't. That's because she was thoroughly pissed off. She'd just had the perfect chance to say something to the mayor about fixing the swimming pool, and the thought never crossed her mind.

Down in the cellar, Colonel Kevin Olorgasele of the Nigerian Finance Ministry couldn't understand any of it. He only began to catch on when the policeman showed up again that evening to ask the woman what the mayor had said about her brother. That was when Kevin actually realized that the guy was a policeman, and this was because he'd started using the same tone that Kevin used when he was putting the screws to somebody without quite bringing his heel down so hard on their toes that they would walk with a limp for a month. What he got to hear was the speech Sergeant Toole had intended to deliver that morning, before all the interruptions, with the cop adding that if she knew where the money was and kept the information to herself, then she and all her children were fuckin' doomed. It was the first time he'd ever heard a police officer speak that way to a white woman, except on the shows on Nigerian TV from England and the United States.

It was also the first time he'd heard a real live woman talk to a police officer the way she did. "You must be fuckin' insane," she'd said. "If I had that fuckin' money, do you think I'd still be in this fuckin' house that somebody is tearing down around my children, and scaring the living shit out of them? Do you think I'd be anywhere near it? What am I, a complete fuckin' moron? If you were any kind of a cop, you'd be protecting us, not threatening us, you fuckin' asshole."

The dollar amount Kevin heard them mention was 1.18 million. To speak the way he had, the police officer had to be interested in acquiring it for himself, while the sister of the dead thief sounded perfectly reasonable. If she had the money, she would have moved back to her family's village in the country, built a mansion, and owned many goats. It would also explain why whoever was tearing her house down was doing it: they believed the money was hidden here. Maybe it still was. And if nobody else had found it so far, why shouldn't he be the one to do it? It was always a good strategy to have a secondary target, and the best thing about the one he'd just lucked into was that nobody in Nigeria had any idea it existed. At the same time, nobody in Nigeria had any idea that the team sent out to acquire the White House gold had encountered one or two setbacks.

With both targets hanging close at hand like big ripe mangoes, it filled him with sadness that his beloved and respected colleague J. Ridgeway Mbunzu was no longer alive to share in the increasingly handsome potential benefits. So profound was his sadness that he laughed out loud and began examining the cellar for a hiding spot that might have been missed by whoever else was after the money, pausing only to puke now and then because the smell hadn't dissipated, despite the holes in the walls and the breeze blowing through.

The way things were going, he was feeling more at home every minute, but he did think he should find a place to live that was less stressful.

TWENTY-THREE

Ed Oataway didn't like the looks of this.

Nina pointed at what she'd written down when she was in Elwell's. He wouldn't even touch the piece of paper. "That's her, though, isn't it?" she said.

"How would I know?" Ed said.

"Maybe because that's where you drove him when he got out."

Dipshit's wife was already bad enough without her getting smartass. His own wife didn't seem to mind, though. "Good guess!" JannaRose said, giving Nina a thumbs up.

"It was her car." Nina tapped the piece of paper. "After the fake robbery, he was driving it around."

Ed didn't like the looks of this because it gave him the feeling that something really bad was coming his way.

"So?" he said.

"So I need you to steal it."

So, he was wrong. What was coming his way wasn't really bad, it was horrible. How many of these vehicles were there in the whole city — two? Maybe not even that. Maybe just this one. A Porsche Carrera GT. Bright fuckin' yellow!

"A car like that," JannaRose said, "it's worth …?"

"New, five hundred thousand," Nina said.

"You're out of your fuckin' mind," Ed said. But he shook his head when he said this, because he honestly didn't think she was out of her mind. He thought she was fuckin' insane.

"No," Nina said. "The Elwells told me."

"I mean about me stealing it."

Ed had been in high-rise apartment buildings before, of course. Sometimes business took him into and out of the towers up at The Intersection two, three times a day. But forty floors that had balconies with patio chairs and tables and nothing else on them such as piles of all the furniture and stuff that didn't fit into the apartment? With nothing on the ground like empty beer cans that had been thrown over the railings? Right along the shore? A place like this he had never been inside, much less cased.

On the other hand, stealing cars was his business. He was a professional. If he didn't steal cars, he and JannaRose would be living on nothing but two welfare cheques, and their kids would be eating nothing but potato chips which, as far as he could tell, was all Dipshit's ever got. But then again, the cars he stole were cars the owners wanted him to steal. Stealing them didn't require him to sneak around and go undetected the way this one did. The owner gave him a key. He made a copy of it. He gave the original back to the owner. Only one thing about this bothered Ed from a professional point of view. That was if the owner waved when he drove away. It made him feel undignified. Like some kind of dickhead. Anyway, the idiot owner then waited a reasonable time before calling the cops, and did they give a shit? A nine-year-old Chevy? Then the owner called the insurance company. The insurance company would be really irritated, but nobody cared about insurance companies' feelings. And they couldn't refuse to pay on the grounds that the idiot owner had lost the key and some thief found it and used it to steal the vehicle.

It was a nice little business that catered to people with real needs.

But a five-hundred-thousand-dollar Porsche?

Not even a drug dealer needed such a thing. Frank's girlfriend, what was she doing with it? He looked the building up and down. Maybe she was good at her work. When that thought whizzed around in Ed Oataway's brain, the sexual overtones made him feel nauseous. He tried to avoid thoughts with sexual overtones because he worried that impulses might get loose inside him and ruin what he had going for him and his family: a nice little business. One of the nicest things about the business was it kept him out of trouble. In fact, the only trouble he'd been in lately was a direct result of Dipshit's lunatic wife. Now here he was skulking around some whore's building because of her.

There were closed circuit TV cameras everywhere. Five at least were aimed at the front door. At least as many on the ramp to the underground garage. There was a doorman in a purple blazer. Ed put him down as a moonlighting cop. Every now and then another guy in the same colour blazer came and shot the shit with him. Another moonlighting cop. Ed figured he was stationed at the desk in the lobby, or else another moonlighting cop who came out for a smoke from time to time was, and this guy was his backup. There were shifts of guys like this day and night. It made Ed feel unsure of himself. He'd spent a few years in places he figured were easier to break out of than this one would be to get into, and almost nobody ever broke out of those places. Since there was no doubt in his mind that all these moonlighting cops were heavily armed, there was only one thing he could think to do.

He went to a pawnshop.

There was something else that he noticed. Almost every day, and sometimes a couple of times a day or more, fire trucks came wailing down the street and into the driveway, and the firefighters rushed into the building. When an ambulance finally showed up, the firefighters came out and drove away. Ed figured that rich old farts who lived in the building would have had attacks of some kind, and the firetrucks managed to arrive before anybody else to do first aid. Whether these things he noticed gave him a good idea or a stupid idea, it didn't matter. They at least gave him an idea, and he needed one.

"Fire! Fire!" he yelled into the payphone, having dialed 911. That was a break right there, finding a payphone when things had gotten so you were likelier to find a winning lottery ticket on the sidewalk. And when he finally got the 911 operator to calm down, he gave her the address. "Smoke is pouring out," he shouted. "People are on their balconies calling for help. They're waving sheets to get people's attention. I see one guy that looks like he's going to jump!"

In no time the driveway was full of fire trucks. More fire trucks were lined along the street. If what the firefighters encountered wasn't exactly the scene Ed described to 911, they didn't seem to care. There were more of them than usual because a fire had been reported, and a lot of them hadn't seen each other for a long time, so everybody was glad to be there, no matter what the problem was. They poured into the building with joyful shouts and high-fives. And Ed, waving a camera, which was what he'd bought at the pawn shop, poured in with them, yelling, "Media! Media!" The camera was a cheapo, but it had an enormous

Jesus flash attachment like the photographers had on TV, and every time he yelled "Media!" he hit the button, and everybody was just about blinded. The lobby was so full of firefighters that hardly anybody could move, and they were all yelling *Where's the fuckin' fire?* And the purple-blazers were all yelling *What fuckin' fire?* It was the first they'd heard of any fuckin' fire. The firefighters had on their helmets and a lot of them wore air tanks on their backs. A lot carried axes. The only person in the whole place who wasn't firefighter- or purple-blazer-related was Ed Oataway with his camera yelling "Media! Media!" and going *Flash! Flash!*

When they noticed this, all the firefighters started yelling at him to send them copies of the pictures so they could put them on the firehouse wall, but it made the purple-blazer guys forget the fire completely. "No media! No media!" they yelled every time Ed Oataway yelled "Media! Media!" Their problem was that they were all out in the middle of the lobby, jammed in by firefighters, while Ed was worming through the mob until he got behind the security desk, where he could hardly believe his eyes. There were maybe twenty-five or thirty TV screens, and he and his camera were featured live on five or six of them. It was really something to just be trying to do your job without anybody noticing and, wham! you turned out to be the star of the Ed Oataway Show!

Later on he thought it was too bad he hadn't brought one of those Identi-Kits along so he could have left an official set of fingerprints in case any of his old friends in law enforcement couldn't tell for sure who he was. He didn't have time to worry about it then, because as soon as the purple-blazers realized the media asshole was behind the desk, they went really berserk. This reminded him that he wasn't back there to wait for them to beat him to a bloody pulp. He was back there to push every button on the control panel as fast as he could, and while he had no idea what all else this did, the lobby lights went out and all kinds of alarms started going loud enough to loosen everybody's fillings. Then he ducked along the wall to a door marked "Emergency Exit" and raced for the basement.

He raced around P1 and had just arrived on P2 when he saw the Porsche. A button on the key unlocked it, and he tried to climb in. He tried again. Climbing in wasn't easy, because the car was so low-slung, it hardly came above his knees. And Ed was so low-slung that every single time D.S. saw him he remarked that it would take two Eds to make a full-sized runt, which caused Ed to want to pound Dipshit to liverwurst every time they ran into each other. Finally he squeezed himself in and turned the key.

The fuckin' car exploded.

If he'd taken the time beforehand, it might have occurred to him that Frank's girlfriend, and where she lived, and what kind of car she owned — that somebody like that could easily have the type of associates who, for one reason or another, would wire dynamite to her ignition. But he never gave it a thought until that instant, and what he thought then was Goodbye Ed Oataway! Then he discovered he was still alive. He was astonished. The car hadn't exploded, it was just very loud. "Five hundred thou," he said, "and you can't hardly get into it, and you can't hardly see out of it, and you can't hear yourself fuckin' think."

As the garage door was opening, two of the purple-blazer security guys showed up in his rearview, running and hollering, so when it was open enough to slip under, he tromped on the gas. And nothing happened. This scared him so much he thought he was going to shit in his drawers. Except not exactly nothing happened. The engine screamed, the spinning tires churned out clouds of smoke, but the car just sat there.

"Back off, backoff, backoffbackoffbackoff!" If he could have heard himself, that's what he would have heard himself saying. And that's what he did. He lifted his foot. Then, with hardly even a toenail, he barely touched the accelerator.

"*Jesus Fuckin' Christ!*"

Coming off the top of the exit ramp three feet in the air scared him so much, he thought he was having a stroke.

"For one thing," he told D.S. in a talking fit induced by his adventure, "there is the normal excitement that goes with stealing a car instead of just pretending to. It is always very stimulating. Add to this the realization that the vehicle I have stolen is totally uncontrollable. When a light turned green, I wasn't just across the intersection before the other cars, I was halfway down the fuckin' next block and standing on the brakes trying to get the fuckin' thing to stop for the next fuckin' traffic light. Which," he said, "I would arrive at with all four wheels still going in a straight line if I was lucky, which I wasn't several times."

You wouldn't have known Ed Oataway had any fuses left that weren't blown by the time he finally arrived at the garage Nina had found. Since it was almost falling down and nobody had used it for years, she figured nobody was likely to pay attention to them being there, and D.S. said he was sure nobody would unless they happened to wonder why the Indianapolis 500 had just pulled in.

Nina and JannaRose poked at the car for most of the day. D.S. said they reminded him of a movie he once saw about some cops who got hold of a vehicle belonging to some crooks, and how the cops had a bunch of mechanics take it apart with cutting torches so they could find the heroin in it. Then they put it back together, and the crooks never realized their stash had been lifted. "In case you haven't noticed," Nina said, "not only are me and JannaRose not a bunch of mechanics, we don't even have a pair of fuckin' pliers."

They couldn't even find a place anybody could hide much of anything, and 1.18 million would take up quite a bit of space unless, as D.S. pointed out, it was in million-dollar bills. Every part of the car was made of such thin pieces, you could hardly hide a five-dollar bill without making a bulge, and one thing Nina could see all too clearly was that there were no bulges anywhere.

It was depressing. She had discovered all these terrific clues: the car key. Where the car was. The business about Frank doing something to it at Elwell's. If he wasn't there hiding the loot in it, then driving it to Elwell's and whatever he did there didn't make any sense. That was the most depressing part of all: thinking she had figured it out. Then discovering she hadn't. Not even slightly.

"Maybe somebody got to it first," D.S. said.

"Could be." Nina sighed as if she finally realized why so many people called him Dipshit. "Especially if it was wrapped in Saran Wrap and lying on the seat."

"Right!" D.S. said, poking her in the shoulder for emphasis.

"Now what?" JannaRose didn't say this the way somebody might say, "All right! We've done Step A and Step B. I guess Step C is next. What is it again?" She said it the way somebody would who knew everything imaginable had been tried, and since the only choice left was to jump off a bridge over the Parkway, then they better get started. It was a fair ways off.

But this time it was her turn to be wrong. Nina had a definite "Now what?" in mind, and when she told her what it was, JannaRose's eyebrows whizzed right up into her hairline. "Really?" she said.

That's not what Ed Oataway said when he got a chance to discuss it with Nina. "Did you know that you're completely fuckin' insane?" was what he said.

"It's got to," she said.

"What do you mean it's got to?"

"Get taken back."

"I meant *why* does it? What if you found the money in it?"

"It would still have to. It's stolen property."

"I know it is. I'm the one that stole it, remember? But it's worth maybe a hundred thou if we can find a buyer. You could put that toward the pool."

"It's not right to fix the pool with that kind of money."

"What about Frank's loot then?" Ed hauled back and pointed a finger at her. "How come you don't give a fuck about it?"

So Nina told him how the insurance worked with money that got stolen from banks.

TWENTY-FOUR

Ed Oataway didn't like anything about this.

Nina couldn't even say what led her to realize the puzzle had a missing piece, other than her obsessive inability to make her mind stop poking through the car. She could still see every bit of it, no matter how tiny. Everything it was made of was thin. Even the seats. The seats were hardly thicker than linoleum. There wasn't a part of anything that wasn't like that. She knew because she had knocked on and poked at every single thing.

Every. Single. Thing.

Knocked on it and poked at it.

Every cylinder and cranny.

Knocked it.

Poked it.

Every ... single ...

"Where's Ed?"

JannaRose just about jumped out of her teeth. She

was dozing with her chin on her fist when Nina burst into her kitchen.

"Ed? Why?"

"No fuckin' way," Ed said when JannaRose told him why.

To be fair, that was his first reaction. It was also his second and third and all the other reactions he had after Nina found where he was hiding and explained how urgent it was for him to steal the Porsche again.

It didn't matter. His reaction never mattered. And it wasn't because Ed was pussy-whipped and had to do whatever his wife decided that it never mattered. He was pussy-whipped, all right, but his reaction never mattered because as far as Nina was concerned he was an idiot, and his wife always agreed with whatever Nina said.

Originally he thought it was ridiculous to imagine they would find the money in the car. Now he wasn't so sure. Stealing it had made him feel that he kind of had a stake in the outcome. Sort of a commitment to seeing things all the way through. And if Dipshit's wife ended up being as big a lunatic as she clearly was, and if there was some lunatic chance the money was where she now decided it was, why not go along with it? What did he have to lose? Who knew but some of that cash might trickle down into his hands. Which would only be right, of course, considering that his dead best friend was a prick who had tried to screw him out of his fair share.

And this time he had a chance to work out a plan that was solid as a rock, because it was based on inside knowledge he'd gained the first time. For instance, when the lobby was packed with firefighters and security guards, he'd stuck out. Not this time, though. Not dressed in a firefighter's coat and helmet he'd rented from a safety supply company. And unlike the last time, he didn't have to call in a false alarm. This time there happened to be a real alarm prompted by a real fire. It was so utterly unexpected that he was stumble-foot stupefied by the sight of firefighters racing into the building and almost forgot to get his firefighter-rigged ass across the street and race in with them. That's when it became clear that his new plan was a good one only as far as it went, which wasn't far enough to take into account a major consideration that everybody but Ed Oataway always did: how truly short he was. Fortunately, if he only came up to the elbows of most of the firefighters, and if the smallest helmet the safety supply had kept joggling down over his eyes so he couldn't see where he was going, there was so much smoke and confusion that nobody paid any attention. There were a whole lot more firefighters, and they were in an even cheerier mood than the last time when it was a false alarm. They were pumping their fists and asking each other if they knew what was burning. Something in the wiring maybe, since besides smoke, so many sparks were whooshing out of the ceiling that each new arrival shouted, "Holy Johnson! Take a look at that mother!"

Ed, doing his best to appear as enthusiastic as the firefighters he squeezed his way through, had just pushed open the door to the garage when the purple blazers went haywire.

"It's him!"

"Who?"

"That little fucker again! There he goes!"

Closed-circuit TVs showed a short guy in a coat so long he kept tripping over it holding a firefighter's helmet with both hands to keep it from tipping over his eyes as he ran down the stairs.

"I've had enough of his bullshit!" shouted one of the blazer guys, pulling an automatic pistol out of his shoulder harness. "This is the last time the little car-stealing cocksucker steals a car on my shift."

"Fuckin' right!" yelled another purple-blazer who was looking at the TV monitors when he took off after Ed and as a result ran flat-out into the gun-wielding security guard, causing him to fire a bullet into the ceiling. Nobody had any idea what it hit up there, but now the sprinklers went off, adding a cascading downpour to the scene. Heedless of their personal safety, the firefighters pushed forward to see what the shooting was all about. It wasn't every day they got a combo of a real fire and gunfire at the same time, something they definitely did here, since the sparks had caused the whole ceiling to shimmer with flame.

Ignoring the firefighters, the blazer guys, including the one who'd fired the shot, did what police officers who moonlight as security guards always did when shooting started, and climbed under their desks. Under his, the senior purple-blazer had an inspiration. Pointing toward several TV screens, he yelled, "*Somebody on the scene is impersonating a firefighter!*"

"What?" There were cries of furious disbelief as the firefighters stopped congratulating each other for being first responders at the dooziest alarm in memory and gathered around the monitors.

"There!" the security guard said, as Ed Oataway, from several angles, scurried through the garage. "See!"

"*He's impersonating a firefighter!*" firefighters shouted.

"The little cocksucker!" gasped other firefighters, standing stone still in amazement as Ed stripped off his firefighter's gear and scrunched into the racy yellow car. "He should be hung by his little fuckin' nuts!

"Stop him!" they chorused. "He's trying to escape!" They all raced out of the building and jumped aboard their trucks, but the last they saw of Ed was a closed-circuit shot of the yellow car going off the top of the exit ramp three feet above the ground. Nevertheless they raced around town for a couple of hours to work off their rage.

Their departure had left the purple-blazers all alone in the immense lobby with flames boiling over their heads.

"Call 911," one yelled.

"I did," another yelled. "I got an answering machine."

While Ed still hollered "Holy shit!" when he touched the gas, it was just force of habit. He was starting to get used to the car's surprises. And while this made him a bit more confident, there was no truth to Nina's accusation that he started thinking he was the King Kong of the Freeways and decided to go joyriding. The route he picked actually was the most direct, except it didn't help that the only one who took his side afterward was D.S., and he said there must have been some good reason for choosing it, because Ed wasn't that kind of an asshole. He followed the shore expressway to the Parkway, intending to get off at the first exit, when the flashing lights showed up in his rearview. Since they were still a ways back, it gave him time to think, and that was part of the problem. Because he thought "Jesus!" In the car-stealing business, it's a rule of thumb that if you're at the wheel of a car you've just stolen, and police come from behind like that, they're on to you.

He reacted instinctively.

He floored it.

Ed Oataway was wrong about the police. But not as wrong as he was about reacting that way. The Porsche had only just started spinning when the police car went past in such a blur that the cops didn't even notice. And if they had, they'd have thought, stomp on the gas in a car as powerful as that and it almost doesn't matter how fast you're travelling, the wheels are going to lose their grip on the pavement. What did you expect?

It kept on spinning until it hit the guardrail, and Ed would have been grateful that this stopped the spinning if it hadn't made the car flip over. Once it started flipping over, it went on doing it for quite some time.

TWENTY-FIVE

Even the idea of this upset Ed Oataway's stomach.

"What kind of a guy steals junk?" he asked.

"It's your own fault," JannaRose said.

Ever since piling the five-hundred-thousand-dollar Porsche into a ravine, he'd had the feeling that his support system wasn't all that supportive. For instance, did he hear even one "Thank God you didn't get killed!" when he survived the wreck? And scrambled up that ravine — *limped* up it? In the pitch dark? That ravine full of garbage and broken glass? With a leg that for all he could tell was broken? That he had to keep limping on for another half hour until he found a subway station? Did he even hear it from his *wife*?

That was okay. Once he got hold of the money, she'd change her tune. Even that son of a bitch Frank would have changed his tune if he was still alive. It wouldn't matter that he'd tried to beat Ed out of what he was entitled to.

Frank couldn't help himself when it came to things like that. It was the way he was. If people everywhere didn't grow up thinking that way, they did in SuEz if they had any interest in surviving.

What kind of a guy steals junk? The lowest of the low. And he was being forced to do it. He had already been forced to push his car-stealing abilities beyond their natural limit, and had almost lost his life as a result. But there was no way he could have avoided that any more than he could get out of what he had to do now. Because what if that was where the 1.18 million really was? And what if he could grab the entire bundle and get a nice place for his family and him to live in? Like, was it his fault that Dipshit's crazy fuckin' wife had never thought to look inside the tires?

Quite apart from professional self-esteem, Ed Oataway had good reason to feel bad about stealing this particular piece of junk. Compared to the two times he'd stolen it before it got wrecked, there were a lot of complications. Locating it wasn't one of them, though. When the cops and insurance company finished with the car, the computer at Elwell's tracked down the wrecker it was hauled to and even identified the row it was piled in, and which pile it was on.

The main complication was Dipshit. He was standing beside the pile the mangled Porsche was on, having just climbed down from the towtruck the Elwells had been kind enough to lend them. And he was saying in a voice that made Ed go all shivery in his intestines, "Oh Christ, Oh God, Oh sweet Jesus, help me!" This complication actually went back to when Ed was informed that Dipshit would be going along with him. It could be it was to make sure he didn't do anything so crazy that it almost led to the death of the dream, like the last time. But even though he noticed that everybody was being careful not to so much as hint at such a thing, he doubted it. The idea that

Dipshit might keep somebody from doing something crazy was *totally* crazy. Ed Oataway could even think of a dozen other reasons D.S. was with him, but once you examined them and threw away the ones that were bullshit, there was only one left, so it had to be the real one. Dipshit was sent on the junkyard job because it would irritate Ed. That's all there was to it.

And did he ever, going on about Christ and God and Jesus in a way that wasn't only irritating, it was scary. Ed quietly let himself out the driver's door and tiptoed around the front of the truck, only to stop cold at the sight of Dipshit with a horrible expression of terror on his face.

Then whatever it was that was terrifying D.S. lunged at Ed! And Ed started groaning "Christ" and asking for help from Jesus, the same as Dipshit had.

A thoughtful person might have asked, "They were in a junkyard. They didn't expect there would be a junkyard dog, for God's sakes?" or "They cut through the lock on the gate in the middle of the night and drove in with a towtruck to steal a wreck and they didn't think the junkyard dog would maybe notice?" Fair enough, but what these questions really show is that the person who might have asked them wasn't the slightest bit familiar with D.S. Dolgoy or Ed Oataway.

The dog was a German shepherd, but all black. When it lunged, it also kind of lurched, so besides being attack-trained, it could be it also had rabies. Drool ran in globs from its jaws.

"Run!" Ed yelled.

"If I run, it'll get me!"

"Jump in the truck!"

"If I try to jump in the truck, it'll get me!"

The dog lurched again. It was close enough that they could get a good look at its eyes. Its eyes looked like it wasn't right in the head.

"We're fucked!" D.S. wailed.
"We're fuckin' dead!
"*Oh God, it's ...*"

TWENTY-SIX

Early the next morning Nina started to realize that somebody had unscrewed all the screws that held the world together and thrown them away. The crumpled heap that had once been the yellow Porsche squatted in the middle of her front walk. The street was quiet, no sign of the ice cream truck. Now that it only travelled with a police escort, it often didn't come by until noon. Things didn't get any noisier when a black Cadillac eased to a stop, the driver's window opened, and the Elwell twins peered out. If looks could kill, the one they gave her would have left nothing but a plywood urn full of ashes on the front steps where she was sitting. They'd never come by before, and she wondered if maybe Ed Oataway hadn't taken back the towtruck they'd been kind enough to lend them for last night's job. Maybe he'd taken off with it the way the average SuEz resident would have. It turned out it wasn't that, though. It turned out to be far worse.

"We are disappointed," they said. "We cannot emphasize how disappointed we are in you."

"In me?" Why her? Except she knew it was only because of her that they'd loaned Ed the towtruck.

"Yes. Because of what happened as a result of the crime you committed," L. Roy said, unless it was L. Ray. It was difficult to tell which was which in the shadowy front seat of the Caddy.

"Or arranged to have committed," the other one said.

"Instigated. Which is a crime in itself."

"Be that as it may. We are not sitting in judgement. We are simply expressing our utter disapproval of you and your associates because wanton violence —"

"— against dumb animals —"

"— against our four-legged friends, no matter how small or large their IQ proves to be is —"

"— deeply offensive to us. Deeply and personally. So offensive that —"

"What the fuck are you talking about?" Nina had come down to the curb so she could hear exactly what they were saying. It was so strange that she grabbed hold of the hair on each side of her head. It didn't sound like one of the Elwells' joking-around routines. For one thing, they weren't laughing.

"About the dog getting shot to death?" one of them said indignantly.

"The junkyard dog?" the other said.

"Not that we intend that as a slur on the poor beast. It is a job description. Junkyard dog was its trade. And as such, it was attempting to do its faithful and honourable duty when the thugs you —"

"— when your thugs blew its hard-working head off."

The Elwell in the passenger seat beckoned Nina closer and turned up the radio. "Give a listen to this," he said. It was Mayor Gladly Bradley, sounding as if his head was on fire. He was raging about "viciousness" and "callousness" and "criminals that would shoot down a dog in the commission of a crime. A brave, selfless dog," he roared, "that worked for a living. They shot it. Killed it dead as dead can be. And if that doesn't call for the death penalty with a capital D and a capital P, then why the hell do we bother having a death penalty anyway?"

"Hear that?" an Elwell said. "Awhile ago he called it 'heinous.'"

"Not often you get to bandy a word like heinous around," his brother said. "But give the man credit, he —"

"— can bandy to beat the band."

"He's a one-man bandy. It was the first thing we heard when we woke up."

"Drove straight over here to tell you that we disapprove. And that herewith and hereinafter we no longer care to be associated with you or your associates in any way, shape, or form. And request that in future you take your business —"

"Your nasty business —"

"Yes!"

"Your *heinous* business —"

"Exactly. In future, you take your vile business elsewhere. And a very good morning to you, sir."

Whichever Elwell it was who said that said it to a chunky man who had double-parked a blue Solara convertible and was approaching the Porsche's remains with a smile so big, it made Nina think he was going to break into a dance. "And farewell to you, madam," the Elwell said to Nina.

Detective Toole grunted "Morning" without bothering to look at the Caddy as it crept away. He glanced at Nina, though, and his smile got even bigger. He circled the wreck as if it was some kind of famous statue and this was the first time he'd seen the genuine article.

"Never thought of you as the dog-shooting type," he said after awhile, his voice filled with sunshine, and this really mystified Nina, because all she'd been able to think when the Elwells and the mayor were going on about it was "Huh?"

"Must've taken me about eight seconds," Toole said, not bragging — more like he thought it was funny it took him so long. "I was drinking my tea in bed, when who comes on the clock radio but our esteemed mayor in an absolute state — an absolute *state* — about a noble dog that had been murdered in the courageous performance of its duty. Then the news came on and said the only thing apparently missing as a result of the break-and-entry at the junkyard where the dog got shot was a wrecked car. Believe it or not, a wrecked *Porsche*. Yellow." With his car key he scraped a couple of flecks of paint off the wreck. "Now I am always interested in crimes that are of special interest to the mayor, and what do I find when I search the records a little bit? I find that the wreck was reported stolen *before* it was a wreck. And then *it turned back up*. And then *it got stolen again!* Almost," Toole said, "like something strange was going on. Does it sound like that to you?"

Nina stared at the ground.

"I also discovered," he continued, "that it is registered to, and was repeatedly stolen from the parking spot of, a woman named Junetta Solito, whose address is —" he clutched his forehead as if he was going to faint "— *whose address is the same one your deceased brother Frank gave as a fowarding address when he got out of prison!* And the second time it was stolen it ended up in a ravine beside the Parkway. And," Toole said, "when I drop around here to see if maybe you can help me understand these things, what do I find in front of your house?" He gave the wreck a couple of raps with his knuckles. "The strangest thing of all."

He raised his eyebrows as if he was interested in hearing what she had to say about all this, but he wasn't really, because he carried on before she got a chance to let him know that she wasn't going to say a word.

"I find it interesting," the cop said, "fascinating even, from an investigative point of view, that a cheap-shit asshole conman like Frank Carson was on such close personal terms with a woman of such considerable means — the owner of one of the most expensive apartments in the city, for instance, and a five hundred thousand dollar Porsche Carrera GT. And that shortly after he meets his grisly end, no sign can be found of the 1.18 million dollars he stole in a put-up job at the main downtown branch of the Great Big One National Bank. Then," Toole said, "not long after that, the automobile in question begins leading an extremely adventurous life, ending up —" he gave the wreck a little kick with the toe of his shoe "— ending up in hardly better condition than your brother. And I can only speculate that somehow he informed you that the money was stashed in the car. But I'm presuming your first search turned up squat. Then you thought of something you'd overlooked." He spread his arms and looked surprised to see the sliced-up rubber all over the sidewalk. "I'm presuming the tires. And was the money in those tires? Wait, don't tell me! I've worked the thing out this far, let me see if I can take it right through to the end.

"In the meantime," he said, "let me advise you of your rights. You have the right to remain silent. You have the right to try to get away with the money. You have the right to try to stay beyond my reach if you do try to run away with it. And you have the right to hand it over to me no questions asked.

"I'll give you —" he was still holding up the fingers he'd counted out her rights on "— some time to make up your mind."

He walked across to the blue convertible. As he was about to climb in, he looked back and pointed at the wreck. "SuEz," he said, "has got to be the only part of town where something like that on the sidewalk is an improvement."

"What do you mean we shot the dog?" D.S. wasn't at his sharpest. He'd only gotten to sleep about an hour after they finally decided that one thing was for sure — there was not 1.18 million in those tires. There was nothing in them, times four.

Sergeant Toole's car wasn't out of sight when Nina steamed into the living room where D.S. was snoring on the busted old couch because he'd been too tired to go and climb into one of the cars along the street, where he usually slept. She kicked his foot and shouted, "You fuckin' moron."

And now he was denying it. "It's on the fuckin' radio," she yelled.

"What's on the fuckin' radio?"

"That you shot the fuckin' junkyard dog."

"What the fuck are you talking about?"

"The Elwells are mad as fuckin' hell. That cop's been here."

"You're fuckin' nuts."

"The Elwells have animal cruelty issues. And the cop heard the mayor and came around and saw the wreck on the front walk."

D.S. pulled a pillow over his face. "This is too much," he groaned.

"You're too much." Nina turned to leave. "None of this would be going on if you hadn't shot that dog!"

"Jesus!" D.S. yelled. This was it as far as he was concerned. This was the limit. He couldn't stand it one second more. He threw off the pillow and got really sarcastic. "We shot the dog? Yeah? Yeah? What with? I mean what fuckin' *with*? Do we have a gun? Did we have a gun? Have we ever had a gun? Where do I keep this gun? Up my fuckin' ass? So what did I shoot the dog with?" He pointed his finger at Nina and wiggled his thumb. "My finger? Blam, blam, blam! And it fell down dead?" He made like he was blowing smoke out of the barrel of a gun.

Nina stopped in the doorway. "So what happened then?" Her voice was very low.

D.S. didn't say anything.

"Was there a dog? Did something happen to it?"

D.S. drooped his head. Because the first thing the dog did, after it lurched at Ed Oataway, was lie down, open its jaws even wider, and give its head a shake.

"It's yawning," Ed said. He couldn't believe it.

"It's a fuckin' killer," D.S. said. "It wants us to drop our guard."

"No. It's just real old and real tired."

"So what the fuck do we do?"

"Load the wreck and get the fuck out of here."

When he heard this, D.S. sagged with relief and yawned so deeply, his whole body shuddered. "See," Ed said, "it's catching." And they were both in the truck, with Ed backing out, when D.S. felt something.

"What?" Ed said.

"What?" Nina said.

D.S. stared at his knees on the couch. "Like a bump."

"A bump?"

D.S. kept staring at his knees.

"A bump?"

D.S. mumbled something.

"What?" Nina said.

Then he said something that wasn't quite as much of a mumble.

"*You ran over it?*" Nina said it as if she wanted to make sure that's what she actually heard.

"I guess it got up from where it was the last time we noticed it, lay down under the truck and went to sleep."

"*You ran over the junkyard dog?*"

"It was an accident."

"It was an accident," she said. "Good! Good! That will calm everybody down. Vicious thieves didn't shoot the hero dog. They ran over it instead. Accidentally. I'm sure the cop will come right back and say he's sorry he bothered us."

"What about the Elwells?"

"D.S.," Nina said. "Get some rest, okay? Your brain is overworked. It needs to take some time off."

D.S. looked at the ceiling, wondering just what the hell she meant by that. It wasn't like her to give him a lot of sympathy. Except he didn't wonder about it for very long, because hardly a minute went by before he was snoring again. And hardly another minute went by before she was back in the doorway yelling at him.

"Where's the spare tire?" she was yelling.

"What?" D.S. mumbled. "What? What?"

"The spare tire for the Porsche," Nina said. "I never saw it. Did you?"

TWENTY-SEVEN

Jarmeel Tolbert got terribly upset when his followers started to burn down the churches of other religions. He had more or less expected that being in space and getting probed would have made everybody calm and peaceful and enthusiastic about doing good work in the community, the way it had with him. He wouldn't have believed anybody who might have predicted a religion of violence would spring from it.

By the time the total got to nine, something else was upsetting him. The police were starting to notice a pattern to the fires and to some other things that were going on. Not all the churches burned right down. The first did, that big Presbyterian one in South Chester, and so did a couple of the Baptists, but a lot of the fires were put out before doing much damage — there were sprinklers, or somebody saw the flames and phoned in an alarm. The Inter-Church Dialogue Crew, which was the committee that handled the burnings, went all the way downtown one night to set the

Catholic cathedral on fire, but they couldn't get anything to catch at all. Some of them took this as a sign from on high, or even higher, to steer clear of Catholic churches until they heard otherwise.

The police determined that in every instance arson was involved or attempted. At the cathedral, combustible materials along with posters from Jarmeel's church were discovered lying around the singed vestry door. There was a great deal of pressure on the police chief and the mayor to do something.

Compounding the problem was that the Inter-Church Dialogue Crew believed in leaving behind a statement of who they were and what they were up to, otherwise what was the point? They chose to do this symbolically, and the symbol they came up with showed an alien space ship flying through the sky, and below that a naked person bent over with a probe that to the non-initiated looked quite a bit like a mechanical duck approaching the naked person's rear end. A halo over the spaceship signified the close relationship between the aliens and God. However, people who didn't grasp the symbolism thought it looked like a bigoted pervert had drawn something dirty on the floor near where the fires had been set or on a wall outside. This would have driven the police chief to get personally involved in solving these crimes, if he wasn't already appalled by the halo, which was an affront to his profoundly Christian beliefs, and by the mechanical duck, which offended the most cherished community standards.

Jarmeel was also touched personally. From the outset, several of his followers had made critical remarks about his qualifications to lead the religion he had founded, based on the haziness of his recollection of having been probed. They whispered that in his case it might have been more of a spiritual experience. But it wasn't until they noticed how nervous he was about the fires that they no longer mostly made these comments behind his back.

They demanded a trial by fire. Jarmeel would come with them the next time they went to burn down an enemy church and do the actual deed himself while they stood around bearing witness and going "Hoooom, hoooom." Jarmeel thought this was an awful idea, and not just because there was a chance he might get caught. It was awful because he would get caught for sure. His fingerprints would be all over everything, and they'd be instantly identifiable. In the army he'd been fingerprinted when he got clearance to handle the classified materials such as brake fluid that the aliens probed out of him. And he'd been fingerprinted when he got arrested before the court-martial. It would take the police two minutes to track him down.

And there would go his welfare cheque.

How would he be able to feed his three children who had been abandoned by their mothers and left with him?

The thing about true religious believers is that when it comes to their leader, they don't take no for an answer, so he had no choice. He had to disappear completely. And not alone, either. He took his kids with him. To get around this obstacle, his followers not only left the mechanical duck symbol at the next fire they set, they tacked dozens of copies of a message around the scene that read, "My name is Jarmeel Tolbert and I am the Blessed Founder of Nearer My God. It was my destiny to burn down this vile place where the defilers of God's interstellar love fulfill their obscene desires." There was a lot more along that line, but this was all the arson squad needed to get on his case. His followers were eager to get their hands on him, too, and Jarmeel was more worried about them, because unlike the police, they were completely deranged.

But his situation wasn't the result of anything he'd done. As far as he was concerned, his liberty, life, and family were jeopardized only because Nina had got him involved when she started raising money to fix some swimming pool or other.

On the other hand, her brother had gotten hold of 1.18 million dollars and then died tragically. Jarmeel had also heard that in order to fix this swimming pool, Nina was leading a big crusade to find that money.

That's when a word popped into Jarmeel's simmering brain. The word was "apparently." Because what if it wasn't true that she hadn't found the money? What if the truth was that she *apparently* hadn't found it? What if now she was only *pretending* to search for it? What if this was *because she had already found it?*

Fuck her.

There were people who needed some of that cash immediately. And who was to say exactly how much they would need? Jarmeel was not a greedy man. It was just that the danger to his life and the lives of his children led him to calculate that 1.18 million was easily how much it could cost to get them somewhere safe and look after them very well when they got there.

As for getting his hands on it, Jarmeel was prepared to do whatever it took. After stashing his children in a secret location, he started to sneak around keeping his eye on Nina. He wore a disguise when he did this, but that wasn't so much to keep Nina from realizing what he was up to. It was so the members of his former religion wouldn't spot him and do whatever they believed their religion compelled them to do, such as lead him back to the fold. When he thought about that, his hair would break out in a sweat.

TWENTY-EIGHT

When Krystal Beach saw her ex-husband Rocky Beach's dick on the floor of her ConGlom Couriers van, she laughed because she realized there had been a horrible accident — she had no idea what. And that she had been — she had no idea how — involved in it. It was the sort of laughter that would result when staggering confusion got mixed together with the feeling that is the biochemical equivalent of being aboard an airplane full of clowns when it crashed into a fireworks warehouse. It was kind of a nervous laughter.

Her previous ex-husband Bonallo didn't know this when he heard it. He took it to mean Krystal had turned cruel and hard-hearted.

She'd heard that Beach wanted to reconcile with her, but she'd had no idea that in order to do this he'd started stalking her, and that when she was climbing aboard her van after making a delivery on the downtown side of the river, he saw his big chance. Unzipping his fly, he had run toward her, waggling his manhood yearningly. Without looking, without even realizing he was in the vicinity, she'd given the sliding door a firm shove that caused it, just as he got there, to slice across like the blade of a horizontal guillotine. Entirely unaware of his anguish, she had driven away.

When Bonallo saw this happen, his heart went out to Beach. Until that moment he had been too focused on his own romantic quest to notice that Beach was also stalking Krystal in the hopes of reconciling. The minute he saw Beach run waggling toward her van, he realized they shared a powerful common purpose. Never had he felt closer to another human being. It was as he knelt on the ground trying to comfort the dying Beach that Krystal came roaring back, slid the door open and flicked the dick out beside them with the toe of her sneaker. And roared off again. What Bonallo would remember more than anything was her hideous laughter. Never before could he have imagined Krystal making such an evil sound or inflicting such a fatal injury, not just on a fellow human being, but on her immediate past husband.

It turned out not to be totally fatal. At the hospital, the doctors stitched Beach's dick back on as good as new, or almost anyway. When he peed, it came out at a ninety-degree angle to the left, so he had to stand sideways to the receptacle. In crowded men's rooms this led to incidents that required him to do a lot of explaining. The important thing, though, was that the bond Bonallo and Beach formed led them to agree that nothing could be more perfect than both of them reconciling with Krystal. So they began stalking her as a team and were more than prepared to devote all their energies to this, because they were both on welfare and didn't have anything else to do.

Krystal Beach had a hard time getting used to the idea that these things actually happened to her, but something else involving her was going on that she didn't know about even slightly, and it was really strange.

When Kevin Olorgasele moved out of Nina's cellar because it was so disgusting, he didn't move too far. He wanted to be able to keep his eye on the White House's agent in the Fort Knox gold deal, so he sized up the van she pretended to drive for a courier service and parked in front of her house every night. One of the things Kevin was taught early in his career with his country's Finance Ministry was how to break into any kind of vehicle without leaving a mark, an approach that was considerably different than the one he'd employed before that, which was smashing a window with a rock. Her van was clean inside, and dry, and smelled one hundred per cent better than his last hiding place.

But he would never have chosen it if he knew how security-conscious ConGlom Courier Services was. The company wanted to make sure its drivers didn't use the vans for their own sidelines after hours and had secretly equipped them with satellite sensors that showed where they were every minute. They could also detect unauthorized changes in the gross weight. That was why ConGlom inspectors were staking out Krystal's van the next night and saw a black man climb into it with some blankets. He opened the rear door so easily, they were certain he had to be using Krystal's own key.

After a couple of hours during which they witnessed no further developments, they drew their guns and used their master key to unlock the van. The man inside came at them hollering and scrambled past in such a windmilling flurry that they hardly got off more than a dozen shots before he disappeared into the darkness. When the security inspectors and the police reviewed the incident, everybody was disappointed that there were no signs of blood to show he had at least been wounded and would have provided a trail they could follow.

Krystal got fired. This infuriated her, and she began searching around SuEz until she caught sight of Kevin, who fit the description of the man her former employer accused her of giving free access to the van. He was also one of the goat-men she'd seen hanging around her house. When she jumped on his back and started pounding him with her fists, Bonallo and Beach saw an ideal chance to get back on her good side. But just as they started beating up the person she was attacking, another person came leaping into the fight. At first nobody paid any attention, because in SuEz it wasn't unusual for an innocent bystander to join in a brawl just because it was there, then, just when everybody was punching and kicking for all they were worth, the fight abruptly stopped. That was because Kevin finally got a good look at the man who was battling for no reason the other participants could see — and his jaw dropped. He backed away. He couldn't believe his eyes. *The interloper was J. Ridgeway Mbunzu!* His beloved colleague. The partner he was sure was dead.

He'd been shot. His body was thrown out a window on the twenty-fourth floor of one of the towers at The Intersection. Kevin was there when it happened. He'd witnessed the whole thing.

For his part, when Ridgeway came upon his principal asset, Ms. K. Beach, getting mugged, he sprang to her rescue and concentrated totally on protecting her. But at the exact instant Kevin got a good look at Ridgeway, Ridgeway realized that *one of the guys he was fighting was his old partner Kevin!*

But Kevin was dead!

There was no question! Because Ridgeway had seen exactly the same thing happen to Kevin as Kevin had seen happen to him! He'd been right there. He'd seen Kevin's body get thrown out the twenty-fourth-floor window.

Now here was each one's dearest and most trusted friend — *alive again!*

They were overjoyed. There was a lot of, "I say, this is rather unbelievable!" and "*Ra*-ther!"

They were also stunned, because, just as Kevin had, once Ridgeway accepted his partner's death as an inescapable fact, he decided to turn the disaster into an opportunity and get his hands on the White House ingots and keep them for himself. The only difference was that he didn't know about the 1.18 million dollars that Kevin saw as a potential bonus. Who wouldn't be stunned when his share of possible billions was suddenly reduced by half?

As these tumultuous emotions jumbled their thoughts, one thing did emerge clearly. Since they were reunited, it would be appropriate to replace the original goat. And they both thought: *the original goat!* And they started to laugh.

It must have been the goat's dead body!

They threw their arms around each in the hilarity of it all.

That crazy man! Throwing a dead goat out of the window!

That was when Bonallo and Beach realized the assholes they'd been protecting Krystal from weren't paying attention and started beating them up again. It snapped Kevin and Ridgeway back to the immediate moment. Their training as colonels in the dreaded Finance Ministry clicked in, and they began to work together like the team they'd been for so long. But this didn't count for zip when Krystal picked up an exhaust pipe that was lying by the curb and hammered Kevin and then Ridgeway over the head with it. Bonallo and Beach stomped on the fallen Nigerians until there was nothing left of them but a bloody mess. Then Krystal told her ex-husbands that if they didn't fuck off and leave her alone, she would hammer them over the head with the exhaust pipe, too. So they ran for it.

Despite all this, Krystal was still furious. She had lost her job. She hated welfare. She hated that she would have to go on it. She hated that it would take months for her to start getting it. She hated that she couldn't live without it. Then she saw a glimmer of hope: Nina's 1.18 million. Where was it? Ever since that wreck showed up on her front walk, Nina had stopped searching for it. Could it possibly be because she'd found it? But if she had, everybody in SuEz would know. Those morons Dipshit and Ed Oataway and JannaRose wouldn't have been able to keep it a secret. Unless ... unless they didn't know! What if she'd kept it a secret from them, too, the bitch.

Fuck her.

If there had been a time in Krystal's life when she really needed to get rich quick, this was it. Nina wouldn't know what hit her by the time she got finished.

If every part of Kevin and Ridgeway's bodies was dripping blood, and if every bone was broken, they were at least together again. Standing up was impossible. But, tugging and pulling at each other, they managed to drag themselves into the cellar where Kevin had hidden before. They climbed down through the busted-out window and burrowed under some rubble. Weary. Barely alive. But at least safe.

They thought.

TWENTY-NINE

To show how the virus of suspicion about Nina and the missing bank loot could spread very subtly and in ways that were painful to her, it helps to begin with a flashback.

When she heard about the junkyard dog, she woke D.S. and gave him grief for killing it. Not even slightly impressed that the dog's death was unintentional, she left the room. D.S. fell back asleep.

The flashback goes like this:

And hardly another minute went by before she was back in the doorway yelling at him.

"Where's the spare tire?" she was yelling.

"What?" D.S. mumbled. "What? What?"

"The spare tire for the Porsche," Nina said. "I never saw it. Did you?"

Remember that?

So D.S. went out and started prying at the wreck. Since Ed Oataway was keeping an eagle eye on everything concerning Nina, he came over to find out what was going on this time. "We never looked in the spare tire," D.S. said. So Ed started prying, too. When they finished, they delivered their news.

"There isn't?" she said.

Nina could get a skeptical tone in her voice, and it sounded like if there was no spare tire it was D.S. and Ed's fault.

"And there never was one, either," D.S. said.

"What do you mean?" She looked at him out of the corner of her eye.

"He means there never was one," Ed smiled, because this time he had Nina right where he wanted her. "That's what he means."

"Yup," D.S. said. "Nope." As if he could hardly believe it himself.

"What do you do if you get a flat?"

Ed handed her an enormous aerosol can.

Nina looked at the label. Fix-a-Flat. "What the fuck is this?"

"You attach it to the valve and spray it in," he said. "It's full of pressurized air and some kind of gunk that plugs the leak and pumps the tire up again."

"That's ridiculous."

Ed didn't say anything, because he thought so, too. Even D.S. did. Nina shook her head and went back in the house, reading the label.

She put the can on the kitchen table. The table was blocking the doorway so people who weren't looking where they were going wouldn't walk into the kitchen and fall straight into the cellar, since there was no floor left out there. She picked up the can and gave it a shake.

After not thinking about anything in particular for awhile, she gave it another shake.

Then she shook it real hard.

Getting the bottom off was quite easy. When she hacked at the edge with the wobbly old carving knife, she worried that a blast of pressurized air and gunk would blind her, but there was no pressurized air in the can any more, and no gunk either. She squinched her eyes and looked inside. She whapped it against her palm a couple of times. Then, with her thumb and forefinger, she tweezered out an envelope. A plain ordinary white envelope.

That was full of money.

More money than she had ever seen in one place.

All in one hundred dollar bills.

Just looking at them made her heart pound. She took a deep breath and started counting. And when she finished, her heart was pounding in an entirely different way. And she knew one thing for sure.

Frank had been fucked.

Totally.

Completely.

Thoroughly fucked.

"Christ," she said.

There were seventy-five one hundred dollar bills. Seven thousand, five hundred dollars. The cash down payment on the fifteen thousand he supposedly was to get for pretending to rob the bank. She had no way of knowing this, of course. But there was no way she could avoid sensing something quite a bit like it, the same as she sensed that in the bank they had just pretended to give him the loot. That they had filled the Nike bag with cut-up newspapers or something and handed that to him instead. He didn't even get to collect the rest of the money they had promised him for the job.

"What a fuckin' moron." She thought she was saying it about Frank until it occurred to her that it ran in the family.

On the other hand, here she had seven thousand, five hundred dollars to put toward fixing the swimming pool. It didn't cheer her up even a little bit.

"That fuckin' Ed Oataway," D.S. roared. Nina was so startled she nearly peed her pants. He'd come in the front door without her realizing it. Her mind must have wandered off, probably because she didn't want to think about what all had happened. "He doesn't have even the slightest sense of humour," D.S. said. He'd been telling a bunch of the latest jokes he'd thought up, and Ed hadn't laughed at any of them. "Can you believe it?" he boomed, stopping right behind her. She felt panicky. She scooped the envelope and the cash and the Fix-a-Flat can and the bottom of the can up under her T-shirt. Then, bent over, she squeezed past D.S. and went into the john yelling that she was sorry, but she was in a hurry.

D.S. narrowed his eyes as the bathroom door slammed. "The fuck was that all about?" he said.

THIRTY

Ed Oataway could have told D.S. what it was all about. It was all about acting suspiciously. But JannaRose had no idea what was going on with her husband when she noticed he was sneaking around, following her everywhere. Nina noticed it, too, because everywhere JannaRose went, they went together.

"What's his problem?" Nina said after a week or so, because she worried that Ed thought JannaRose had a boyfriend. She would have said something earlier, but she didn't want to put JannaRose on the spot in case she did have a boyfriend and was hanging out with Nina to make it look to Ed as if everything was normal.

"Why are you following me around?" JannaRose said when Ed came in that night.

He looked at her as if she was out of her mind. "I'm not following you around," he said.

Since she'd seen him doing it, and so had Nina, she said that was a big fat lie. This hurt Ed's feelings. Was it his fault that she was always with Nina? How was he supposed to find out where Nina hid the money if he didn't follow her everywhere? If JannaRose didn't believe this, all she had to do was follow him when he stormed out indignantly and did what he'd started doing whenever Nina wasn't out and he wasn't following her.

He circled her house.

And it was on one of those circles that he collided with somebody who was peeking through a crack in the wall. Ed had no idea who it was, but the other person was pissed off. "What the fuck are you doing on my turf, you son of a bitch?" he hissed. "Go find your own fuckin' welfare queen."

Ed still didn't realize it was the welfare inspector, or that the inspector had taken it for granted that whoever bumped into him was an inspector from some other branch of the welfare department. Competition had become so fierce that welfare inspectors no longer reported what they found, because their reports would attract a whole lot of inspectors from other branches who wanted to get in on the action. The welfare inspector who'd made the original discovery would end up squeezed out. It's why they were mostly happy just to get on the nerves of the people they spied on and make their lives miserable. So it was understandable that he started punching Ed Oataway in the nose.

Ed had never won a fight in his life, except that time he'd whanged D.S. in the face with a hubcap, and D.S. said that wasn't a fight anyway, it was a discussion. He always disappeared the minute things got physical. This time, though, it was different. He disappeared, but not for days the way he usually did. He only disappeared long enough to run to the pile of stuff behind his house that included the back door of Dipshit's kitchen, and to scrabble around under it to find a suitable weapon. As soon as he grabbed something that felt right, he ran back to where whoever attacked him was peeking through the crack in the wall again, quite relaxed because as far as he was concerned he'd chased away the bastard who was trying to horn in on his case. And this time it would be a fairer fight, because while the welfare inspector only had one arm, Ed Oataway now had three.

He'd first found the other one when he was snooping behind Dipshit's house the night Nina threw it at the bad-tempered home wrecker digging the hole by the foundation, and it seemed to him like the kind of thing he could pawn.

Sneaking up behind the welfare inspector, he poked him on the shoulder. "Who you calling a fuckhead?" he said, making the inspector jump and angering him because he'd never called anybody a fuckhead in his life. Spinning around, he swung his only available fist and caught Ed Oataway between the eyes. After he stood back up, Ed clonked his antagonist over the head with the artificial arm. He clonked him so hard that he sank to his knees, where Ed kept on clonking him until he stretched out flat on the ground and stayed there.

Ed had been in such a rage that he didn't realize what he'd grabbed from his pile in the dark was the artificial arm. As far as he was concerned, it was simply an object with enough heft to do the job. He'd had no idea that the individual fighting him was a welfare inspector. He didn't know the welfare inspector only had one arm. And so there was no way he was aware that it was the welfare inspector's other arm he used to knock him cold. It was just the way things worked out.

And when he threw the artificial arm back on the pile in his yard, it never crossed his mind that the welfare inspector hadn't moved — that he'd just kept on lying there. He was still lying there the next morning when Nina noticed him. She knew who it was because of his plastic windbreaker and assumed that he'd been tired after spying on her all night and had fallen asleep. A couple of hours later, she noticed he was gone.

That was because when the welfare inspection branch he worked for didn't get a call from him at the end of his shift telling them everything was in order, they sent somebody out to check. And when they found him unconscious they took him to the hospital. He never emerged from a coma that had been induced by severe brain injuries, and a couple of days later he died. The marks on his head showed he'd been beaten with an artificial arm. When the artificial fingerprints were examined, they showed it had been his own artificial arm, the one he'd lost in the scuffle with Nina.

In no time, Sergeant Toole was back on her porch telling her that a brutal murder had taken place right beside her house and that the murder weapon was an item she'd been connected with in official reports. An item that, as a matter of fact, she had chopped off the body of the future murder victim himself. Was that part of her long-term plan? To move up from shooting junkyard dogs to knocking off municipal civil servants?

After Nina told JannaRose about this latest Toole visit, and JannaRose mentioned it to Ed Oataway, it occurred to Ed that he was in possession of a murder weapon. The next thing that occurred to him was he better get rid of it quickly. The third thing that occurred to him was to leave it on the back seat of the car that D.S. had started sleeping in on a regular basis.

While the fate of the welfare inspector followed its tragic course, Ed took every opportunity to talk to JannaRose, and what he talked about was the money. The money and nothing else. He explained to her how he deserved a considerable chunk of it because of all he'd done for Frank at the time of the pretend robbery, but also during their life together as best friends. Not only did he deserve it, he knew where it was. Nina had it. Not only did Nina have it, she knew he'd never been paid for crashing into the getaway car. But that wasn't the worst part. The worst part was her pretending she didn't have it because she didn't want him to get what he was owed, much less receive his fair share. This didn't surprise him, he told JannaRose. Nina was so much like her brother, he could hardly stand it. They never thought about anybody but themselves. In her case, she wanted to use the money to fix the swimming pool so everybody would start bowing down to her, and she'd get interviewed on television and could go around acting like the Queen of Fuckin' England, which she thought she already was from everything he could see.

But this would be impossible if Dipshit found out she had the money, because he would go killer-gorilla crazy. This was another reason she was keeping it secret. Because Dipshit would never let her throw money away on something as idiotic as a swimming pool.

"He always said he was happy for her to do whatever she wanted with the money she raised," JannaRose said.

"Sure, but that was when it never occurred to anybody that she'd get any. Once he finds out that she got some after all, and especially when he finds out how much she got, and that she's hiding it from him and from everybody else — there's going to be blood on the fuckin' moon."

JannaRose didn't believe a single thing Ed Oataway told her. She had never been closer to another human being than she was to Nina. It was more than if they were sisters. It was like they had their own reality show on TV and they were on it together all the time, sending the same thoughts and feelings out to all their viewers. When they did this, the viewers could see it was love and respect for each other that made both of them beautiful and strong. If Nina had that money — if she had even one cent of it — okay, there could possibly be certain circumstances that might make it impossible for her to tell JannaRose. For instance, if her life was in danger. But it didn't matter, because if she did have it she wouldn't have to *tell* JannaRose. Because JannaRose would be able to *tell* she had it. And so far she couldn't. So Nina couldn't. So she didn't.

"Explain that again for me, will you?" Ed said.

He did get JannaRose thinking, though, and what she thought was that no matter how sure you might be, with some people you could never tell.

She started to watch Nina as closely as possible to see if there was anything different about her. Anything like maybe having 1.18 million tucked away somewhere and not telling her closest friend. She started being around all the time instead of just most of the time. She never took her eyes off Nina for one second, and when she wasn't able to keep her eyes on her friend, she followed her right to the bathroom door and waited for her to come out. Then she whipped into the bathroom to see if anything had been rearranged. And little by little, it became apparent that something was definitely going on. One thing she noticed in particular was that Nina started looking up all of a sudden and saying, "Why the fuck are you staring at me?"

"I'm not staring."

"You are so."

"I don't know what you're talking about."

"I've been keeping my eye on you and caught you."

JannaRose would have looked astonished if she hadn't been taking care not to let on that anything surprised her. *Why was she keeping an eye on me?* she wondered. Was Nina nervous about something? Was it because she had something to hide? Was it possible she was worried that she'd do something that would give herself away and somebody would notice? It must be she felt guilty about something. Why else would she be doing it?

"You don't honestly think she's got the money," JannaRose said to Ed.

He gave her a look like the last drop of sanity was seeping out of her mind.

It made JannaRose feel sad. "I guess it could be that it's — you know —"

"True?"

"— possible."

"Fuckin' definite is what it is."

JannaRose sat there not looking at anything, not moving. "Shit," she said.

THIRTY-ONE

Somebody tipped off the cops.

D.S. certainly didn't tell anybody he had the murder weapon. He didn't even know it was a murder weapon. Not that he wouldn't have loved to tell absolutely everybody that somebody had stuck an artificial arm on the back seat of the abandoned car he was sleeping in if the subject happened to come up. He would have said something like, "People always give me the finger, but this is the first time they gave me all of them. Plus the hand and the arm." That's why most people tried to avoid having subjects come up with D.S. Besides, finding something like that ditched in an abandoned car you were sleeping in hardly counted as interesting in SuEz. It had to be a whole lot worse than that for anybody even to notice.

Other things were going on that got him wondering, though. One was Jarmeel waking him up by banging on the window of the car. Jarmeel was dressed sort of like

Zorro and shouting that he wished Nina would give him a shitload of that stolen money she had so he could take his kids someplace that was safe from the religious maniacs who were chasing him. Another was Krystal coming up to him when he was looking for a place to take a leak saying that if it hadn't been for his wife, she wouldn't be out of work and broke. For that reason alone, shouldn't Nina give her some of her brother Frank's loot to help her get back on her feet?

Something that impressed him was JannaRose yelling from across the street that Ed Oataway was at least entitled to a fair share of it. Was that too much to ask? D.S. thought she looked weird when she did this, like somebody had shoved the third rail from the subway up her ass and turned on the juice.

It was a good thing he wasn't the kind of person who automatically thought that where there's smoke there was fire. He said exactly that to Nina, but without letting on that it had to do with what everybody was telling him about her.

They had to have been tipped off. Otherwise it was impossible to explain all the undercover cops who thought nobody on the street knew that's what they were or that they were watching the car D.S. slept in, six of them per shift, twenty-four hours a day. But when nobody came near it for a week, and even though the doors weren't locked, one of them smashed a window with the butt of his gun and grabbed the arm. Then the car got towed.

Pretty soon word started going around that a warrant was out for D.S.'s arrest.

When Nina tried to discuss this with JannaRose, she found she couldn't. JannaRose just stood there, not saying anything. This pissed Nina off. "Why are you standing there like that?" she said.

"Like what?" JannaRose said real fast, hardly moving her lips.

"What the fuck is going on around here?"

"Nothing!" JannaRose said even faster. "You'll have to excuse me. I forgot something." She ran into her house.

"You'll have to excuse me?" Nina said this to herself three or four times and shook her head.

"Ahem!" a voice said. "Ahem!" Nina turned. D.S., in his blond wig, had stuck his head around the corner of their house.

"Come here." He looked around to make sure nobody was watching.

"What do you want?" She stayed where she was.

"Come *here!*"

"What do you *want?*"

"They're trying to arrest me for murdering that welfare inspector," he said. "The one with the artificial arm you hacked off that spied on us through the bedroom window."

"I know. What are you going to do?"

"Make a run for it."

"You should turn yourself in. You didn't kill him."

"Who's going to believe me? So I'm getting out of here, and if someday they catch me, I'll plead innocent."

"Good," she said. "For sure they'll believe you then."

"But if I'm going to get away, I'll need a lot of money. Give me some ... please."

"I haven't got any money. You know that."

"Don't fuck me around," D.S. said. "I don't have time to put up with your shit. Everybody knows you've got Frank's 1.18 million, and right now," he said, "I need a bunch of it. You hear me?"

"I haven't got it, D.S. Believe me. I don't know where it is."

He edged toward her. She backed up a step, two steps. He ran to grab her then realized he was out in the open where anybody could jump him.

"You held out on me," he snarled.

She hurried up the street, checking over her shoulder. So D.S. was after her, too. That made everybody. Everybody she knew believed she had the money, along with how many others she didn't know. She never would have thought D.S. would act like this after all they'd meant to each other. On the other hand, she would have thought he would if she'd thought about it. Like, it wasn't as far from impossible as anything she could imagine. When you got right down to it, if anybody was going to be bone-fuckin' stupid enough to figure she had Frank's loot, it would be D.S. So it was going to occur to him sooner or later. And when it did, he was bound to want her to give it to him, even if he didn't happen to be desperate to get away from the police. Not because he was greedy or anything like that. Or selfish. It was just the kind of person he was.

She kept out of sight the rest of the day. And she decided she'd better not sleep in the house that night. It turned out to be a smart idea.

THIRTY-TWO

Victor didn't believe that Raoul had prospected for oil way up north in the Arctic regions. But he didn't believe he'd been at Abu Ghraib or that he'd been an expert in torturing the prisoners there either. When he got right down to it, Victor didn't think there was anything Raoul might say about himself he would ever believe, but those were the only two things he'd ever heard him say, so it was all he had to go on. Victor still didn't believe his name was Raoul, either. What kind of an individual would go around with a name like Raoul? The same kind of individual who would barbecue Frank Carson's guts when Carson was right in the middle of telling them where the money was. The way Victor saw things, it took a major asshole to do that. If Raoul ever called himself a major asshole, Victor would have believed him. So there actually was one thing Raoul could have said about himself that Victor would have believed. But then, it was the only thing he had proof of.

Raoul had phoned Herbert, the human resources consultant who had teamed the two of them up and given them the job of tracking down the loot from the fake robbery of the Great Big One National Bank, and filled him in on his expertise in using explosives to find oil. He told Herbert he believed it would work better than anything else when it came to locating the missing 1.18 million dollars in Carson's sister's house.

It was Herbert's first departure from his normal way of doing business, which was supplying ex-convicts to contractors who needed certain work done. He was employing Victor and Raoul himself because he was going to get out of prison soon and thought that if he got hold of the money, he could use it as a stake in whatever line of work he went into as a civilian. Neither of them was a terrific example of the personnel he usually offered to clients, but Herbert hoped that if he put them together they would cancel out each other's personality disorders. He also didn't have a lot to choose from at the moment. Clients at both ends — looking for employers, and looking for employees — had been steering clear of him ever since his last bright prospect, Frank Carson, decided right in the middle of the Great Big One job to become an independent operator, and then went up in smoke.

If Raoul was absolutely convinced the money was under the cement floor in Carson's sister's cellar, and that nobody had found it because they didn't have his expert knowledge of the latest seismic exploration techniques used in underground searches, and if he could do it, fine. That was how Herbert saw it. And if Herbert was prepared to sign off on such a stupid fuckin' idea, that was all Victor needed to go along with it, because if they came out with nothing, what did it matter: he was on a retainer. And if they came out with the cash, he would disappear the hell out of there with all of it before Raoul's body even stopped twitching. Victor figured blowing the asshole's brains out the instant they saw the money was the best idea, because the scheme Raoul would have come up with to knock Victor off would be so totally fuckin' complicated that by the time he got it underway, it would be too late.

Victor couldn't believe anybody still lived in the house. All that was left standing were the living room, the bathroom, and part of one of the bedrooms, which was no longer connected to the other rooms. The stairs to the cellar only went halfway down. Victor looked things over down there, scraping at the floor with his shoe. "I can't see where anybody has dug up any of this," he said.

"You wouldn't be able to tell," Raoul said.

"What do you mean I wouldn't?" Victor was getting a little tired of Raoul telling him what he wasn't able to do. "I can see that nobody has dug into this fuckin' floor since the concrete was poured, whenever the hell that was. So how's he supposed to bury the money under it?"

"You forget he was a paving contractor." Raoul flashed a smile that was even bigger than the one he'd been smiling.

"What?"

"That's what Herbert said."

"Herbert said he was a fuckin' con man."

Raoul's smile got brighter still. "A fraudulent paving contractor can make anything look perfectly paved. It is a skill the good ones acquire."

Victor closed his eyes. "You really do have —"

"What?"

But Victor decided it was the wrong time to say "snakes in your head" to somebody who had as many snakes in his head as this wacko.

"You really do have ... this all worked out. I'm very impressed."

"Think nothing of it," Raoul said.

Back in the car, he handed Victor something that Victor took one look at and handed back so fast he hardly touched it. "This is the baby that will do the job for us," Raoul said.

"It looks like a fuckin' bomb," Victor said.

"Now here, my friend," Raoul said, "is another example of you not being familiar with the state of the art. It is a seismic charge —"

"Isn't that a stick of dynamite?" Victor pointed nervously at something long and skinny wrapped in what looked like red waxed paper. It stuck out each end of the device.

"— and is designed to send precisely calibrated vibrations deep into the earth. The echoes from these vibrations will be picked up by these sensitive microphones" — he held up a Baggie full of round black things — "that I will plant around the site to transmit the signals from the seismic echoes to this computer." He patted a laptop. "Any unusual formation under the concrete will be delineated, and that will be the thing we're after."

"Is it a fuckin' stick of dynamite or isn't it?" Victor said.

"In this instance," Raoul beamed, "not having had time to acquire the specialized charges used in petroleum exploration, I have been obliged to use this somewhat cruder material. But there's no need to be afraid of it. Unless an electrical charge is applied to the detonator —" he pointed to a thing that had wires coming out of it "— dynamite is completely inert. You could hit it with a hammer. You could even," he said, lighting up so much that Victor wanted to shield his eyes, "you could even eat it and not do yourself the slightest harm. Would you care to taste a little bit and see?"

"Fuck you," Victor said.

The only person who was ever in the house any more was a woman they took to be Carson's sister who sometimes slept on the living room couch. Tonight, though, there was no sign of her. They climbed down inside with tiny flashlights and cleared a space in the middle of the cellar floor. That was where Raoul placed the seismic device. He connected a switch to the detonator wires. He put a bunch of microphones around the walls and ran wires from these to the laptop.

They climbed out and moved back a ways. "Now I'll just give it a little prune juice," Raoul said.

"Like you used to say at Abu Ghraib," Victor said, getting dazzling glints of Raoul's smile from the streetlights.

"What?" Raoul said. "We never said anything like that in Iraq. It was a term that was used exclusively while exploring the Arctic petroleum fields." And he turned the switch.

It wasn't loud.

Not much more than a thump.

There weren't any flames.

Victor felt the thump under his feet, but it didn't jolt him around or anything.

Then the entire rest of the house crashed down into the basement.

A gigantic whoosh of dust rose up, turning the night foggy, dimming the streetlight, and when it finally cleared they saw that the whole cellar was piled with the walls and floor and roof and all the other stuff that collapsed into it, piled entirely full, like a swimming pool filled to the brim with trash. If the loot did happen to be buried under the floor, now it was buried under the floor and an enormous heap of beams and slivery boards and plumbing and shingles.

Raoul typed at the laptop. "I'm not getting a reading," he said. "Very strange."

"You fuckin' cocksucker," Victor said.

"Hmmmmm," Raoul said, as if trying to figure out if some calculation had been overlooked. He shone his flashlight on the switch to see whether it might be wired incorrectly.

But the "Hmmmmm" was the last sound he ever made, because Victor pulled a gun out of his pocket, stuck the end of it in Raoul's ear and pulled the trigger.

The police came the next day after somebody noticed his body lying beside where the house used to be. Since the Dolgoy family had abandoned it, nobody bothered to phone 911, even though when it fell down Ed Oataway called JannaRose to come and see. Nina's daughters followed her out the front door, and Fabreece and Gwinny started crying, but Lady told them Nina wasn't in the wreckage, so they shouldn't worry. They said they weren't worried about Nina; they knew full well that she wasn't in it when it happened. They were crying because the only home they had was gone. Lady told them to suck it up. It wasn't like there weren't lots of other places around just as good.

It didn't take long to identify the body, and it turned out his name really was Raoul. But it was more than a year before anybody discovered the other two dead people. That was when the foundation was dug out so apartments could be built. Kevin Olorgasele and J. Ridgeway Mbunzu of the Nigerian Finance Ministry, having just been reunited after believing each other was dead, and having been severely beaten, were just starting to get a little of their strength back when Raoul exploded his seismic device and the house fell on top of them. They never really got a chance to form a good impression of what life was like in this country.

THIRTY-THREE

Merlina and Lady headed over to Elwell's on their own one afternoon. They wanted to make it clear to both the Mr. Elwells that what happened to the dog in the junkyard was an accident. They wanted their family name to stop being a swearword as far as the Elwells were concerned, and they wanted them to stop thinking terrible things about their mother and father. The accident was caused by backing up over the dog in the dark, they said.

L. Ray said he wasn't especially surprised. "I never figured either Ed Oataway or your dad was smart enough to be able to kill a dog on purpose," he said.

L. Roy sat up straight and said it surprised him to hear hear L. Ray say that. "It wasn't the least bit funny."

"Wasn't trying to be funny," L. Ray said. "I believe these young ladies shouldn't hear anything but the serious truth."

"Is that because they represent the future of the whole human race?"

They looked at the girls for about a minute then turned back to the TV set above the counter, that was showing a weather lady giving the report on the big screen, and in a little picture down at the bottom, a weatherman on a different channel also giving a weather report.

"That's not funny either," L. Ray said.

"Watching two weather persons fight to the death on TV?"

"No. About these children being the future."

"You could try looking on the bright side."

"What bright side?" L. Roy said.

"That by the time the future gets anywhere near to where we are —"

"— we'll be —"

"— long gone. Long, long gone," they said at the same time, then shouted "Yeah!" and gave each other high-fives. While they sat there laughing, Lady wandered out into the shop. Merlina yelled at her to come back, but L. Roy said it was okay, so Merlina sat and watched TV with them while Lady went around and watched what the mechanics were up to.

"Let's go back. It's neat there!" Lady said the next day. So they started visiting a lot. On the way home, Lady would tell Merlina how that particular day she'd learned how to replace a catalytic converter, for example.

"What the fuck's that?" Merly said.

"A thing cars have," Lady told her.

"Having you girls around civilizes the place," L. Roy said one day.

"The guys out back even watch their language," L. Ray said.

L. Roy looked at Merlina. "So it seems only fair if you children did the same."

"I've got to tell you, there's a lot of Frank in that little lady, Lady," L. Ray said to L. Roy another time.

"Not to change the subject," L. Roy said to Merlina, "but how is your mama's fundraising campaign coming along?"

"Raking in the millions?" L. Ray said.

"She quit that," Merly said, not taking her eyes off the TV.

"She quit it?"

"Now she's hiding. She says everybody is out to get her."

"Out to get her?" L. Roy said.

"Everybody?" L. Ray said. "I'll be goldarned."

"That makes both of us," L. Roy said.

The girls still lived at the Oataways'. D.S. showed up in the yard from time to time and yelled at them through the back window to tell Nina he needed a whole lot of that stolen money she had so he could get himself to safety for a crime he hadn't committed. "Why is she making it so difficult for me? I never expected her to turn into a selfish bitch."

Ed and JannaRose told him he was right. Nobody deserved the money more than D.S. did, except for Ed. They were about equal, the one having been forced to work and suffer at Total all those years, and the other having been Frank's friend through all those years that Frank was screwing him. Although, it also shouldn't be forgotten that Ed had been Frank's close associate in carrying out the actual crime that resulted in all that wealth Nina had hidden away.

"We can talk about this later," D.S. said.

"Who's talking about anything?" JannaRose said. "I'm just saying what's fair."

Nina snuck around to see the girls when the other adults were busy somewhere else, such as when the ice cream truck came by. That's when they would disappear, because they didn't want to feel guilty about not giving her kids any money for treats. Now, when it saw them, the truck said things like, "Here's Guinevere! Hey, Guinevere! Why don't you come down and get some of these delicious frozen dog turds. We don't know anybody who loves dog turds more than you." And, "Merlina! Hello! We know you've been waiting for this. A Puke Slushy made with real puke we threw up just for you." For Lady it would be, "Lady, Lady, Lady! Your dream come true! Snotsicles! Snotsicles in every flavour you want — dirty snot, filthy snot, snotty snot, and shit snot." Then, "Fabreece! Our sweetest, very, very favourite Fabreece! Here's the sweetest, sweet treat you've been wanting for so long: A Hundred-Below-Zero —" and made a noise that sounded like a fart.

That's when Nina would poke her head around the corner and crook her finger for them to follow her. She'd give them money to buy chips at the Korean's store so they wouldn't put pressure on JannaRose to feed them and get her even madder at Nina than she already was.

After a couple of weeks, Nina's chin was drooped down between her shoulders. "We can't live like this," she said. "It's awful."

"Daddy says we can't live like this either," Guinevere said. "And he wouldn't have to if you gave him that money."

"I haven't got it." Her tone said, *How many times do I have to go over this?* "I don't know who has."

Lady said she didn't think D.S. would kill Nina, even if he got the chance, but it must be hard with so many other people out to get her.

That was when Merlina said why didn't they all go and hide somewhere together — the four sisters and Nina? Except nobody could think of a place. After they gave it quite a bit of thought, they couldn't think of one the next day, either. Then something started going on in Merly's mind. People later said it was like something they'd seen a long time before on TV. She couldn't remember anything like it, though. All she thought was there had to be some way to protect Nina and the rest of them, and they wouldn't be protected if they hid somewhere in some dark corner of an alley, because what if somebody found them there and nobody else knew where they were?

"What?" Nina said.

"If you hide out somewhere and nobody knows where you are," Merly said, "then whoever finds you could do bad things and nobody else would ever find out. If you're going to hide out —" she had to work through this kind of slowly "— then it's probably better to hide out where everybody knows where you are."

"That's stupid," Guinevere said.

"I don't know," Merlina said. It did seem kind of confusing.

"It's so fuckin' like you," Gwinny said. "You just have to talk, even if everything you say is the stupidest shit."

"I'm just —"

"Do you really think that if you've got a big fuckin' diamond ring or something and you hide it on the middle of the sidewalk —"

"I don't — I think it isn't —"

"— that the first person that comes along and sees it lying there isn't going to take it and run like hell. What do you think people are, complete fuckin' —"

"Gwinny," Nina said. She looked like somebody who was thinking harder than their brain was certified for. "Shut up for a minute, okay?"

And they all shut up until Nina gave a twittery laugh. "Maybe I should steal another one of Ed Oataway's cars," she said.

"Why not a bus?" Lady said.

"A bus would be perfect." Nina looked kind of forlorn when she said this.

"No!" Lady was looking at Merlina. "Me and Merly. We know where one is."

"Elwell's have all these old cars and things out the back," Merly said. "One of them's this old school bus."

"A *yellow* one," Lady said. "Who's going to kill you if we're all riding around in it?"

"You want us to drive around for the rest of our lives in some dirty old fuckin' wreck of a school bus?" Gwinny said.

"Gwinny," Nina said.

"What?"

"Fuckin' shut up. Like I already asked you. I'm trying to think."

THIRTY-FOUR

The plan called for Merlina and Lady to go to Elwell's with Nina. Nina told Fabreece and Guinevere they would pick them up at five thirty in the morning, before it was light. But a little after five, D.S. clomped through the front door of Ed Oataway's and JannaRosc's. When he could only find two of his kids, he started muttering, "Where the hell is everybody? Where'd they all go?"

If he noticed they were already dressed when he yanked them out of bed, he didn't say anything. Instead he kind of sang, "Come on guys, going for a picnic. Come on for a picka-nic, a picka-nicka."

It's hard to say whether Fabreece and Guinevere were more scared or confused. Nobody had mentioned the possibility that D.S. might appear and drag them away to do something they'd never done before: have a picnic. "Daddy, it's dark," Fabreece said. If he suspected something was up, or if he'd instinctively decided the time had come to spring into action, not even he could say for sure. And if two out of four daughters were all he could round up, they would do. He'd tell Nina that if she wanted to see them again, she better stop holding out.

He was rushing them through the front door as a police officer was climbing out of a blue convertible. If Sergeant Toole had suspected something was up, or if he'd instinctively decided it was time to increase surveillance on the girls, he wasn't exactly certain. The only thing he was interested in was Frank's loot, and if Nina got away with it and her daughters, he'd have a hard time tracking it down.

He was surprised to see a big fat blonde woman pulling two of the girls out of the house. "What's going on?" he yelled.

"Mind your own fuckin' business," D.S. yelled back.

"Who the fuck are you?" Toole yelled.

"*Me?* Who the fuck are *you?*" D.S. yelled.

D.S. started to move around him, and Toole was just about to yell that he was the fuckin' police, that's who, when the most amazing thing happened, at least from the point of view of everybody else in her family. It amounted to the first time anybody could think of that Fabreece was paying attention. What she did, though, was crouch down. Then with all her might she sprang forward and butted her head into Robbie Toole's crotch. This caused him to fall down and roll around in a ball, groaning.

D.S. hollered, "Let's go!" and started pushing Gwinny and Fabreece past the detective, who was making noises like he was going to be sick. But just then Toole stood up and threw a punch that knocked D.S. over backwards.

"Hey!" Toole said, picking up the wig. "You're no fuckin' woman." Then he took a closer look. "*Wait!* You're the asshole that's wanted for murder." And he kicked D.S. in the crotch. Now it was D.S. rolling around in a ball, groaning.

That's when the second most amazing thing happened from the point of view of anybody who knew Fabreece. Gwinny was standing there looking at Ed Oataway and JannaRose's house as if she was frightened and might run back into it. Merlina's theory was that she'd forgotten all the lipsticks and makeup she'd shoplifted over the years and wanted to go back for them. It didn't matter, because Fabreece wasn't taking any of her shit. She grabbed her sister by the hair and started dragging her up the street, making her go faster and faster.

Nina arrived with the school bus while all this was going on. Fabreece dragged Guinevere in through the open door.

"Here we go," Lady said.

"I guess so," Nina said, and pulled away from the curb.

THIRTY-FIVE

At first they stuck to streets in the east end of the city, east of SuEz, and after the sun had been up for awhile, Nina nosed the bus into a plaza because everybody was hungry. "No stealing!" she shouted after the girls as they went into a store to buy chips and drinks. "This won't work if we do anything illegal."

"What won't work?" Fabreece said.

"What we're doing," Merlina explained.

"Oh," she said.

Because of what had gone on between D.S. and Sergeant Toole, the police would know by now that they'd taken off. This meant it hadn't been necessary to ask the Elwells, when they got to work that morning, to call the cops and tell them their school bus had been stolen. Nina thought it was still too soon for word to have gotten around, though, so they were safe stopping for breakfast.

She'd been sort of surprised to see it really was a school bus. Five rows of two seats each on both sides of the aisle.

Maximum Capacity twenty. And while it was yellow like most school buses, instead of having the name of a school district or whatever on the side, it had "Metropolitan Alcohol Rehabilitation Centre." The Elwells said that before it got old and they bought it, it had been used for picking up drunks and taking them to the detox. The big red lights on the front and back worked the same as on regular school buses, though, and Nina kept them flashing all the time. This threw a lot of drivers for a loop, because they'd only seen school bus lights flash when one was stopped, and they were supposed to stop, too, both ways.

The Parkway was jammed with people going to work when Nina squeezed on to it. Then, after it was starting to feel like they'd be creeping along forever, she said, "Okay everybody, here comes one," and a police car with its own lights flashing pulled up alongside. The cop motioned for Nina to pull over, but instead she pointed to the dashboard of the bus, and for a long time he couldn't figure out what she meant. Then he pulled ahead a bit until he could look over his shoulder. And what he saw Merlina.

She was standing at the front window holding two wires with bare ends. At the same time, Nina kept pointing over and over at the dashboard — not at the dashboard itself, but at a thing that the wires Merlina was holding were attached to. Nothing happened for a minute, then the cop dropped back really fast and stopped all the traffic behind them.

"Jesus!" Nina said. "It worked!"

"What worked?" Fabreece said.

"This." Merlina tapped the thing the wires were attached to. "It's like what they used to blow up our house." Exactly like. It turned out that Raoul, the bomber, had become a firm believer in redundancy after electrocuting Frank. If one system didn't work, he insisted on having another that would do the job right. "Me and Lady found it in a bag behind our house after they took the body away."

"So you're going to blow up our bus?" Fabreece said.

"Don't be fuckin' —"

"No, sweetie," Nina said. "But the police will be real careful about how close they get if they think we might."

"Especially with us on it." Fabreece nodded approvingly.

Getting this point across was a very important part of the plan. So was the next part. They needed a cop off by himself with nobody else too near. In the meantime, they were stranded between traffic jams — one behind, where the cops were holding all the traffic back, and one in front where the cops were waving all the traffic off at the next exit. They didn't move until there was nothing ahead but a clear highway, except for the line of police cars that stretched from one side of the Parkway to the other, all their lights flashing and travelling at the same speed as the bus. Then they saw one cop all alone on the shoulder. It was a lady cop, and she was standing beside her cruiser as if waiting until everybody went by, but Nina signaled and pulled over.

When the door opened right in front of her, the cop looked definitely unprepared for anything like that. "Ma'am," she said, "I have to ask you to let the children off. And to get out. And —"

"Hold on, officer," Nina said.

"You see this?" Merly said, holding the two wires close to each other and pointing with them at the thing on the dashboard.

"Ma'am —"

"In case you wonder about it," Merly said, "this here is its twin sister." It turned out Raoul didn't just believe in redundancy, he was weird for it. There were two extra bombs in the bag the sisters found.

"Catch," Lady said, and tossed the other one to the cop, who caught it easily. Then she looked at it, her mouth dropped open, and she held it as far away as she possibly could. "It's — it's —"

"Dynamite," Lady said.

"Now listen, please." Nina held up one hand like she wanted the cop to be calm. "I'd like you to please tell anybody that wants to know that the money they're looking for is right here with us. We put it in the tires."

"It's in the tires!" Lady said.

"Money?" the cop said.

"Yes! The *money* everybody is looking for. It's in the *tires!*" Nina shouted, pulling away.

"Hey, ma'am?" the cop shouted.

"It's in the tires! It's in the tires!" Nina and Lady shouted.

The bus was dirty and old except for the tires. That's how they looked, anyway. At first they looked as old as the rest of the bus, but then Lady had an idea. She borrowed a jug of Armor All from the Elwells and wiped it on them and they turned shiny black, just like in the ads on TV. Anybody looking at it would think, *Shitty bus. Nice tires, though.* And they'd figure somebody must have done some work on them lately. Certain people would think that for sure, especially once the money got mentioned.

"I got to pee," Gwinny said.

"Everybody's trying to help," Merlina said. "But not Gwinny. Gwinny only cares about Gwinny. And Gwinny's got to pee."

"Shut up, Merly," Nina said.

"I got to pee, too," Fabreece said.

So did Merlina. She'd had to for about an hour, but she was absolutely not going to let on. Anyway, Nina hauled off at the next exit and gave the entire police department a brain hemorrhage. They had to race around until they got a bunch of police cars in front of the bus again, but Nina only drove along for about a block before pulling into a parking lot. "*McDonald's!*" Fabreece shouted, like it was the most beautiful thing she'd ever seen in her life. "It's a *McDonald's!*" They'd only been in one a few times — except to go to the bathroom. Nina said it cost too much to eat there.

"Okay, Gwinny, you go and take Fabreece to the Ladies," she said. "Merly, you stay right there in the window holding those wires."

"Fuck," Merlina said.

"What?" Nina said.

And when they came back, Merly went and Lady held the wires — they were wrapped around the dynamite, not actually attached to anything. None of them had any idea how they could make it explode. After Merlina, Nina took Lady.

They were gone for a long time. A long, long time. The McDonald's was surrounded by police cars, and even though the sun was out, so many lights were flashing that Merly thought it was like being in the middle of a lightning storm. Finally they came out, but with a McDonald's lady who was carrying a great big box full of McDonald's stuff. Lady was so astonished she could hardly talk. Nina thanked the McDonald's lady and closed the door, and it wasn't until they were back on the freeway with the police cars racing to get out front again that she told them what happened. What happened was they were on TV.

"They have pictures from helicopters and from overpasses that show the bus and us and where we are," she said. "On the TV over the counter you could see us right down in that McDonald's parking lot. And the manager looked at me and said, 'Is that you folks? You're famous!' And she told us we could have anything we wanted for free."

"But we couldn't think what to get," Lady said.

"So they gave us this box full of everything."

"*McDonald's*," Fabreece sighed, and she touched all the stuff in the box.

THIRTY-SIX

The bus lurched. Sharply.

It lurched again. It swung toward the centre guardrail. "Mom!" Merlina yelled. Nina's chin was on her chest and her eyes were closed.

"Mom!" Merlina and Lady yelled at the same time. Nina snapped upright and looked around, yanking the wheel so hard the other way, the girls were thrown across the aisle. "What?" she said over and over, steering back and forth, toward the guardrail, toward the shoulder, until she finally got settled down and going straight.

She blinked a couple of times, using her whole face. "We've got to get off." She sounded dazed. "I'm almost falling asleep." There was an exit right ahead that she followed on to a street. They'd been making big loops, one after the other, following the freeways and expressways and the parkway around the central part of the city, and just along the street was another McDonald's. She pulled into the lot and stopped. Her face was white, as if she was going to be sick. She dropped her head on to the steering wheel.

"Mom?" Merlina said.

Nina didn't answer. She was out cold.

"Now what?" Lady said. She didn't sound hopeful. They watched police cars zip around until this McDonald's was surrounded, too. They dragged Nina out of the driver's seat and got her on a couple of passenger seats, where she could stretch out a bit. She didn't notice. None of the girls spoke. It was as if they couldn't even talk. Or think. Or feel anything except maybe an ache that was wired directly into Lady's question: Now what? Until this, Merlina and Lady had at least felt like they were doing something. Now nobody was doing anything. And not doing anything felt a lot like the whole thing was falling apart. More than a lot. It felt awful.

Fabreece pointed to a McDonald's kid who came out and waggled his arms over his head. "What does that man want?" she said.

Merly opened the door. "What do you want?" she yelled.

"Take a —" the kid yelled, then he paused and changed his approach. "That bomb you've got isn't going to go off or nothing, is it? Blow us all up?"

"No way!" Merly yelled. "We're real careful. We don't want anything bad to happen." Behind her, Lady waved the two wires to show how far apart she was holding them.

"Good!" The kid looked relieved. "So then, take a look up there!" He pointed at the big McDonald's sign where big gold letters were winking across it that said, "Welcome Nina and Girls! McDonald's Welcomes You! We Love You Nina!"

"McDonald's loves Mommy?" Fabreece said.

"I got to pee," Guinevere said, and opened the door.

"Here we go again," Fabreece said when she and Gwinny came back with bags full of McDonald's stuff. Gwinny was looking a little bit happy for the first time in weeks. She said everybody in the restaurant was watching a TV that had live pictures of them. When she and Fabreece got to the counter, the manager showed them what was on the other channels.

"It was us!" Gwinny said. "We were on all of them!" She floated around the bus, hugging herself.

"What an asshole," Merlina said.

"You'll be sorry when I'm a star," Gwinny said.

It was another hour before Nina woke, and when she got them back on the freeway, she asked what they were going to do once it got dark and they all needed to sleep. Nobody knew what to say, except Gwinny.

"It's awesome," she said, spreading her arms and waving at the crowd at an interchange. Everywhere they could get a view people were gathering, waving at the bus. Some held big signs. "We Love You Nina!" and "Burger King Loves You & Girls — Next Exit & Turn Right!" and McDonald's with its own signs telling the exits where they could be found. And Popeye's and Arby's and all kinds of other places telling them they'd get all the food they wanted for free if they'd only stop there. Sometimes Ronald McDonald would be by the freeway, blowing kisses.

The police cars behind them were followed by a solid stream of ordinary cars that stretched back as far as Nina could see. They had their blinkers flashing. Flags streamed out the windows.

"Why are they doing that?" Merlina said.

"Because they want the money," Lady said.

"Because they love us," Gwinny said. "We're on TV!"

Signs started showing up that said, "Nina the Bandit Queen!" and "Long Live Bandit Queen Nina!" Nina had no idea what that was all about unless it was because the Elwells reported the bus was stolen. They had no way of knowing that reporters on TV had been saying that, according to police sources, Nina Dolgoy wanted to save her local swimming pool. To do this, she had been going around robbing the gangsters and drug dealers in SuEz of their criminally gotten gains. And she had hidden the money in the school bus's tires for safekeeping, millions of dollars stuffed into each one. Then the TV would show close-up pictures of the tires that were no longer as shiny as when they'd started out, but still were a bit.

It was nearly dark when one of the police cars up ahead stopped and left an orange traffic cone on the pavement. They stopped and read the note tied to it: the police would clear a parking lot at a mall and put in a Johnny-On-the-Spot that they could park beside. They could stay there till morning. The police would leave them alone. The police needed a rest, too. She should blink her lights if that was okay. She blinked her lights and was led to an exit, then up to a mall where a huge lot had been cleared. All alone in the middle was a Johnny. The door was open so they could see that nobody was inside waiting to jump them.

When the police surrounded the lot, hundreds and hundreds of other cars swarmed up behind them, honking their horns and blasting music. Every now and then the yelling would coalesce into a chant. "Nina! Ban-dit Queen-a! We love Nina! Bandit Queen-a!"

"That should be Nina the Welfare Queen-a," was all she said when she heard it.

Blankets and pillows had been left beside the portable toilet, and while they were getting them arranged, Fabreece yelled, "Look who's coming! Look who's coming!" It was Ronald McDonald himself. He'd gotten through the line of police cars and was carrying bags of McDonald's stuff. He stopped halfway to the bus and waved a kind of Hiya! then started forward again.

"What's the matter with Ronald?" Lady said.

"What?" Merlina said.

"Ronald is skinny," Lady said.

"Skinny?"

"Ronald is always skinny. Except today he's not. He's real big!" And she ran out the door yelling at him. "You stop right there," she yelled. But he didn't, he just slowed down. "Don't you move!" she yelled. "Blow the horn at him, Merly!" Merlina started blasting on the horn. Finally he stopped.

"Get away from here!" Lady shouted.

He leaned in their direction. "We don't want you any closer," she said. He made a kind of who, me? gesture. Then after a minute or two, somebody at the police cars with a loudspeaker said, "Okay. Leave the food. Come on back." Ronald turned and did a well, you can't win them all thing, and walked away on his big flapping shoes.

"Why's Ronald leaving?" Fabreece said.

"He's a fake," Merlina said.

They'd been lied to. The police would trick them if they could. Somebody was going to have to stay awake all night to keep guard. They decided they'd each do an hour, then sleep until it was their turn again, except for Fabreece.

"I think it was the real Ronald," she said. "This food he left is real."

Some of them wondered about that later on. Maybe it had some kind of sleeping drug in it. Or maybe it was what they had to expect when they put their faith in a fuckin' idiot like Gwinny, Merlina said. Because when it was her second time to hold the wires while the others slept, she fell asleep, too.

The next thing any of them knew, the motor started. Merly sat straight up. The bus started to move. The parking lot was lit almost as bright as day, and she could see Nina sprawled on the seat across the aisle. Cops were moving cars out of the way, other cops were waving the bus ahead, through the opening.

Merlina looked at the man in the driver's seat.

"Fuck," she said.

He was waving thanks to the cops. Merlina's sisters were sitting up and saying "Oh my God!" and making screechy noises.

"Did we get arrested?" Lady yelled.

"No!" It was Nina. The others got real quiet. "He's not a cop."

The driver nodded, as if she couldn't have been more right about anything.

"What do you want?" she said.

"Let's everybody take it easy," he said. "We're all going to be fine, okay?"

THIRTY-SEVEN

"Who is it?" Guinevere whispered.

"James G. Bradley, at your service," he said.

"It's Gladly Bradley," Lady whispered.

"Who's that?" Guinevere whispered.

"The mayor."

He gave a big goodbye wave to the cops who had let them through.

"Fuck," Merlina said.

The next very important part of their plan had been to drive around the freeways for twenty-four hours. If they could do that, they figured everybody who needed to know where the money was — or where it was supposed to be — would know it. So when daylight came, they were going to ask the cops to get the police chief to come and talk to them. When he got there, they'd give up to him, and everybody who needed to would see them getting led away empty-handed from the bus with the shiny tires. Nina the Welfare

Queen and her girls, as poor as ever. This part of the plan was actually the most important part of all.

And whatever was going on had totally screwed it up.

Since he was the mayor, when Gladly Bradley showed up and told the cops he was going out to the bus to talk to that woman and settle this thing, nobody was about to tell him he wasn't. And he started right in as soon as they were out of the parking lot. "Mrs. Dolgoy," he said, looking at her in the rearview, "I believe we can all profit from this, even if nobody that I personally have in mind ends up with the eighteen million dollars you hid in the tires."

"It was one 1.18 million, and you know it," Nina said. "And my brother got set up and didn't get it."

"Whatever you like, Mrs. Dolgoy," Gladly said. "Myself, I never argue with the media. What matters now is that you and me get a chance to benefit from it in a way that's profitable to both of us. If you end up getting to keep the money —"

"There is no money."

"If you get to keep the money," he continued, "that's fine with me. And if I get some small bit of recognition —" he held his thumb and index finger so close they almost touched "— as the man who saved this dangerous situation from turning into a bloodbath, or worse, then it will be worth more than eighteen million —"

"I don't fuckin' believe this," Nina said.

" — it will be worth far more than mere money to me. So," he said, "if you will kindly shut the fuck up, we'll go somewhere that isn't quite as public and discuss our arrangements more fully."

Gwinny put up her hand. "I got to pee," she said.

"Who gives a shit?" he said.

All the people who had been partying all night on behalf of Nina were pretty quiet until they saw the bus go by. This got them cheering again about how much they loved her and the girls. The girls were so nervous, they started waving back. The chant started again. "Nina! Ban-dit queen-a! Nina! Ban-dit Queen-a!" She and the girls could hear it all the way down the ramp and onto the freeway, where everything was the same as before.

The line of police cars in front. Another line behind. The ordinary people racing to get into formation behind them, honking their horns. But Gladly was driving really, really slow, not even half as fast as Nina had.

He gave her a big wink in the rearview. "Just waiting until there's enough light so they can get a good look at us." He meant the helicopters, since he pointed toward the roof.

When the sun did come up, there were even more helicopters than the day before. Some flew right alongside with their cameras aimed at the bus. Gladly waved like crazy and gave the thumbs up. He opened the driver's window and leaned way out so they could get a better shot of him waving. He even blew kisses like the Ronald McDonalds along the expressways had. Then, after about half an hour he pulled over to the side the way Nina had when she needed a rest. The police cars stopped. He turned sideways on the seat. Let's see what you and me can come up with, Mrs. Dolgoy."

"Like what?"

"Exactly," he said.

They would drive to City Hall. Nina and the girls would get out and tell the media how the mayor talked them into stopping their campaign ... their crusade ... their reckless, endless drive around and around the city ... their whatever it was they'd been doing. That if it hadn't been for him and how much they trusted him, they would still be driving around recklessly, endlessly, maybe forever.

"Yeah?" Nina said. "You really don't care about the money?"

"Money? I wouldn't know what you're talking about. So —" He looked out the side window. They all did. A police motorcycle that had rumbled up behind them swung past the bus and parked in front of it. When the cop climbed off, he removed his helmet and put on a police officer's hat.

Then he pulled out a gun. "Open the door," he shouted.

"What the fuck is this?" Gladly Bradley shouted back.

Nina was wondering the same thing. It turned out it wasn't a police motorcycle, just an old blue Honda. The police uniform was way too big, all baggy around the middle. The hat came down over his ears. His hair stuck out over his collar. When he shouted "Open the door," his accent made it hard to understand. It sounded like "Hobben de doe."

"What the fuck is going on?" Gladly shouted, looking out the back window where the police officers had piled out of the patrol cars that stretched across the highway. They were standing in a circle, waving their arms, pointing at each other, pointing at the bus. Up ahead, the other police cars were getting tangled up as they jockeyed to turn around so they'd be facing the bus.

The cop-type person with the gun shouted again. "Hobben de doe."

"Shit," Gladly said. "I know that guy." Then, "Who are you?" he shouted. "Where do I know —"

There was a bang. The bullet made a hole in the windshield just above Gladly's head and went zinging out through the roof behind him. Gladly vanished under the steering wheel. But Nina didn't think the cop-type had been trying to shoot him, or to shoot anything. Because when the gun had gone off, he stepped back, staring at it like he was trying to figure out what happened.

A siren up ahead started screaming and a police car came tearing down the road. "Hold it! Hold it!" Gladly started yelling, and maybe he thought of making a run for it, because he opened the door. But instead of rushing through it, he dashed to the back seat. The cop-type climbed aboard. The police car rocked to a stop and the driver jumped out.

"Fuck me," Nina said. It was Sergeant Toole.

He was terrifically agitated. To him it looked as if some kind of clown cop had shown up and was horning in on top of the mayor who had already horned it to get Frank's money before he could. The clown cop had his back to Toole because he was waving his gun at Gladly Bradley, who was yelling at him not to shoot.

"Drop it!" Toole was aiming his own gun at the middle of the clown cop's back. "Drop it!" he yelled. "Drop that fuckin' gun."

The clown cop whirled around. He must have recognized Toole's voice. His hands were shaking. It was Carlo, Toole's new boyfriend. "What the fuck are you doing here?" Toole demanded. "Why are you wearing my old uniform? Why have you got my old fuckin' gun? Didn't you hear me tell you to drop it?"

Carlo opened and closed his mouth a couple of times. But instead of dropping the gun, it looked as if he thought he was supposed to hand it to Toole. Maybe it was a language problem. He started holding it out. Cops always take a narrow view of guns in other people's hands, no matter what their relationship is, especially if they're staring at the barrel. They take them very seriously. They don't take their eyes off them. They get scared.

Toole's first shot hit Carlo in the middle of the chest. The next two missed, possibly because Carlo fell down, possibly because Toole was so upset, possibly because he wasn't all that good a shot. They missed Carlo, that is. One of them caught Gladly Bradley in the thigh.

Toole collapsed on top of Carlo, yelling, "What were you doing? What were you doing?"

Gladly Bradley, on the other hand, was shrieking in pain. "You crazy fuck! You fuckin' shot me!"

By this time, cops were all over the place. When they rushed the bus, they had to hold Sergeant Toole down and take his gun away because he was trying to put the barrel in his mouth and blow his brains out. Then the paramedics carried the mayor out on a stretcher. "Sit me up so I can speak to my people," he told them. There were only two or three cameras and a couple of microphones around so far, but he started going on about how it had been worth it, facing death in the line of public service. It was worth it because he so terribly much wanted to bring to a safe conclusion — safe for all but himself, he said, pointing bravely at his bandage — the ordeal of this poor woman and her children that had captured the world's attention and brought this great city to a complete standstill.

The instant Gladly Bradley had run to the back of the bus and Carlo jumped aboard, Nina herded her girls behind Carlo's back and out the door. They ran until the shooting stopped, and the next thing they knew they were standing beside the Elwell's tow truck with its yellow lights flashing as if there had been a traffic accident and they were looking for customers. L. Roy and L. Ray were telling the police that Nina hadn't stolen the school bus after all. There had been a clerical error. Somebody in middle management got overexcited when they saw it wasn't in the yard and called 911. To tell the truth, they had loaned it to the Dolgoys so they could go down to the beach for a swim. Little did the Elwells dream what might happen as a result.

Then they told Nina they were retiring from the service centre and, out of gratitude to her for being so community-spirited, and because of their affection for her late brother Frank, they were letting her have the tow truck for her own personal use for as long as she wanted.

"What?" Nina kept saying.

"What?" Even the cops were saying it.

But the Elwells said they'd cleared everything with their attorneys, led the sisters over to the truck, and boosted them into it. Because it had four doors and a back seat, they all fit in with room to spare.

"Now get the hell out of here," L. Ray said to Nina.

"While the getting's good," L. Roy said.

"And this is as good as it's ever going to get."

"Don't listen to him," L. Roy said. "He says that to all the girls."

Nina didn't leave right then, though. She parked the truck out of the way a bit and told her daughters to be quiet. She wanted to make sure. And before long, a police department hauler hooked on to the school bus, pulled it up on its flatbed, and drove off with it, the tires still a little blacker than they had been.

"There," she said.

Then they got the hell out of there. For a long time nobody spoke. For one thing, nobody but Nina knew she had the seventy-five hundred dollars socked away that her brother Frank had hidden in the tire-repair can and, what with one thing and another, it didn't occur to her to mention it. For another, it never occurred to anybody that they were about to get into the tow-truck business until Nina asked, out of the blue, "I wonder how you tow something with one of these?"

"Ask Lady," Merlina said.

Lady had been leaning forward studying the dashboard with its dials and buttons and switches and toggles and levers and police-radio scanners. She looked very intense. "It's so not a problem," she said.

MORE GREAT FICTION FROM DUNDURN

Halbman Steals Home
by B. Glen Rotchin
978-1459701274
$19.99

Haunted by the memories of his former home and life, Mort Halbman risks everything in a daring attempt at a last shot at redemption. Halbman is a crotchety, divorced, sixty-five-year-old garment manufacturer who laments losing the one true love of his life, the Montreal Expos. Now the dream home he built in the late 1960s in the exclusive Montreal suburb of Hampstead, where he lived with his family for twenty years, has burned down under mysterious circumstances, and Mort finds himself the prime suspect in an arson investigation.

Meanwhile, his estranged gay son has announced that he's getting married and wants Mort to participate in the rabbi-officiated same-sex ceremony along with his ex-wife and her insufferable boyfriend, Canada's book reviewer extraordinaire. It's the last thing Mort wants to do. He feels compelled to continually return in his Jaguar to the burned-out ruin of his former home, and to the memories the place still holds for him. With pathos and humour, *Halbman Steals Home* tells the story of Mort's daring attempt to risk everything for a last shot at redemption.

Waiting for Ricky Tantrum
by Jules Lewis
978-1554887408
$17.99

Jim Myers is a painfully shy kid living in Toronto's west end Bloorcourt Village. Rarely is he able to muster enough courage to say anything beyond "ya" or "dunno." After school he hangs around with his neighbour and only friend, Oleg Khernofsky, playing basketball against a NO PARKING sign in a laneway. In the evenings, he haunts Nicky's Diner, a restaurant owned by Oleg's uncle.

On the first day of junior high, Jim crosses paths with Charlie Crouse, a brash, mouthy kid full of wild stories about his past. Charlie takes Jim under his wing and introduces him to the electronic strip poker machine at the Fun Village Arcade in Koreatown, a Queen Street hooker who calls herself Steffi Graf, and the diverse sounds and utterances of his landlord's three lovers. As Jim and Charlie's friendship grows, however, the realities of looming adulthood seep into their lives with surprising consequences.

DUNDURN
www.dundurn.com

What did you think of this book?
Visit www.dundurn.com for reviews, videos, updates, and more!